A
GENTLEMAN
for
LADY
JUNIPER

A
GENTLEMAN
for
LADY
JUNIPER

CLAIRVOIR CASTLE *Romances*
BOOK SIX

SALLY BRITTON

Published by Pink Citrus Books
Edited by Emily K. Murdoch
Cover design by Blue Water Books

Sally Britton
www.authorsallybritton.com

First Printing: November 2024

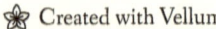 Created with Vellum

For Emma, Krystal, and Lydia:
Thank you for the bookstore quest.

CHAPTER 1

JANUARY 5, 1822

H alf a dozen men dressed in the finest clothing from the finest tailors in England ambled about the gardens of Castle Clairvoir, the family seat of the Duke of Montfort, on a chill winter's afternoon. Puffs of steam left their mouths and noses as they spoke, each one of them bundled against the cold in wool coats, leather gloves, and top hats which made them easy to track even from the other side of the well-trimmed hedges.

A man dressed in the livery of a footman, John Sterling—Jack, to those who knew him best—stood guard over them. He posted himself on a slight rise on the other side of the hedge, watching as their hats bobbed and dipped like ducks on a pond. They spoke in low voices, and he listened for tone more than word as his eyes darted from them to the trails outside the garden where they'd ambled about in the cold morning air.

A few of them puffed on pipes, including the duke. He was easy to spot, given he stood a few inches taller than his guests. It was to the top of his hat that Jack looked most often. The duke was his employer, his to guard and protect, above all else—and while the duke trusted the men accompanying him, Jack still kept himself ready to pounce at the slightest signal.

The duke had called his closest political allies to visit him at Clairvoir in the weeks leading up to their removal to London for the next parliamentary session. His Grace was in the final part of planning sessions designed to help his party take immediate action when they arrived in Town. In the six years Jack had worked for the duke, he'd watched the way Montfort planned and strategized with the precision and acumen of a field marshal.

Unexpected motion at the edge of the statuary gardens immediately caught Jack's eye. He didn't tense up. The inexperienced tensed. He relaxed, released a slow breath, and evaluated.

Not a gardener. Not another guard. But—ah. The duke's youngest son, creeping along the path, holding something flush against his chest.

Jack's gaze flickered from the top hats to the boy. Little Lord James, all of eleven years old, moved in the opposite direction from his father's meeting. Sterling took a few steps around a hedge into the boy's path, surprising him.

Lord James yelped, and held whatever prize was in his hands tighter to his chest. His eyes grew wide as he whispered, "I wish you'd teach me how to move that quietly."

"Practice, my lord," Jack said coolly. "You are not supposed to be out here this afternoon, Lord James. Did you slip your guard again?"

The child grinned broadly. "Yes. Everyone thinks I'm in bed with a sick stomach." He held his hands out. "But I went to fetch this to pack it for Eton." He held out a jar full of multi-hued stones.

Though tempted to ask, Jack needed to get back to his post. He held his hand up above his head and signaled with two quick hand movements for another guard to join him.

"Norton will take you back to the nursery," he told the child.

The boy's eyes widened. "Sterling, are you going to tell my father?"

Jack sighed. "I am going to put the event in my report to Rockwell. As I am required to do, my lord—as you well know."

The lad sulked. Truthfully, he slipped by the schoolroom guards with enough frequency to alarm everyone. The child was worryingly adept at timing his escapes from the watchful eye of his governess and the guards assigned to the duke's three young children.

The guard acting as Jack's support for the afternoon arrived, dressed in a footman's livery and wearing a warm coat. He chuckled when he saw Lord James and his gaze flicked to Jack. "I'll see him back to the nest."

Jack gave a quick nod, bowed to Lord James, and returned to his post. Back on that slightly elevated rise, his eyes on the top-hats, he settled in for as long as necessary. All six men remained present. Hats still bobbing. Low voices still discussing the politics of the kingdom.

Watching over the ducal family, and at times their rather extended kin, hadn't struck Jack Sterling as an especially difficult job—not when he'd first been approached by Captain Rockwell, years ago, when Jack came home from the war with France. The work had appealed to him on multiple fronts: he wouldn't have to depend on his family for a home or income, and he wouldn't have to tuck himself into an office somewhere doing work considered respectable for one born into a family from the north of great respectability but modest income.

Yet over the years, he'd found himself keeping the family safe from kidnappers, rioters, thieves, and once—so far—an assassin. He'd guarded the unsuspecting children from rough hands and unkind words. He'd stepped between the duchess and a runaway horse. He'd patrolled the duke's lands and assisted in local emergencies, be it floods, fire, or snowstorms.

He'd found purpose, post-war, which had been a necessity on several fronts.

A movement from the corner of his eye brought him into a quick turn. From the approach, he knew before looking that another guard arrived. They had been trained on how to move into one another's spheres, to avoid alarm or accidental firing of weapons. One thing the guards never did was surprise one another.

"I am to relieve you from your post," the man in deep blue livery cut like a soldier's uniform—if not for the cursed snowy cravats—said with a touch of surliness. Rollins didn't particularly like the cold. He wore a dark coat over the servant's unassuming uniform, concealing both his bulk and any weapons he held. "Rockwell wants you in his office."

Jack raised an eyebrow, gave a brief account of what he'd observed of the duke's guests, and left the garden for the nearest entrance to the castle. Once inside, coat slung over his arm, he slipped into one of the many hidden passages within the labyrinth of Clairvoir Castle.

A footman who was in truth only a footman passed him in the narrow corridor and took Jack's coat from him with a friendly remark on the weather. The servants in the household knew the duke's guards were unique. In truth, the two dozen men were the equivalent of a private militia—yet they'd often filled the dual role well enough that the true footmen, maids, butlers, and the rest, had built a camaraderie with the guards. After all, they all served the same master.

Jack and his fellow guardsmen were the human equivalent of a weapon, hidden in plain sight, ready to spring to use at a moment's notice.

The office of the head guard had the second largest room afforded to a servant, only somewhat smaller than the steward's quarters. The duke took exceeding care to ensure those responsible for the safety of his family and his lands had everything they needed.

As Jack walked into the room with its walls papered with maps, he never failed to admire it. Of course, it sometimes felt more like a field tent on the eve of battle, depending on the duke's movements and plans. On days before traveling or large parties, the guards received orders about carrying weapons and defensive positioning while they polished shoes, buckles, buttons, and sometimes combed their blasted white wigs.

Today, though, Captain Rockwell stood alone behind his desk, hands clasped behind his back, his fierce stare fixed on a piece of paper on the flat surface that held almost nothing else.

He glanced up when Jack entered and gave a small nod. "You never lollygag, Sterling. Always liked that about you."

No one beneath the captain's command would have dared to fall short of his expectations, but Jack received the compliment with a confident, "Thank you, sir."

The captain motioned to one of the stiff-backed chairs on the other side of his desk. "Sit, Sterling. You'll need at least four legs under you for the news you're about to learn."

Somewhat alarmed, though he kept the emotion reined in, Jack obeyed the order. "Is it my family, sir?" No point in delaying any ill-tidings. If it wasn't a family issue, everything else could be dealt with.

"Yes, this is about your family."

Damn.

Rockwell picked up the paper on his desk and revealed a folded, sealed missive beneath it. He read the open paper aloud.

Dear Sir,

I find myself compelled to request, with immediate effect, the release of my son, John Sterling, from his current service within the esteemed household of His Grace, the Duke of Montfort. As the nuances of social standing have recently shifted greatly in our favor, I must declare that his role as a footman no longer aligns with our family's newly elevated station. It is with great fortune and no small amount of solemnity that I have come into the inheritance of the title Earl of Benwaith. I entrust you to convey this significant change in circumstance to my son with all due haste, along with the enclosed missive bearing my new seal.

Yours, with the utmost respect,

Richard Sterling, Earl of Benwaith

Jack blinked and slowly shook his head at the awkwardly formal wording. "That's...that's impossible. I have never even heard that my father was in line for such a thing—or known anything about who held the Benwaith title before. This cannot be right."

Rockwell handed Jack the sealed letter. "Best read your father's explanation before you declare it impossible, man."

Jack's stomach twisted, and it was likely only his military training which kept him from breaking into a sweat. This wasn't right. It had to be a mistake, a jest, a ploy—

He took the letter and broke it open to find his father's handwriting and a more familiar, informal tone.

Jack,

I know you will not believe it, son, but the best of fortune has fallen upon us. Some far-flung cousin of mine died, four months back, and they have only just traced the roots of the family tree to discover I'm the closest living male heir to someone who held the title a hundred years ago. The toff who came to inform us said no one wanted the lands and title to default to the Crown, so they went to all the bother of tracking me down to our ramshackle little cottage. When you get this letter, we will be on the way to a house in London. We have a house in London! What a thing to say. I have written to all the family—your brothers and sisters are coming. Your sisters are all Ladies now! How well it sounds to call them such. Lady Mary, Lady Anne, Lady Emily. It is the very best of news. Why are not sons of earls called lords? Seems *strange. Richard will have the honorary title of Viscount. I am sorry there is nothing to offer the rest of you. But we need you here, lad. You can help us work all of this out. Come at once— leave your servant's trappings behind. It is a new world and a new start for us.*

Yours ever,

Father

Jack stared at the paper and read it over again. The nausea grew and his head felt thick with a fog of disbelief. He held the letter out to Rockwell. "This sounds more like him."

Rockwell accepted the paper and narrowed his eyes with concentration as he read. The less formal letter also came with less tidy writing. "I have heard of stranger things happening with inheritances. I suppose I had better get your pay together."

That statement startled him enough that Jack frowned. "What? Captain Rockwell, are you dismissing me? Because of *this*?" He was a fourth son. Nothing about his father's sudden change in status would truly change Jack Sterling's place in the world. He would never inherit the title; he wouldn't even be changed in address, he was still Mr. Sterling, not Lord John.

Besides, he enjoyed his work—he was good at it. He liked the routine. He liked sparring with the other guards. The pay was more than adequate, too.

The older man raised his thick graying eyebrows. "We couldn't possibly employ the son of an earl, not even in a duke's household. Perhaps especially not in a duke's household. Not only is it unprecedented to do such a thing, but it would elicit judgment from both His Grace's political rivals and his allies, once it becomes known...and it *will* become known. Things like this cannot be kept secret."

Nothing about the situation was fair. Everything about it felt like a bad dream. Jack shook his head in denial again, though it made his insides twist to speak in such a way to a man he respected and had always obeyed without question. "I have no wish to join my family in London. What would I do, lounge about drawing rooms and speak of the weather? I am a soldier. My purpose is here. Not in Society, having dull conversations."

Rockwell's jaw became hard. "Not anymore, son. Things have changed. Think of it as a battlefield promotion—perhaps not what you want, but it is necessary."

Battlefield promotions occurred when a commanding officer died, in the thick of things, and it fell to the man next in line to take charge no matter his rank. Unfortunately, Jack was familiar with the practice. He'd been young during the war with Napoleon...perhaps too young. Now, at nine-and-twenty, he faced a more complicated and less life-threatening form of promotion. A promotion in Society.

He cursed again under his breath. Military life didn't make a man's vocabulary gentler. Serving in the duke's household had cleaned up his language and his uncouth habits to the point he'd lost most of his rough ways, but this situation merited several four-letter-words.

He had no choice in the matter. He had to forfeit the only thing which had kept him sane after coming home, worn and battle-scarred at the end of the war, and instead take up a life he'd watched others live for the last six years.

The life of a noble.

Jack rose from his chair and looked Rockwell straight in the eye. "As you say, sir. There is no choice in the matter. Before I go, I wish to express my heartfelt gratitude for all you have done for me, for all you have taught me, and for the opportunity to serve alongside you to protect the safety of an honorable man and his family." It was a succinct speech. One he may have made better, if he'd had any time to prepare for such a moment.

Rockwell's solemn gaze softened somewhat. "You are one of the best men I have trained and worked with, inside this duty and the military. It has been an honor to know you, Sterling. I will order a carriage for you in the morning to take you as far as the first coaching inn. As of this moment forward, you are relieved of all duties. Say your goodbyes, son. Know that we will all miss you, sir."

Jack winced at the acknolwegement, however slight, that he now outranked the man who had commanded him during his time in the ducal household. He did not voice his discomfort as he bowed, then left the office with a heavy heart and his father's letters—both of them—clutched in his hand. He hated this feeling, one he knew well from when he'd returned home from the army. He was untethered, a kite without string, a sword which no longer knew which direction to point.

Purposeless.

Sons of earls didn't do much with themselves, unless they were the heirs, did they? They merely managed estates or tried to marry well.

He thought of his oldest brother, Richard, named after their father. Richard, now an heir to an earldom, needed to be home. But the rest of them? They all had careers...and not exactly noble careers, either.

Realization struck him hard as a hammer to the head. He stopped walking abruptly and rubbed at his temple. No one in his family knew the first thing about being part of the gentry, let alone what it meant to be peers of the realm. He'd grown up in a cottage! His mother had one maid of all work and a cook, and his father had been the one to hitch up the horses to a plow to work the land. His older sisters had married tradesmen!

None of them knew a thing about London, either—except maybe Arthur, who'd worked at the London docks until he found himself a merchant ship that needed additional crew.

Jack swore again, then bit his tongue. He'd never heard the duke swear. Not ever. And though not at all close to the duke's position, he made up his mind in that moment to model his behavior after the noble he held in highest esteem.

He looked around the corridor he stood in. Down at the rug

he'd walked across thousands of times, up at the elegant painted ceiling, around at the masterpieces hung in their gold gilt frames. He'd miss all of it.

He said his goodbye that evening in the servants' hall during dinner. His brothers-in-arms jested with him, called him a toff, a noble, along with a few less savory words reserved for the upper classes. He laughed through it, their pats on the back, their congratulations. Those were more difficult to bear.

But as he rose to go to bed, Rockwell caught him one more time. "His Grace wants to speak to you, sir," the old guard informed him. "Said to inform you before you turned in. He's in his study."

Jack straightened immediately, tension shuddering through his shoulders. There was that *sir* again. From a man he always considered his superior in all things. It rankled. "I wish you had told me before, Captain. I have no wish to keep His Grace waiting."

"Aye, I'm certain that's why he ordered me not to tell you until now." Rockwell's smile was brief but sincere. "He'd want you to enjoy your last evening, wouldn't he? Off you trot now, Mr. Sterling."

Mister instead of simply Sterling. How was he ever to bear it?

It took all his self-discipline not to actually break into a trot. Walking as efficiently and quickly as he could through the halls would have to suffice. He wished he could change back into his footmen's uniform, but he'd taken it off before dinner in favor of his own clothing.

He passed one of the other men outside the library and study and nodded.

The man gave him a grin. "Lucky devil, aren't you? He said to tell you to knock."

Though tempted to respond to the remark, Jack went through the library without saying a word. The familiar scents of rich tobacco, books, and leather offered him paltry comfort. He came to the door disguised as shelves and knocked on the wooden frame.

"Enter," came the duke's voice.

Jack entered the duke's study—a room he'd stood in many times to brief His Grace about matters, or to stand guard during delicate moments. He found the duke inside, sitting before the hearth with a book in hand.

The duke stood when Jack walked in—a thing the man had never done before—and gave a shallow bow. "Mr. John Sterling. Thank you for coming."

Everything within Jack revolted at the idea of the duke acknowledging him this way—as the son of a peer rather than a soldier. He bowed more deeply. "Your Grace. You have been informed of my change in circumstances."

"Indeed." His Grace gestured to the chair across the hearth from his own. "I must insist that you sit. For a moment, at least."

Jack immediately hated it. Sitting in the presence of a duke? Had His Grace asked rather than commanded, Jack would've politely refused. As it was, his movements were stiff, his legs like iron, his knees bending reluctantly.

He sat. Unhappily.

"Thank you, Your Grace. May I be of service to you in some way?" The question was habitual, he couldn't hold it back.

The duke smiled at him almost fondly. "I cannot count the number of ways in which you have already served my family, Mr. Sterling. You have protected them many times. You have shepherded my children when they were on their worst behavior, and you have suffered the indignities of some of my guests when they thought to abuse a common servant."

A memory of a specific lady asking him to model for a painting exercise came to mind, but he quickly dismissed it. That certainly hadn't fallen under mistreatment.

"You have done your duty with honor and dignity. I have

come to trust your judgment, along with your abilities. I have not invited you here to ask more of you, sir. Instead, I mean to offer my services to you."

Immediately, Jack was on his feet again. "Please Your Grace, that is not necessary—"

"No, I shall brook no objections," declared the duke, his hands thoughtfully steepled before him, his eyes twinkling with good humor. "Your service has been marked by steadfast loyalty and unwavering honor, qualities which bespeak a man of great virtue—uncommon qualities. Now you and your family ascend to a more distinguished station within Society. Such transitions are fraught with both opportunity and peril."

Here the duke's brows drew together, his expression changing to one with more seriousness. "You will find yourselves in need of allies, of friends well-versed in the intricacies of our world—your new world. It is with both pleasure and purpose that I offer my support and goodwill to guide you through this labyrinth. My friendship. You, who are adept at discerning the subtleties of human nature, must surely appreciate the value of forming the right alliances swiftly—and let us not disregard the less savory characters, those who might seek to exploit your family's newfound prominence. It is in our mutual interest to shield your good fortune from such predations."

Jack's heart hammered and his mind sorted through the formality of the duke's words. He relaxed. The gesture was more than benevolent. It was not sympathy; it was strategic. And Jack always appreciated a good strategy.

Taking a moment to collect his thoughts, Jack's posture remained rigid with military precision. Finally he spoke, his voice steady and reserved, despite his inner turmoil. "Your Grace, I am...overwhelmed by your generous offer. To say I am grateful would scarcely cover the breadth of my appreciation. You have always been a commander worth serving—wise and just. I had imagined continuing in your service, safeguarding the legacy you are building here. This...this new role, it is not one I had ever envisioned for myself."

He paused, looking towards the hearth, where flames danced like the thoughts flickering across his mind.

"However, I understand the importance of strategy, both on the battlefield and within the walls of Society. Your guidance would be invaluable, and frankly, necessary for my family as we navigate this unfamiliar terrain. I accept your offer with a hope that I can continue to give you my loyalty and aid where it is needed."

Jack's gaze met the duke's, a silent acknowledgment of the shift in their relationship. "I only ask for patience, Your Grace, as my family learns to walk this unexpected path. This will be entirely new to them, in every way conceivable. I would not have your reputation sullied should we fail to rise to the occasion. And perhaps...perhaps I can help them, though I feel like little more than a soldier borrowing a noble's cloak to wear."

The duke's warm smile reappeared. "Good man." He rose from his chair. "I will see to it that my family calls upon yours at the earliest possible moment, and there will be invitations from Her Grace to your mother and sisters when we return to London ourselves."

That would not be for some time, Jack knew. The duke's eldest son and his wife were due to have a child, their first and the possible future heir of the dukedom, in two months' time. The whole family planned to remain at the castle until that event occurred.

"Lord Dunmore will arrive in London sooner than my household. I already dispatched a message to his home in Town, along with a few other men I trust to make introductions to your father." Dunmore, Teague Frost, was brother to the duke's expectant daughter-in-law, and a close friend to the duke himself.

Jack bowed. "Thank you, Your Grace."

"You had best get your rest, I understand you leave early in the morning. The road to London can be miserable this time of year. I hope your journey is swift and safe. Until we meet again, Mr. Sterling."

Taking his leave like a gentleman instead of a footman or soldier proved difficult, and Jack had to clench his jaw to get through it. Everything in his life had changed in the space of a single day. He'd hoped a dozen times or more that it was all a dream, yet the knot of worry in his stomach and the weighty burden of his father's two letters in his pocket assured him every moment that this was all too real.

In the space of a few hours, his life changed forever. His purpose gone, he'd have to rededicate his life to something new. He hoped he found it soon. There was nothing he loathed more than feeling directionless.

CHAPTER 2

FEBRUARY 4, 1822

Lady Juniper Amberton woke to a maid politely standing at her bedside with a lamp in hand, whispering, "My lady? Lady Juniper? It is time to dress for dinner."

Perhaps taking a nap immediately after arriving at her brother-in-law's townhouse hadn't been a perfect plan. Though she had executed it without the slightest guilt, Juniper woke completely disoriented.

Blinking groggily, Juniper sat up and her novel tumbled from her bedding to the floor. The maid picked it up and handed it back to her, not even glancing at the novel's spine for the title.

"Oh, thank you. How—how much time do I have until dinner?"

"Half an hour, my lady." The maid bustled away and turned up a gas lamp, then went about lighting a few candles, too. February in London was a gloomy, dark month.

Juniper slid out of the sheets, peering after the young woman in the lessening darkness. "I'm sorry—what was your name?

"Hettie, my lady. I will be attending to both Lady Betony

and you during your stay. My mother is the cook here, and my brother, Henry, is one of the footmen."

Juniper nodded blearily and made her way to the dressing table. "Hettie. Hettie."

When she'd finally walked through the doors to her brother-in-law's London townhouse, she'd felt like falling to her knees in gratitude. They'd traveled several days from Ireland's coast to London's bustling streets: coach to ferry, then a coach again, and stops along the way to London, with five other people in the same vehicle as herself.

No one had been demanding or annoying, but the complete lack of privacy for a week of travel had made her itch, body and soul. Although her brother-in-law Teague Frost, Lord Dunmore, had ensured they stopped at the most comfortable inns and houses of friends, she'd shared a room with at least her younger sister every evening.

Thoughts of her sister prompted Juniper to ask, "Is my sister ready?"

"Indeed, my lady. The baroness instructed me to allow you to sleep as long as possible." Hettie looked over Juniper and gave a slow nod. "Your hair is dark, which means it will be forgiving, but it's also slightly mussed from your sleep. We will smooth out the rough bits. The baroness also wished me to inform you that tonight is informal, so you ought to dress comfortably. Your trunks arrived yesterday, so I have already prepared a few gowns for you."

"Whichever you think best will be fine," Juniper said as she yawned. "Goodness. One would think I hadn't slept at all—but it's been hours."

"Indeed, my lady. Travel will do that to a person." Hettie bustled about the room, retrieving things from the wardrobe and helping Juniper with a gentle efficiency the lady immediately liked. As promised, the maid smoothed out the rough places in

Juniper's coiffeur after settling a simple blue evening gown upon her frame.

"I haven't the slightest idea where I am supposed to go." Juniper met the maid's eyes in the looking glass.

"Lady Betony is waiting, and I believe she has already had a tour of the house."

Nodding, she completely submitted herself to the maid's ministrations. Hettie had her ready for dinner in quick order and promised to be waiting when Juniper returned for the evening. As always, Juniper plucked a novel from her stack of favorite stories to carry with her. Her brother's wife, Fanny, had disapproved of such things, but Teague and Ivy never minded in the least.

Betony was indeed waiting, right outside of Juniper's door, and wore her large smile and sparkling eyes beautifully. Fiona, the eleven-year-old sister of the baron, stood with her dressed for bed, it appeared, with a robe over her nightgown.

Betony, the youngest of the three Amberton sisters, was speaking with animation to the girl. "Your tour was wonderful, Fi, but I absolutely insist on you giving me all the best secrets of the house later. You will know all the best corners and hidden places, I think, and the sneakiest routes to the pantry and garden."

Fiona, a sprightly girl with a particularly impish view of the world, tossed her head of dark curls. "You needn't be sneaky in the slightest. Our cook here adores giving out sweets. I will introduce you first thing tomorrow, and once she knows your favorite treats she will make certain to have them on hand." The girl beamed up at Juniper. "You missed my first tour during your nap. Was your rest nice, at least?"

"It was lovely, yes. And it sounds as though I must be part of tomorrow's expedition, if you will have me."

"Of course," Fiona said with wide eyes. "You both are practically my sisters now. I will show you everything." She wrinkled her nose. "I have to go to bed now. I really don't think it's fair. Our first dinner back ought to be a family dinner. Not a grown-ups-only dinner."

"Teague wanted Ivy to practice right away," Betony said with a good-natured shrug. "You know how the two of them are about each other."

The three of them exchanged grins.

The happy couple had been married since September and their small acts of affection had become a normal sight. It seemed every time the two stood near one another, Teague found one reason or another to show his wife his adoration. Anyone watching could easily see his love for her, whether it was when he wrapped his arm around her waist or brushed a kiss to her temple.

Juniper cleared her throat, a smile on her lips. "I am certain we will have an informal family dinner soon and you will join us then—if only to give you the practice you need, Fi."

"I know." Fiona rolled her eyes, then gave a curtsy. "Good night then, sisters. Enjoy your evening."

As Fiona left, Betony turned her full attention to Juniper. "Is this not a lovely house? Though I suppose you have only seen your room. And what did you think of Hettie? She is so quiet, I felt almost like a ghost waited upon me."

"I rather like her." Juniper reached out to straighten the clasp of Betony's necklace. "She has a calming way about her."

"You two will get along then." Betony glanced at the book in Juniper's hand. "And which companion do you have with you this evening? That is a rather familiar purple cover."

Juniper held the spine of the book toward her sister. *The Bandit of Bleakhollow* was a favorite of hers. She owned every book written by the author, who had revealed his true name but a few years ago. Erasmus Grey was more popular now than he'd been even five years before, one of the few gentlemen authors in the genre that Juniper liked.

Betony shivered. "Why you insist on reading stories with bandits and ghosts, I will never know. There must be pleasanter books."

"I like the anticipation of things going horribly wrong," Juniper said with a grin, "and then turning out all right in the end."

Her sister rolled her eyes before she took Juniper's arm and tugged her down the corridor. "You would not like it if such was your lot in life."

She started chatting away at once, telling Juniper all about the house, her favorite rooms, where she hoped they would spend their time, all about the music room, the garden, the kitchens, and more things that Juniper couldn't possibly remember until she saw it all for herself. Still, she didn't regret her nap. She had ages to get to know the house, but her mind had needed to reestablish some semblance of calm.

Joining the others in the drawing room, the sisters realized they were the last to enter, yet no one seemed in any great hurry to go through to the dining room. The dowager baroness sat near the fire, speaking to her son, while their sister Ivy sorted through letters at a small writing desk. She looked up as they entered and grinned at them both.

"It seems I mistook the time for dinner. We are all early." Ivy appeared completely at ease over a mistake that once would have rattled her to the point of being over apologetic. "You both look livelier than when we all parted."

"I am completely refreshed," Betony said as she stepped to the hearth. "Lady Dunmore, Fiona gives the most enthusiastic tours. I felt I was on an adventure this afternoon."

"She has a delightful imagination, doesn't she?" Lady Dunmore seemed particularly pleased.

"Oh, heavens." Ivy's quiet exclamation drew Juniper's attention away from their third sister's conversation. "The duchess's letter is full of surprises."

"Is something wrong?" Juniper leaned closer. "There isn't anything the matter with Isleen? Or the baby?"

"No, nothing like that. They are still waiting for the babe to enter the world. Everything is fine there," Ivy hastily reassured Juniper. "There is some wholly unexpected news, and it is surprising. Quite surprising." Ivy looked up at Juniper with wide eyes. When she spoke again, she raised her voice for everyone to hear. "Her Grace writes to update us on Isleen's health, gives a list of events she hopes we will attend in her stead, and shares the most interesting turn of events. Do any of you remember that footman, Sterling? He was often assigned to look after the young ladies or the children at the castle. A well-mannered fellow."

Warmth instantly flushed into Juniper's cheeks. With all eyes on Ivy, however, she doubted anyone noticed. At least, she hoped not.

"Oh, yes." Betony perked up brightly. "We painted him. Remember, Juniper?"

She remembered Sterling quite well. She'd kept the water-color portrait she'd done of him, too, even though it wasn't her best work. Every time she looked at it, Juniper imagined she could hear his deep voice, sense the aura of protection that he bore, feel the security his mere presence offered.

Thinking of Sterling that way made her honestly wonder if she ought to put aside her Gothic novels for at least a few weeks and read something factual and dry. The man had fulfilled his duty, nothing more. For a lady of her birth to admire or fantasize about him in any way was unbecoming, inappropriate, and highly dishonorable. An earl's daughter had no business daydreaming about a footman, even if he was part of the Duke of Montfort's respected private militia.

Ivy tapped the letter on her writing desk. "The duchess says his family has inherited a title. His father is an earl now, and

Sterling—Mr. John Sterling, I should say—is here in London with them."

Juniper's knees weakened, leaning her hip against the writing desk for at least some small measure of stability. Her mouth went dry and her heart hammered loudly in her ears.

What? That couldn't possibly be true. She'd slipped into a daydream. Her novels had finally overcome her soundness of mind.

She put *The Bandit of Bleakhollow* down.

"An interesting shift in fortune. I had a letter from the duke about it, I meant to tell all of you," Teague said from across the room, sounding amused rather than shocked. "It is quite the change to go from servant to gentleman, soldier to noble."

That was all he had to say on the matter? Juniper had questions. Dozens of them. She looked down at Ivy and her eyes darted to the letter, but despite the duchess's neatness of hand, reading upside down was impossible with her thoughts swimming like deranged tadpoles.

"Quite." Ivy lifted the letter closer and read aloud, "'It is the wish of His Grace that our family and our closest friends make an effort to welcome Lord Benwaith—that's Sterling's father—and his family into their new position in Society.' How interesting. Do you think it is for the guard's sake that Their Graces wish for such a thing?"

"He has risked his life for their safety on several occasions," Teague said, perhaps privy to more information than the rest of them due to his sister's role as wife to the duke's heir. "I liked him well enough. The duke's letter mentioned the same desire. I see no trouble with following through on Her Grace's suggestion—I will call on his father tomorrow, in fact. It will take but a moment to learn the address from one of the clubs."

Ivy waved the letter in the air. "Oh, the duchess included it in the letter. When you pay your call, you must invite the whole family to dinner, as soon as possible."

Juniper found enough fortitude to speak, at last. "H-How kind of you, Ivy. That will be a lovely way to get to know them."

The son of an earl. Sterling was now *the son of an earl*. And she, the daughter and sister of one. They were now equals in rank, if nothing else. The tall, handsome, dark-haired, blue-eyed soldier who'd existed like a shadow on the edge of her awareness for an entire summer would enter her home as her social peer. And she could speak to him without worry of saying something that would cross an invisible line between their classes. He'd not need to confine his responses to those of a respectful and distant servant, either.

An *actual conversation* might occur.

She had to bite the insides of her cheek to keep from grinning at this change in his fortune—and hers.

"I wonder if they feel like they are living a fairy tale," Betony remarked from where she sat, eyes glowing.

Teague's mother shook her head and spoke in her thickly accented English. "Let us hope not, dearheart. For as much as we may enjoy the happy parts of such tales, there is always much darkness to pass through or villains to thwart before one finds their happy ending."

"New blood in an old title is always looked on with suspicion." Teague tapped his fingers along the mantel. "And it brings out the predators of the *ton*. There will be many who will seek to benefit from a stranger's good fortune. I hope Sterling's father is as level-headed and stoic as his son."

For the sake of the former guardsman, Juniper hoped so, too. She'd been at the mercy of the nobility at home and in public. Her brother's wife, Fanny, had come into their lives as a physical manifestation of snobbery and prejudice. If Fanny disapproved of a book, an event, a person, those things were kept far from the Amberton sisters—or ripped away from them. If Fanny saw opportunity for herself or the family's reputation in obtaining an introduction or a fashionable item, she pursued it relentlessly. And as a countess, she had power and influence among a large circle of other women. Her likes and dislikes trickled through her network and came back to her, intensified and pricklier than before.

With people like Fanny in the upper classes, in the peerage, Sterling's family navigated nothing short of a medieval gauntlet of harsh words, cutting opinions, and precarious reputations. The pitfalls of Society would be twice as dangerous for them as it was for someone like Juniper.

Her initial shock and excitement at the news of Sterling's elevation transformed to worry. He and his family would need all the help they could find.

Perhaps even Juniper's.

CHAPTER 3

J ack Sterling counted backward from twenty to calm himself. He'd tried counting backward from ten, at first, but never achieved sufficient equilibrium by the time he came to 'one' for the counting to be effective. Twenty seemed the better number to try in this particular circumstance. Twenty, nineteen, eighteen, seventeen—

"But who is Lord Dunmore?" his father asked, staring at the letter he held with narrowed eyes. They were in the study of the family's inherited townhouse: a fine study, though thirty or forty years marked the furniture as out of date, and the books on the shelves were likely all out of print. Not a modern author existed among them.

Emily, the youngest and only unmarried sister Sterling possessed, stood next to her father's desk. She picked up his spectacles and handed them to him. "Here, Papa. It is all explained in the note. Put your spectacles on." At five-and-twenty, Emily ought to have found herself happily married and seeing to her own little family's needs, yet their parents had never minded the idea of keeping her close.

Now, Jack hoped, she'd at least benefit from their rise in

station by finding a man she deemed worthy of her hand. Miss Sterling, a poor man's daughter, would never fare so well as Lady Emily.

Their father, now styled Lord Benwaith, perched the spectacles on the end of his nose and continued glowering at the expensive stationery in his hand. "An Irish baron. House of Lords. Friend to the Duke of Montfort." He snorted. "Why do all the duke's friends keep calling on us?"

Jack had to interrupt his counting. "His Grace has bestowed on our family a favor, Father, by telling people of the highest honor and rank to pay visits to us. Such notice will put all of us in a better position. We will be invited to the best clubs, parties, and events—Mother, my sisters-in-law, and Emily will all receive calls from ladies of importance. The duke is paving the way for our family's success."

With a grumble, his father put the letter down again. "It's all a lot of stuff and nonsense—pretense! At home, I knew Benjamin Greers was my friend because he'd loan me the use of his good mule and send over a barrel of cider at the end of every harvest. I was his friend because I loaned him my best dog and gave him a share of the winter pig."

Perhaps Jack should start counting down from fifty next time.

As though she sensed her brother's patience wore thin, Emily gave her father a soothing pat on the shoulder. "There we traded possessions as favors and tokens of friendship. Here, people trade notice. Visits. Invitations. It is the same thing, Papa. Lord Dunmore will visit us here, and then we will visit his family. It is the visits that build relationships."

Sterling gave her a grateful glance and she grinned at him. Truly, of the family, she seemed the most suited to their change in fortune. Emily had always been a pleasant child. Jack, only four years her senior, knew that much about her. He'd gone away to war when she'd started to sprout into young woman-hood, and had rarely ever returned home.

Honestly, he looked forward to coming to know his sister better. The two of them needed to join forces to keep everyone else from causing an uproar—or worse, a scandal.

"He will arrive soon, Papa," Emily added, picking up a stack of books from the desk and returning them to their places on the shelves. "I will see that Mama, Katherine, and Susan are well. Our new gowns arrive from the seamstress today, so be certain to compliment all of us when you see us at dinner."

Their father tutted, allowed her to kiss his cheek, then sank into his chair when she left. "If Emily is the only one who bene-fits from this kerfuffle, I will be mighty pleased."

Jack nodded his agreement, then added, "Everyone is bene-fitting, Father. My sisters who are not here now have generous annuities so their families will want for nothing. Richard is a viscount. George and his family have a house and land. If we ever track down Arthur, he will have the option to invest in his own merchant vessel rather than act as first mate. Emily has a dowry that ensures her happiness. All is well."

"And what of you?" his father asked, raising bushy white eyebrows. He needed to find a barber but had yet to concede such a thing, despite Jack and Emily's insistence. "Here you have been, shepherding all of us about, nipping and growling like a collie, yet you seem remarkably displeased with the whole situation."

"I am not displeased," Jack countered, turning to pace to the window, looking down at the street. A carriage had arrived bearing the crest of the Dunmore Barony. "I am..." He tried to find the right word for it. "Resigned, to my obligation as a member of this family."

His father chuckled. "Displeased."

Jack smirked and shook his head. "The nobility will devour us,

Father, unless we make a good showing. Even if you would rather return to the cottage and the farm, Richard needs you here to help him build something of the earldom. Richard's children need to hold their heads up in Society, to be on level with their peers."

"And dear Emily," the unready earl added quietly. "She can have a good life. Better than anything the rest of us have dreamed."

"If she makes an advantageous marriage, she will find happiness and security the likes of which no gentleman farmer could ever provide," Jack said with a frown out the window. "Her children need never know want. The world will be open for their exploration, their choice in what they do with their lives."

"Unlike what my own children went through," his father said, voice quiet in the stillness of the room.

Jack looked up at his father. "We have not turned out so terribly. My choice suited me, as the others' have suited them."

"Liked going off to war as a boy, did you?" his father asked, tone somewhat gruff—yet Jack didn't miss the regret in his father's gaze, even turned as it was toward the surface of the desk.

"I have appreciated growing into the man I am," Jack said, no less solemn for his father's display of feeling. "And I did have a choice, Father. One I do not regret. I merely want more— something different, for Emily and for my future nieces and nephews."

"As do I." His father heaved a sigh. "I suppose that means we keep putting our best foot forward."

Nodding his agreement, Jack left the window to stand beside his father at the same moment a footman opened the door to announce the arrival of their guest. The family had agreed that Jack, with his close observation and understanding of the noble classes, would take lead in the unfamiliar matters whenever possible. Leaving his father and brothers to learn more of their station and their duties from land and estate agents, lawyers, and those who managed the previous earl's vast wealth and holdings.

Jack, therefore, often stepped into the role of advisor. Acting as guide for his family as well as protector.

"My lord, Lord Dunmore to see you."

The earl stood and tucked his hands behind his back as the Irish baron entered. Teague Frost, Lord Dunmore, immediately put on a friendly grin after his bow. Jack almost relaxed. He was familiar with the somewhat informal and optimistic Irishman from the man's time visiting Castle Clairvoir.

As a member of the duke's staff, Jack had liked Dunmore at once. The man was honorable, kind to a fault, and not nearly as stuffy or demanding as some of the duke's other guests. Given that Dunmore's sister had married into the family, the man had a more comfortable place at Clairvoir, too, and was a more frequent visitor.

After Jack made the introductions required, his father gestured to one of the chairs on the other side of his desk. "Please, Lord Dunmore, make yourself comfortable. My son has told me little enough about you, though I know you have his good opinion."

Dunmore settled into the chair with a wide grin. "Mr. Sterling is too kind. I think I must have annoyed him on more than one occasion in his past life." He appeared completely at ease as he sent an amused glance toward Jack. "How open will you be about your former place as the duke's guard? You will likely find yourself in polite company with many who you knew and served while in that capacity."

"I have not given it much thought," Jack admitted, glancing at his father. It was the truth. He'd been too busy preparing his family for what was to come to focus on any awkwardness his former occupation might bring. Still, he continued with some confidence, "I doubt many of them will have bothered to remember me. Most thought me a mere footman. Who among the upper ranks bothers to know a servant's name, let alone his face?"

His father chuckled. "It is almost as though you have been a spy all these years, gathering information on behavior and persons of interest, all to our benefit now." He sighed and gave Dunmore a measured look. "You are the first who has openly spoken of Jack's former work, though you are not the first sent to us through the duke's good graces."

"Likely the others have better manners than I do," Dunmore quipped, his grin widening. "I see no need to pretend I haven't met Mr. Sterling before. I benefitted from his astute observations. While all of this must seem something of a dream, I have seen reversals in fortune before—in both directions. It is imperative that you have allies, from the beginning, to ease your way into a Society that can be as cruel as it is exclusive. I know this from personal experience."

"And you will be one such ally?" Jack asked as his father remained silent and thoughtful.

"Absolutely." Dunmore tapped the arm of the chair. "My family is prepared to stand by you and assist in whatever way we can. My wife, Lady Dunmore, remembers you fondly, Mr. Sterling—as do our sisters, hers and my own. If there is anything we can do, you have but to ask it. To begin with, Lady Dunmore and I request your family join ours for dinner. As soon as you can, in fact."

Jack had watched over Lady Dunmore, formerly Lady Ivy, and her sisters Ladies Juniper and Betony, while they stayed with the duke. The sisters had been as fascinating as they were entertaining, and he'd come to rather like the three of them.

That is, like them as much as a mere guardsman could. Of course.

Lord Benwaith relaxed. "There are eight of us that trot around together. I hope that will not put the baroness out?"

"Not in the least. I look forward to meeting the rest of your family." He glanced from father to son. "Have either of you found a club to your liking yet? I imagine you have been invited to preview a few by now. I am a member at Brooks's. I am on my way there next. Would either of you, or other gentlemen in the household, wish to join me?"

Jack glanced at his father, who visibly withered at the idea of leaving the house. Yet one shouldn't reject invitations by peers, even if they were as accommodating as Lord Dunmore. It fell to him to make the decision, and his military training assisted him to make it in an instant. "I wouldn't mind joining you, if you can do without me for a time, Father?"

"I think we will manage not to burn the house down in your absence," his father said with a dry smile. They both knew Jack had put out several metaphorical fires in the weeks since he'd arrived from Clairvoir. No one had prepared his family for living in a house which needed more than a dozen servants to keep it running. The housekeeper had quit in a rage the day before he arrived, the butler had threatened to do the same, the maids were confused by the vague instructions the new countess gave them, and the cook tried to spend double the allotted budget for the kitchens to pocket half the funds for himself—though not for long.

Were all nobles cheated so swiftly by their servants?

"Excellent." Dunmore took his leave of Lord Benwaith and Jack followed him out of the house and into his waiting carriage. The moment the door of the conveyance closed behind him, Dunmore folded his arms and gave Jack a solemn look.

The frank appraisal made Jack stiffen, his posture so straight his back did not touch the seat cushion behind him. "You look as though you wish to say something, Lord Dunmore."

"Several somethings. I arrived last evening, and it only took a few pointed questions this morning to hear handfuls of rumors about your family. I am going to be blunt, Sterling, because I believe you are a man who appreciates plain-speaking." He gave a slight shake of his head. "Your family needs help, and a lot of it, if they are going to survive this elevation, let alone this Season."

Nothing about the statement held cruelty, and the sheer honesty of it startled a laugh from the former guard. "I must agree."

"Did one of the women in your household truly try to hang laundry in the garden?" Dunmore winced in sympathy. "That must be a gross over-exaggeration."

"She hung a dress out from her window, which overlooked the garden." Jack hadn't seen it but had been informed by a scandalized member of the staff. "Rinsed out a spot. Thought it would be faster to go about things that way rather than send it out to the laundress." He wanted to groan and drop his face in his hands, but he stayed upright and kept his face a mask of calm. "They are not used to this. Nor am I, in all honesty. But we are doing our best."

He'd hired a governess to act the part of lady's companion to his mother and social instructor to his sister and sisters-in-law. The woman had accepted the generous salary in return for her slightly unorthodox duties. He'd also found a housekeeper with thirty years of experience in a former military commander's home. He'd given the woman the control of a general on the battlefield, and she'd had the rest of the staff in hand in less than two days, to everyone's mutual relief.

But there was still much to do—many mistakes that could be made.

Lord Dunmore appeared thoughtful a moment, his fingers tapping on the seat beside him as the carriage made its way over cobbled streets. "I want to assist you, Mr. Sterling. You were there when my sister and Farleigh were in danger. You have watched over Fiona, kept her and Lord James from harming themselves with their less-than-safe flights of fancy. You are a good man. Even had the Duke of Montfort not suggested it, I would offer you my friendship. Let me help you."

The offer pricked at Jack's pride, but his family needed people like Dunmore. The women in his family needed the friendship the ladies of Dunmore's house would supply. Despite being a younger son, he was the only one present. Jack held the weight of the household on his shoulders.

The baroness and her sisters understood better than most the importance of keeping up appearances, a thing he had heard them bemoan on more than one occasion when he served as little more than a protective shadow.

"I accept your offer, your lordship. With gratitude." Jack bowed his head slightly.

"Then no more 'lording' me. Dunmore is good enough, in company and out of it."

"Then I prefer Jack." He sighed. "Though I find it easier to answer to 'Sterling' than what I was christened with, I think those days are over." He would forever be Mr. Sterling now, and when in company with his brothers Mr. *John* Sterling, or Mr. John.

"I imagine years of service in the military and as a member of the duke's rather unique household would make that the more familiar thing to answer to." Dunmore grinned and folded his arms, leaning back. "We will get you through the ensuing battles of Society, Jack Sterling. Eventually, we will win your family the war, too."

Jack had every hope that was the truth, even though he didn't think his troops—his family—ready yet for any kind of enemy engagement. With the allies the Duke of Montfort kept sending his way, it seemed less impossible than it had in the beginning.

Juniper paced for the better part of the morning. She'd seen her brother-in-law off on his visit to Lord Benwaith and she'd tried to read in the morning room that faced east. She had a delicious Gothic novel in her hands, with a highwayman and a young lady who needed saving, trapped by a wicked uncle in a dilapidated cottage, yet she'd been unable to focus.

All she'd thought of, all morning long, was the former guardsman. What would Teague find when he met Sterling on more equal footing? Would the stoic guard have turned into a horrid rake, like the men of her favorite novels did when their fortunes turned? Or would he have softened and become a gentleman of sophistication overnight?

She'd dared to say such a thing to Betony, while her younger sister carefully mended a beadwork reticule.

Betony had snorted. "This is why I do not read your sort of novels. I would be up every night fearing an evil uncle come to take me away."

"Life is not in the least like novels, of course." Juniper cut her sister a wry look. "As often as I have heard people say that real events and true stories inspire fictional tales, I doubt there are dozens of evil uncles holding hundreds of unfortunate and morally perfect orphans in crumbling towers throughout England."

Betony's smile turned into a crooked smirk. "In Scotland, perhaps, but not England."

Juniper paused in her pacing as she laughed at that, just as Ivy walked in hand-in-hand with Fiona. "Look who I have kidnapped from her governess!"

Betony and Juniper exchanged a quick glance and both burst into a fit of giggles. "No cruel uncles, then, merely lovely baronesses."

"What are you talking about?" Fiona asked, dark eyebrows raised at them before she looked at Ivy.

Clearing her throat, Juniper answered with amusement, "Novels, mostly. How are you doing today, Fi?"

"I am well enough," the girl said, her Irish lilt somewhat fainter than her older brother's and certainly less than her mother's. "Despite being kidnapped." She released Ivy's hand and went to study Betony's work. "I cannot stand to work with such tiny things as the beads you use, but it's awfully pretty."

"Thank you. If you like, I will bead a reticule for you." Betony pointed to her box of tiny compartments, each little box full of sparkling glass beads of all colors. "Tell me your favorite colors."

While the two of them discussed colors and beading, Ivy settled on a couch and patted the cushion for Juniper to join her. "I hear you were awake and up to see my husband off this morning. Is something troubling you? Normally, you lay abed as long as you can. *Reading*." Her playful words, accompanied by a tilt to her head, told Juniper her sister sensed something amiss. Ivy's curiosity was always fully pursued of late, thanks to the encouragement of her new husband.

Juniper settled onto the couch and folded her hands in her lap, pulling her posture and expression from every lesson about 'proper ladies' their overly concerned sister-in-law used to give them.

"I wanted to wish him well before he went to meet with the new Lord Benwaith and his family, that is all. Though I cannot think of a man better suited to putting others at ease than Teague, I thought he might appreciate a little encouragement."

"Why the interest in that family?" Ivy's eyebrows pulled together softly, not fully contracting to make the line between them appear. This matter appeared to be of light interest to her, thank goodness. "Besides the fact that we will all do our part, should they allow us, to help them grow accustomed to the dangerous topography of our Society, all its plains and pitfalls."

Tightening her grip on her own hands, Juniper adopted an

unconcerned tone. "It is something one rarely hears of, is all. An entire family elevated at once, unexpected by anyone including themselves, to such a position. It is the stuff of fiction. Of my novels."

"I suppose." Ivy reached down to the basket beside the couch. She'd left her sewing things there earlier, and she picked up an embroidery hoop already occupied by a swath of deep green material. "Though these are real people, Juniper. Not characters in a work of fiction. I do hope you will curb your imagination when it comes time to meet them, and assist where we can, without looking for anything untoward in their past or present."

"Untoward?" Juniper repeated with raised eyebrows. "Oh. Like wives in attics or pirates in cellars, wicked uncles and decrepit towers. Those sorts of things?"

Ivy choked on a laugh and narrowed her eyes playfully at her sister. "Is that where your flights of fancy immediately go? No, dear. I was thinking more about the two single members of the family. It is a good thing so many of Lord Benwaith's children are already wed. Two sons and two daughters, the duke's letter informed Teague, already with their own spouses and homes. But he still has two unmarried sons, the youngest of our acquaintance the former guardsman, and a daughter near my age, who will now be swarmed with suitors."

An immediate poke of disappointment assailed Juniper's heart, trying to pop her pleasant daydreams of Sterling as a sewing needle popped a soap bubble. She hadn't given that situation much thought—that was, she had thought greatly of him, but not of all the other young ladies who would, as her sister said, soon swarm.

She grimaced. "Oh. Suitors. You wish me to avoid...what? Matchmaking?"

"I wish you to avoid spectating." Ivy shook her head a little. "*Gossiping*. Romance is all well and good for one to eavesdrop upon within a novel, but in real life it is a shame so many study and dissect people's relationships as though they have a right to. I am grateful beyond words that Teague and I had the chance to court and fall in love away from the eyes of Society." She shuddered. "They will already be watched by many. Be a friend. Do not contribute to or pass on suppositions about their prospects. That is all I wish to suggest."

Juniper let her gaze trail away to the window letting in the late-morning sunlight. "I will avoid romanticizing what will surely be a trial for them." And for her, she supposed, as she watched an imaginary Mr. John Sterling navigate ballrooms full of ladies, all eyes on him, as both their newest and most intriguing option for ensnaring a husband.

He was new to their set, new to London, and entirely too handsome to be ignored. Juniper's visions of him surrounded by elegant ladies in bright gowns was likely to come true.

Blast.

Why hadn't she considered there would be competition for his attention? And when, precisely, had she decided that he was what she most wanted? Not merely to reacquaint herself with him, but to—for lack of a better term—set her cap for him?

Her heart gave a stutter at the realization.

"When we meet the whole family for dinner," Ivy said, tone no longer one of concern, "we will know how best to help them, I am certain. At that point, we will likely need all the ideas you can spare for the best way to make them comfortable. I hope you are up for that challenge, Juniper."

"So do I." Among other things.

CHAPTER 4

"Father, you simply cannot wear your daytime clothing to dinner." Jack felt the twitch in his eye an instant before it moved. "You must listen to your valet. Tobbs has your best interests at heart, he knows what is and is not appropriate for every given situation."

"It's a waste of time, changing clothes for every activity," his father, Lord Benwaith, looked somewhat mutinous. "Not to mention a waste of good cloth. That tailor we went to will be richer than the king himself with the coin we paid him."

Jack gritted his teeth and looked to the rest of his family. All of them had gathered in the drawing room so he could look them over before leaving for the dinner at Lord Dunmore's London house. His mother, his eldest brother's wife, his second-eldest brother's wife, and his only unmarried sister Emily were well-turned out in their frocks and fripperies. His two brothers appeared stiff and uncomfortable in their formal evening wear, but at least they looked the part of gentlemen.

And then there was the new earl himself.

"Someone else please explain this to Father," he said, his

temples throbbing with an oncoming headache. "I will check on the status of the carriages."

There were too many of them to take one carriage, so he'd had to send word to a stable to hire out another for the evening. The baron's family had no idea the chaos about to descend upon them, but Jack could hardly do anything to stop it.

Eight adults, with the barest understanding of London Society's expectations, about to dine with a baron. After a mere week with them in their newly inherited townhouse, Jack had pleaded with his father to take them all back to the country house. They were not ready for London, not ready for the *haute ton*—not ready for any of it.

Jack's mother had wept and declared that he was ashamed of his family. His father had turned purple with indignation. His older brothers present, Richard and George, had started teasing about their younger brother thinking they were dunces, and Emily had looked at everyone with the wide eyes of a frightened doe.

And so Jack stormed down the steps of the house and stood before the carriages, barely seeing them.

All their remonstrances together had meant they still remained in London, a full month later, little better than they had been before. All Jack had managed was to bring a governess into the house to act as a genteel tutor to his mother, sister, and sisters-in-law.

Though his breath made puffs of steam appear in the air, he didn't feel the cold. His thoughts were too preoccupied to notice the weather, even if it made his skin prickle.

The men could be idiots if they wished, but Jack wouldn't stand for the women in their family to go unprepared into the claws of Society's matrons. They had reputations to lose now.

How often had he seen even the duke's family express concern over rumor and gossip? If a ducal family didn't have immunity to such things, his family was especially vulnerable.

He'd witnessed the harshness of the matrons on several occasions; most recently, when the very ladies he would see that evening had been subjected to the harsh dictates of their sister-in-law. Lady Dunmore had fought for their freedom the previous summer, winning it through marriage and a genuine affection with the Irish baron. He hoped the sisters were happier now. They were kind. They deserved better than to remain beneath the scrutiny of their harpy of a sister-in-law.

The frigid February air bit at his skin, the fog of his breath disappearing into the night. Jack's eyes fixed on the waiting carriages, a flare of irritation warming his cheeks. The tension coiled in his muscles was a familiar sensation, a ghost from his days in the army when the weight of a saber at his hip provided a reassuring presence. Now instead of the practical garb of a soldier, he was draped in the ridiculous finery of a gentleman.

His current attire made no sound as he moved; there were no sabers to rattle, no pistol close to hand, only the whisper of soft, sleek fabrics that fitted along his frame. The deep blue of his waistcoat, embroidered with subtle, intricate patterns, meant to glimmer in the gaslight of proper parlors. It was a far cry from the utilitarian military uniforms he'd been accustomed to, yet as he had dressed earlier that evening, a surprising sense of satisfaction had washed over him. The clothes, crafted by a tailor who wielded a measuring tape with the precision of a cavalryman handling his blade, fitted him perfectly, enhancing both his form and his confidence.

When he'd examined his reflection before leaving his room, a spark of unexpected pride flickered within him. The garments were a declaration that Jack Sterling belonged in his new role. That his family belonged in theirs. He cut a more than decent figure—a realization that, despite his initial reluctance, pleased him more than he would care to admit.

The door opened and closed too rapidly to allow his entire

family to exit the house. He didn't turn, instead counting down again from twenty. Twenty, nineteen, eighteen, seventeen…

His youngest sister's voice interrupted him. "He is trying, you know," she said softly, appearing at his elbow in her fur-lined cloak and fresh finery. "We all are. It has been a long day, and all Papa wants is to smoke a pipe in front of a warm fire."

"I know." Jack gritted his teeth around the admission. "He has never been afraid of working a full day in his life until now, though, when it matters most to Mother, to Richard, to you."

"And to you." Emily leaned into his shoulder. "I understand you are quite the catch now."

He snorted and barely refrained from rolling his eyes. He'd been told gentlemen didn't do such a thing, which would take breaking a habit of a lifetime. "Trust me, Emily. No one thinks such a thing after more than a moment's conversation with me."

"Perhaps when you were a footman at an assembly or one among many other servants, but now you are a gentleman." She gave him a teasing grin. "Your silence will strike ladies as mysterious rather than stand-offish."

"Is that a word? I believe you invented a word."

"I am a lady. I am fairly certain we are allowed to invent words, or at least not have our attempts commented upon." She raised her little nose imperiously in the air and pulled a chuckle from him as only she could.

"You will come through this better than most of us, I think," Jack said, fondness in his voice. "You are indeed a lady."

"And I will do my part, Jack. I know you worry about all of us—let me help. My role is to find a good husband now, is it not?" She smiled brightly when he gave her a sharp look. "Oh, come now. That's always a woman's primary concern, is it not? Rest assured, I am happy to give my full effort to finding a devastatingly handsome and impossibly rich gentleman, marrying well—giving you one less thing to concern yourself about."

"Emily. Yes, I hope you find an advantageous marriage, but there is much you do not know about this world. About the men within it."

"I am certain you will help me learn," she said softly. "I want you to understand that I am willing and able to do my part, though. I promise."

The door behind them opened before he could make his answer, and this time Jack looked over his shoulder to see his family coming out in a line down the steps...not in order of precedence, despite him advising they practice such a thing at every opportunity. At least his father had changed, thank goodness.

Once they had settled into the carriages, their travel under-way, Jack turned his mind to the rest of the evening.

A formal dinner with Dunmore's family.

Richard and his wife, Katherine, were of similar mind, as they both said at the same moment, "Tell us about the baron—" Then looked at each other and laughed. Richard gave his wife's hand a squeeze then they both turned expectant gazes to Sterling.

For all his family's quirks and stubbornness, they were each of them good people. Jack wanted the best for Richard as the future earl, for his nephews and nieces, for all of them. None of them had asked to be thrust from their comfortable, inconse-quential lives in the country to the whirl of London life.

With this reminder at the forefront of his thoughts, Jack answered their query with patience. "The baron is a good man. Honorable and fair. He is one of the least pretentious people I have ever met. I also think that, while he was born to his posi-tion, he will have the most understanding and sympathy for our family's need to adjust. As an Irish peer, he has had to fight for his place, for acceptance, among the British elite. Just as we must do."

Katherine nodded along with all he said. "What of his wife?

The baroness—she is the daughter of an earl, I believe you said?"

"Indeed. From what I observed of Lady Dunmore and her sisters, Lady Juniper and Lady Betony, they are warm-hearted. Friendly." One specific memory came to the forefront of Jack's thoughts and he smiled. "They painted me once, when I was a footman. They were not unkind, but asked sincerely if I would mind posing for them. An artistic exercise, they called it. Most of their rank would have made it a demand, an order, for a servant to do their bidding. Yet they ensured I did not mind before they made their arrangements for the activity."

Emily, sitting beside him, raised her eyebrows. "That still seems a mite high-handed to me. How could you have said no?"

"They gave me every reasonable way to excuse myself." He remembered well how Lady Juniper had repeatedly expressed concern that they not interrupt his duties. "And they did nothing to make me uncomfortable with my agreement."

Truly, Lady Juniper's shy smile had been more than enough for him to acquiesce.

"Uncomfortable?" Emily repeated, head tilted to the side.

Richard was the one who answered, voice low. "It is not only the female servants taken unkind advantage of in wealthy households, my dear sister, and in ways we prefer not to think on or mention in decent company."

Emily's soft, "Oh," made Jack wince for his sister's innocence. What made it worse was when she asked quietly, "But Jack, you were never...?"

He patted her hand. "The duke's household was safe for all who worked there, Emily. On one occasion, I witnessed the duke himself turn out a guest who dared express an inappropriate interest in a governess."

Katherine cleared her throat. "It is safe to say, then, that all those who come to us through the Duke and Duchess of Montfort are well-vetted and apt to be the good sort."

"Quite safe to say so, yes," Jack agreed, some of the tension leaving the carriage with his lighter tone. "There are decent folk among the *ton*, and I will do my best to navigate us away from those who would take advantage or seek to do harm."

"Father is right about you," Richard murmured with a crooked smile. "You are like a shepherd dog, nipping at our heals so we behave, growling at anyone who comes too near your precious flock. I only hope we do not prove as stupid as sheep."

"Not all of us, anyway," Emily teased, grinning at her brothers. "Goodness, I hope this evening goes well."

They spilled from the carriage shortly after that, hardly speaking another word. Everyone seemed nervous, it rose in the air along with their steamy breaths. It was the first time Jack had allowed the whole family to accept a dinner invitation. Oh, he'd gone with his father and brothers to a few smaller things, less formal with only men in attendance, picking and choosing carefully where he let the men in the family try their new skills—but this was the ladies' first venture out into Society. He would have to hope they'd return home with their reputations intact.

As they gave hats, cloaks, and coats to the Dunmore servants, Jack again took in his family's appearance. His father had begrudgingly put on a fine evening suit of clothes, his mother wore a gown appropriate for a matron without it being overly gaudy as some older women might choose, his brothers looked well, his sisters-in-law stood close together in gowns of similar color but different cuts, and Emily was the very picture of a wholesome, unwed lady.

Their entirely appropriate attire gave him a moment of hope. Not a long moment, or a particularly satisfying one. But it flickered, nevertheless. Perhaps if they dressed well enough, people would overlook other issues.

They ordered themselves easily for entering the drawing room, where their hosts waited, and Jack held his breath. He escorted Emily into the room behind the others as Lord

Dunmore made introductions. Jack kept his eyes on his father and Richard most often while Dunmore introduced each member of his family, all the way down to his two unmarried sisters-in-law.

"...and my wife's sisters, Lady Juniper and Lady Betony Amberton."

Jack's gaze flickered to them, hoping they would take an interest in Emily and befriend her, though his sister was of course a few years older than them both. His attention immediately returned to the older of the two with curiosity, seeing Lady Juniper's eyes focused on him. Staring, in fact, rather intently—until she realized he stared back. Then she lowered her eyes quickly to the carpet, her expression neutral.

Lady Juniper looked as well as when he'd last seen her the morning after her sister's wedding. He'd been on duty when she'd climbed into the Dunmore coach to accompany her sister to Ireland, her eyes aglow with excitement at her coming adventure. She'd even made eye contact with him through the window of the carriage, smiled brightly, and waved. Her happiness had rippled out like water, and he'd nearly forgotten himself and smiled at her.

That she avoided his gaze now seemed...odd.

A momentary concern pinched his heart. Did she not like seeing a former servant as one of their guests for the evening? It was entirely possible, and he could think of no other reason for her stare and then avoidance. Unless...she found the sight of him in something other than livery strange? Perhaps that was all it was—taking her aback by presenting her with something familiar in a new context.

He'd choose to think that, rather than the former possibility, so when she looked up again, he tipped his head forward in acknowledgement. *Yes, I am an unexpected sight. But I hope not necessarily unpleasant.* He would do his best to set her at ease, if the occasion allowed for it.

He was, after all, a gentleman.

EVERYTHING IN JUNIPER'S MIND CAME TO AN ABRUPT HALT, a clatter and a crash of a stop, the moment Mr. John Sterling met her gaze and returned her stare without so much as a flicker of interest, recognition, or even a pleasant smile. Her initial shock twisted into disappointment.

He didn't care in the least about seeing her again. He appeared as stoic and solemn as a gentleman of means as he had when he'd stood at attention as guard and footman both.

She'd averted her gaze to compose herself before she blushed with her realization, but when she looked again to see him still staring, her mouth went dry.

Then he nodded, the movement slight and slow, yet it somehow set off a whole flock of geese in her stomach. Miniature geese, to be certain, but given the cacophony of wings beating and wild thrumming inside her, it could only be geese that caused such a thing.

Thank heavens for Betony, who took Juniper's arm and brought her across the carpet to speak to Sterling's sister, a lovely, delicate looking creature named Emily.

"It is such a pleasure to meet you at last, Lady Emily," Betony said, taking the lead as she so often did in social gatherings. "The moment I learned of you, I wished to know everything about you. I hope you will forgive my forwardness, but I have so many questions for you."

Juniper peeped up at Sterling—Mr. John Sterling—as he stood protectively beside his sister. She experienced a difficult time adjusting to calling him his correct name even in her own mind, as it seemed both inefficient and strange. Goodness, but he'd somehow grown handsomer. The suit he wore was incredibly well made, and the deep blue of his waistcoat drew out the dark blue of his eyes. His jaw was still clean shaven—his dark hair, though, looked different. The cut sharper, still short and military-like, but elegant.

Admiring the man's hair was ridiculous. She hastily gave her full attention to his sister, speaking to her. "I hope you will forgive our eagerness to come to know you, Lady Emily. Being an earl's daughter is not without its challenges, and we are happy to share anything we have learned with you if it will make your path easier to tread."

"You are too kind. I confess, I wanted to meet you the instant I learned of you both." Lady Emily's eyes darted between Juniper and Betony. "My brother told me a delightful tale about modeling for you while he was a footman with the duke. Is there any chance one of your paintings was brought to London? I would love to see it." She cast an impish smile up at Mr. Sterling, whose reaction was a mere raise of his eyebrows.

The word Juniper focused on, though, was 'footman.' Perhaps his family did not discuss his true purpose in the duke's household when they were in mixed company? An acceptable practice, and a detail Juniper tucked away.

Betony answered the question before Juniper could. "Oh, yes. My sister kept hers. Mine was lost in the shuffle from one house to another, but Juniper's painting is in her portfolio. She keeps several things on hand, no matter where we go. We will have to fetch it after dinner. Is that all right, Juniper?"

Blushing, and not entirely certain she wished to have her work on display, Juniper gave a brief shake of her head. "I-I cannot be certain I know where it is at present. Perhaps another time. It certainly isn't all that critical to view, though. My skills aren't enough to make it worthy of study or appreciation."

The painting's subject appeared as neutral and uninterested as ever. His eyebrows had even fallen back to their normal position. Another moment passed before he seemed to realize the ladies looked to him and expected him to say something.

Mr. Sterling cleared his throat. "I assure you, Lady Juniper, my sister wants only to find a new reason to torment me. Beyond that, she will have nothing critical to say of the piece."

Did the man have any idea at all how charming he sounded? The man had a voice her books would describe in all manner of creative, and ultimately impossible, ways. Rough. Solid. Deep. Level. Dark. It wasn't quite fair that a real man sounded like that and then refused to give answers longer than a sentence or two.

She wanted a monologue; preferably a passionate one which grew in volume until he declared something impossible, such as his wish to court her. Or that he would do anything for a single smile. She would even settle for something less dependent on her as its subject.

Oh dear. Perhaps she *had* been reading too many novels of late.

Ivy drifted near, serene as ever. "Ladies, I have come to explain the order of precedence for the evening. As we kept the party to our two families, we do not have even numbers of ladies and gentlemen, and the variety of ranks among us will feel rather strange." She glanced up at Mr. Sterling. "I have already explained to the other gentlemen in your family how we will best practice one of the stricter rules of Society's evening events. Tonight, as host, my husband escorts the highest ranking woman present in to the room." She nodded to each lady as she named her. "This is Lady Benwaith, your mother, as a countess. Then your father escorts the next highest-ranking lady who is not his blood relative, your sister-in-law, the viscountess." She went on to explain that her mother-in-law, the dowager baroness, as an Irish noblewoman, ranked below everyone but those without a title present because the titled Irish went lower in the order of precedence, than the English. "It isn't ideal, as a more even party is easier, but it is still within appropriate bounds."

Lady Emily's eyebrows climbed higher with each word. "It is so much to remember. How will we ever manage in an even larger party?"

"Oh, it gets so much worse once you have to know who is the grandson or granddaughter of someone important, their names won't match so it can get complicated." With a calming touch on Lady Emily's wrist, Ivy reassured her. "But never fear, my dear. The more complex the party, the more likely you are to have the hostess or master of ceremonies come whisper in your ear to whom you ought to look for as your escort." Then she tipped her head toward Mr. Sterling. "Your brother likely knows as well as any who goes before whom."

Juniper glanced up at him from the corner of her eye. It seemed no matter how she fought to keep from staring, her attention drew back to him again and again. Unfortunately, he hadn't met her gaze again. Presently, he was devoting all his focus to Ivy.

Why had Juniper let herself imagine that when he saw her again he'd not be able to take his eyes from her?

"That leaves your sisters unescorted," Lady Emily protested a moment later, looking to Betony and Juniper. "That doesn't seem fair."

"Indeed. That is why for most parties there are careful arrangements made to ensure there are as many male guests as female," Ivy said with a smile. "My sisters will manage on their own. We are only going across the corridor."

"This is why there are entire volumes of books dedicated to delineating who is descended from which noble house," Betony remarked with a little smirk. "We have several in the library of this house. You are welcome to borrow them, if you would find them helpful."

"I have ordered several for our collection," Mr. Sterling

rumbled beside them. "Thank you for your thoughtful offer, Lady Betony."

Why hadn't Juniper thought to make that offer? And why did she feel so incredibly foolish about everything this evening? She was neither a flighty woman, nor without wit, but she felt she'd become quite silly over a man who had barely said a word to her.

Best to prove to herself she hadn't lost all her senses. She turned a pleasant smile to the gentleman. "How have you enjoyed London thus far, Mr. Sterling?"

Then immediately berated herself for the inane question.

Yet it worked well enough to get his attention focused on her for a moment. A flash of something in his eyes, something which didn't appear positive in the least, appeared before his mask of indifference settled again. "I find London as busy, crowded, and large as ever, Lady Juniper."

The pause that followed his words made her want to turn and flee. He didn't like London. He didn't seem to appreciate her attempt at polite conversation, either. Why couldn't she have said something clever?

"My brother is like my father in that he prefers the country, but he will never admit as much." Lady Emily gave her brother a glance that read as something between warning and amusement. "For some reason Jack seems to see a threat behind every streetlamp and ruffians in every shadowed alleyway."

Watching as closely as she was, Juniper noticed the slight brightening of the man's eyes when his sister said the more familiar version of his given name. Not Mr. Sterling, or John; Jack. It suited him.

The allusion to him seeing danger everywhere, however, made her again question whether his sister knew of his work as a guard. Surely they knew?

"I prefer something between the two," Betony said, speaking of London and country life. "Give me a smaller sphere, a village

SALLY BRITTON

with enough people to make for good company, and I am content. My sister is happy so long as she has access to a well-stocked library. But London? I find it fascinating only in the smallest of helpings."

A bell rang, calling everyone to order for dinner. As they all carefully took their places in line, Juniper and Betony standing side by side behind Jack Sterling and his sister, Juniper tried to recover her sense of self.

Her younger sister leaned in close to whisper, "Are you all right? You look as though you are fighting away a headache. Your expression is pinched."

"If only that were the problem," she whispered back. "No, no. I am well." Even if nothing had gone the way she had dreamed it would.

At least she had an entire season in London to gain Mr. Sterling's friendship. He presented an interesting challenge. What would it take to make him take notice of her? Precisely what she would do when she had it, she wasn't entirely certain. She only knew she wanted it; wanted him to look at her with something other than his dutiful expression of stoic responsibility.

Dinner went well. All the conversation remained polite, on topics of food or fashion. Juniper sat between the older brothers and directly across from Lady Emily. That didn't stop her from sneaking several looks at Jack—*Mr. John Sterling*, across and down the table from her. He sat with perfect posture, hardly speaking except to murmur direction to his mother or answer whatever it was Betony said to him.

Why had Betony been placed beside him? It made Juniper somewhat envious of her sister, but she kept up her own cheerful conversation with the gentlemen at either side of her who were passably pleasant.

When at last the meal ended, the ladies stood and went across the corridor to the drawing room. The baroness, dowager baroness, and countess all sat together, along with the future Countess of Benwaith. Those four ladies immediately spoke of upcoming events and who had invitations to what, the better to align their social calendars. It looked exhausting.

"Your sister is kind, going to so much trouble to assist my family," Lady Emily said to Juniper as the two of them settled at a table with cards.

Mrs. George Sterling, whose given name was Susan, joined them and nodded her agreement. "We are most grateful that so many of the Duke of Montfort's friends are eager to help, though it does strike me as somewhat curious."

Juniper picked up a deck of cards and shuffled them, looking about for Betony. Her younger sister had slipped away without a word. Hopefully she would return soon and make a fourth for their game.

"Why does it strike you as curious?" she asked as she cut the deck. "His Grace is a remarkable man. I think he rather likes helping the people he cares for."

"That is just it, isn't it?" Mrs. George Sterling said with a raise of her eyebrows. "Jack was merely a footman to His Grace. I certainly appreciate the kindness, of course, I am merely surprised that a man with such power would go to any lengths to help a former servant's family. Even though my father-in-law is now an earl, he cannot hope to have much influence any time soon."

Lady Emily put a hand on her sister-in-law's arm. "Forgive us, Lady Juniper. We do not have an understanding of this new world we find ourselves in, and I have been told that people of the duke's power would only form connections in places where it would be of benefit to his interests. Thus, our agreeable surprise."

They truly had no idea that their brother had served as a guard in the duke's household, then? That he had even saved the duke's family from injury or worse in his time with them? How strange.

"You needn't apologize." Juniper dealt out four hands of cards and looked again for Betony. "Most people of higher rank are what you say—looking out for their own selves and their immediate family with nary a care for anyone else. Whatever His Grace's reason for it, I am glad we are coming to know one another better. It can be difficult to make close friends while in London." She hoped her words and smile were reassuring to the two newly-minted ladies.

The door opened again and she turned in time to see Betony dipped down by a table, as though putting a thing down or picking it up. She narrowed her eyes at her sister as Betony approached the card table.

"Where have you been? I began to despair of your arrival to play a game with our guests."

Betony batted her eyes with false innocence that immediately raised Juniper's suspicions. "I had to fetch something for later. It is of no consequence at present. Shall we play Whist?"

Less than a quarter of an hour later, Juniper and Lady Emily had lost the game of Whist, and the men of the party rejoined them.

John Sterling came directly to his sister's side, his brows drawn together as though concerned. Did he not trust Lady Emily to their company? Perhaps he merely worried after her comfort. Whatever the reason, that stern look of his brought to mind more than one instance when he had given disapproving looks as a guard.

"Emily. How was your game of cards?" he asked, his voice low and deep.

Juniper had to pinch herself to keep from shivering. It was such a charming voice.

"I am afraid I kept Lady Juniper from victory," his sister said, turning an apologetic smile in Juniper's direction.

Juniper glanced away before the gentleman caught her staring at him, giving her full attention to his sister. "Please do not concern yourself on my account, Lady Emily. I am not the best at cards, you can ask my sister."

She turned to have Betony corroborate her words—but her sister was already out of her chair, going to the table where she had tucked a thing away. Perhaps she had another game to play, or an object to show their brother-in-law, Teague, now he had entered the room.

"Lady Juniper," Mrs. George Sterling said, drawing her attention again. "When one especially enjoys a particular aspect of a meal, is it polite to ask after how to make it?"

"Oh, yes, of course. You would let my sister as hostess know that you enjoyed it, and ask if her cook would be willing to share the recipe. If the cook is willing, as you know some recipes are guarded like national secrets, our cook will send it along to yours."

The other woman frowned somewhat. "I will never see it, then?"

"Likely not, unless you ask after seeing it. Which you are certainly permitted to do once the recipe arrives at your home," Juniper reassured her hastily. "Though no one will ever expect you to cook it yourself, of course, or to know all the details about how it is made."

"My sister-in-law is a most excellent cook," Lady Emily said. "I can attest to her skills in the kitchen. It seems a shame that ladies do not cook if they wish to do so."

"Some ladies likely do," Juniper said, glancing briefly at Mr. Sterling again. *Egad.* She needed to call him something other than the surname he shared with his whole family. John Sterling. Jack? No, that felt far too familiar, even in her own mind. "Though I admit I have never heard a lady attest to such a thing in company."

Betony returned to the table, holding a large, thick paper.

"Lady Emily, you wished to see my sister's likeness of your brother, did you not? I thought I had best show you when he rejoined us, the better to see how well Juniper executed the task with her watercolors."

Juniper's face immediately flooded with heat, and she stood hastily. "Oh, Betony, you should not—"

Betony's smile was full of mischief, not malice, as she turned the thick art paper around to show the watercolor painting to both its subject and his female relatives at the table. Juniper winced and turned her attention to Mr. Sterling... whose cheeks looked fine, but the tops of his ears were now somewhat red.

She swallowed an apology, then stumbled over a hasty explanation. "It is only a watercolor, done somewhat hastily so as not to bother Mr. Sterling or take him from what his duties were at the time—"

Lady Emily took the paper in her hands as she stood between her brother and sister-in-law, and studied it closely. "Oh, but the details are marvelous. You captured his chin perfectly. The look of his eyes, too. Who is he meant to be, with the sword and shield?"

The man's eyebrows were drawn together again as he looked at the paper, and Juniper realized he had never seen the final work. Why had she not showed it to him?

She cleared her throat. "A medieval soldier. Wearing leather armor, rather than metal." If her cheeks would cool and her heart would calm, she might find a way to make light of exactly how much time she had spent getting the details of his face and hair exactly right. She may have spent a little too much time studying him after the initial painting was done.

"I think it is one of Juniper's better pieces," Betony said, the pride in her voice unmistakable. "My own rendering was so wholly unremarkable that I did not even bother to pay attention to where I had laid it down."

"Oh, we must show Mama," Lady Emily said, looking up at her brother. "It is a lovely painting of you. She will admire it."

Mr. Sterling finally looked up at Juniper, one corner of his mouth pulling upward. "Indeed. I think Mother will enjoy it. Lady Juniper has done a fair job of making me look far more interesting than I really am."

His sister-in-law scoffed. "All of the Sterling men are quite handsome, you cannot help but look interesting." She rose from the table. "I will come with you, Emily. Perhaps we can talk your other brothers into having their likenesses painted—though we will spare Lady Juniper the trouble of putting up with their company by finding another artist."

Juniper looked up at Mr. Sterling as they walked away, Betony with them. "I...I am terribly sorry. I did not know my sister retrieved the painting, nor that she intended to show it to the whole gathering."

The furrow disappeared from his brow, and he tipped his head toward her as he spoke. "It is of no matter, Lady Juniper. Your talent overrides the poor subject you worked with to create the painting."

Oh. He thought her talented? Her cheeks felt warmer than before, somehow.

"Jack," his eldest brother said loudly. "I didn't know you went to battle with sword and shield."

The jest made Mr. Sterling sigh. "Excuse me, please." He nodded to her, then joined his family members studying the painting.

Teague wandered to the table where Juniper stood, frozen in place by mortification and compliment alike. Her brother-in-law folded his hands behind him. "Shouldn't the artist be with her painting, to explain the thoughts behind her work?"

She shook her head, watching as the earl held the painting and looked from it to his son, then said something in a low voice which made everyone laugh.

"I think this is less about the painting and more about a family teasing one another," she said quietly. "I cannot understand why Betony had to fetch it."

"I think it was wise of her." Teague grinned when she turned a frown in his direction. "Truly. They have been doing their best all evening to behave properly. There has been an unnatural stiffness to every word, look, and motion. But now see, they are more relaxed. I think, too, it gives them yet another link to our family through your familiarity with one they love, as innocent as it may be."

Juniper looked up at her brother-in-law who was one of the cleverest and kindest men she knew. "You really do want to help them."

"Of course I do." He winked at her. "I could use more English allies, for one thing. I find I like them a great deal, for another." He offered her his arm. "Now come. You must at least accept his mother's compliments, as I am certain she wishes to give them and hasn't worked out how to approach you yet."

"Oh, very well." She let him escort her over to the crowd, where most of the teasing had ended.

Lady Benwaith did have quite a few kind words to say. All in all, the evening seemed a successful introduction of their two households—and though Juniper caught herself glancing at John Sterling throughout the evening, he said nothing more to her about the painting. Or anything else, for that matter. It was not the stirring success she had hoped for upon their reintroduction, but nor was it a complete disaster.

Perhaps she ought to reconsider her approach to coming to know him better.

CHAPTER 5

Avisit to the house of the Ambassador of the Kingdom of the Two Sicilies hadn't been something Jack expected to perform. Yet there he was, in the drawing room with his sisters-in-law and Emily, sitting in a chair with a plate of biscuits in one hand and a cup of tea in the other, utterly bewildered as to how one was supposed to eat a biscuit whilst retaining a hold of the cup of tea. He was only here because the *contessa's* note to the ladies of his household had mentioned the *conte* wanted to speak to him about a particular matter.

The *conte* had yet to join them. He was, apparently, in meetings that morning.

Before her marriage Emma Arlen had been ward to the Duke of Montfort and remained the dearest friend of his eldest daughter—which explained how his sisters had obtained the invitation in the first place...even if that didn't clarify why the couple had included Jack.

"I understand you had dinner with Lord and Lady Dunmore's family last week," Lady Atella said with a wide smile behind the rim of her cup. "They are lovely people. I am planning to host them here soon."

Jack shifted in his seat the moment that evening's memory rose in his mind. A successful evening; even if he had been mercilessly teased for being the subject of a young lady's painting, in a somewhat heroic pose that his brothers thought ill-suited to him.

When he had posed for Lady Juniper and her sister all those months ago, Jack never dreamed his family would one day see the painting. Even if he had, he would have agreed to stand as model for them. He had liked all three Amberton sisters, even then.

"Oh, we truly enjoyed our time with them," his eldest brother's wife Katherine said, seeming to feel more confidence when speaking of the mutual acquaintances. "We hope to return their generosity soon." As Viscountess of Tenby, after all, she was a mere touch below the contessa in rank.

"The balance must always be kept," Lady Atella said with a shrewd raise of her eyebrows. "But know this, Lady Tenby. You are among friends when you are with us. My husband and I have agreed to do all we can to ease your way into London's elite circles. If ever you need help planning parties or dinners, or returning invitations, or anything, please do not hesitate to call on me. I absolutely delight in arranging social events. It is one of my favorite things about being married to an ambassador."

Jack nearly smiled at that. He'd known the *contessa* for years, even if it had been a formal and distant knowledge. He'd joined the household before she'd come out into Society along with the duke's eldest daughter, and she'd always been lively in spirit. Her enthusiastic offer didn't surprise him in the slightest.

"I have a question, then, your ladyship," Emily said with a little raise of her hand, as though reluctant to draw attention to herself. "As an unmarried lady, I know entertainments I organize must be smaller and given with the permission of my mother. But am I permitted to do more than invite other women to tea or on an errand?"

"As long as you are not planning parties, of course. And you cannot invite men to spend time with you without parental approval and chaperones."

Emily blushed and laughed softly. "I have not met a man I would like to go to all that trouble for. Yet." Jack's protective instincts stirred briefly. "However, I would like to have Lady Juniper and Lady Betony join me of an afternoon. Merely to talk, you understand. I quite like them."

"They are of equal rank to you, too, so it would be beneficial to you to do something in public with them." Lady Atella gave an enthusiastic nod of her head. "They are enchanting women. You could not ask for better friends. That all three of you are out in Society is excellent, too. They may go wherever you are permitted in your shared unmarried state."

"Would it be permissible for someone like my brother to join us, should we wish to wander about in shops or go to Gunter's for ices?" Emily slanted a look toward Jack. "As an escort, of sorts."

Something about her tone made Jack take notice and focus on her expression. The question seemed pointed. Specific. What was she up to?

With a shrug of her shoulders, Lady Atella answered, "I do not see why not. Brothers accompany sisters all over London, when they are not getting up to their own mischief."

Katherine gave her brother-in-law a well-meaning grin. "I am not certain Jack knows how to get into trouble."

"I think he would laugh at the mere idea of being involved in any sort of ill-doing," Emily agreed. "Or any sort of amusement, too, which is why I wish to drag him about with us. He will think himself a particularly effective escort, but I am secretly forcing him to enjoy himself."

"Not so secretly it seems, given you are plotting right in front of him." Lady Atella chuckled with amusement. "You sound as if you mean to torture your poor, well-meaning brother, Lady Emily."

Susan, his brother George's wife, had been shyly quiet for the visit thus far. But here she perked up somewhat. "I think it a good idea. Especially if you include the Amberton sisters. They are pretty ladies. Perhaps they could encourage our brother-in-law to be freer in his comportment."

His eyes narrowed, but Jack calmly took a drink of his tea. He didn't mind in the least that they talked about him and around him as though he were not present. He almost preferred it—it was hardly a new sensation. But hearing plots against him was somewhat disconcerting.

"Lady Juniper would certainly try," Katherine said somewhat dryly, drawing Jack's attention to her as she nibbled a biscuit.

Whatever could she mean by bandying about Lady Juniper's name that way? He needed to say something, even if he disguised it with confusion. "I am uncertain what you meant to imply with that remark, Katherine."

She smirked and made eye contact with Emily, raising her eyebrows. "Merely that she seemed quite invested in whether or not you enjoyed yourself at dinner last week."

Had she? Jack sorted swiftly through his memories from that evening again, this time as rapidly as he'd once rehearsed battle plans to himself. *Try to remember every detail; discard the unimportant.* He had to slowly shake his head. "I cannot think what you mean. She paid particular attention to Emily which I thought kind of her."

Lady Atella's eyes sparkled with delight. "I wonder if you were focused on the wrong details that evening, Mr. Sterling. Knowing what I do of your former life, it would not surprise me if you were too occupied with assessing for threats that you missed a lady offering an allyship, of sorts. I do not know Lady Juniper as well as I know her older sister, the baroness, but I do believe she's regarded as a quiet, steady sort. You would do well to secure her friendship."

He almost responded, almost contradicted a countess in her own home to say, *I would have noticed someone as lovely as Lady Juniper casting her eyes in my direction, surely.* Yet he'd spent most of the previous summer in her presence, assigned to watch over the Amberton women during their stay at Clairvoir, and had actively reminded himself on a daily basis that he couldn't stare at her all day. He hadn't any right to smile when he saw her or chuckle at her quips.

He had closed every part of his mind to her except the dutiful, protective part...or tried to. A man would have to be blind to avoid noticing how beautiful she was, how softly she spoke, how brightly she smiled. A servant—even a guardsman—and an earl's daughter couldn't have the barest of acquaintance without crossing dozens of lines.

Except... He wasn't a servant anymore. Nor was he a guardsman.

Jack's mind was doing something strange. It shifted, his thoughts realigned, settling rather firmly in the knowledge that Lady Juniper and himself were now...equals.

No. That was ridiculous. She'd always be a touch above him, no matter their stations in life.

Susan raised her eyebrows and murmured softly, "Jack, assessing for threats? Goodness, you do know him well."

That brought him back to the conversation as nothing else would. His circumstances had changed, and so had his duty. His family needed him. "I have a responsibility to keep my family from harm. All sorts of harm."

Emily tapped her finger to her chin. "Lady Juniper offered to assist us. Well—she and her sister offered." She looked to Katherine. "And I agree with you. She paid pointed interest to Jack, too."

"And heaven knows he needs help," Susan muttered behind the rim of her teacup. "Poor old soldier."

What could she possibly mean by that? He was clearly the most well-equipped in the family to make it through their coming social trials. London was filling up to the brim with lords, ladies, and gentry, the first round of balls beginning in a week's time. He'd secured a dancing master, at high cost, to begin working with them two days before. What had they done?

Jack stiffened somewhat and put his cup down.

Perhaps they had seen Lady Juniper paying attention to him. Perhaps he'd missed it, and she had looked at him with pity due to his lack of experience in the world she'd lived in all her life.

A humiliating thought.

"I think you have offended him," Lady Atella remarked with a teasing grin. "He looks more fierce than usual."

He fought to appear more relaxed. "I am not in the least offended, Lady Atella. Merely perplexed by the observations made by my sisters."

All four ladies started to laugh or giggle, and he had to shake his head in complete confusion. Fortunately for him the door opened and in walked Lord Atella, the ambassador. He greeted them all politely, his wife warmly, and then motioned to Jack.

"Ah, Mr. Sterling. Again, it is good to see you. I am grateful you have come. Ladies, I must steal this gentleman away. I have wished to discuss matters of embassy security with someone as knowledgeable as Mr. Sterling for months now."

Jack winced and looked at the ladies from his household, and all of them raised their eyebrows at him. As far as they knew, he'd been nothing more than an upper-footman in a duke's house. His military career long in the past.

He cleared his throat. "This old solider is happy to be of assistance in whatever way I can, Lord Atella." He would have to tell the ambassador to avoid speaking of his former occupation, even if it was among people who had reason to know the duke employed a private militia in the guise of servants.

He'd never seen a reason to make his family worry over his safety. After all, they'd done enough of that during the war with the French. All anyone needed to know was that he'd worn the duke's livery for several years. No further details were necessary.

He followed the *conte* out of the drawing room and to his office and attempted to put the idea of Lady Juniper showing him any sort of extra attention, be it critical or otherwise, out of his mind.

"You like John Sterling."

Juniper froze where she stood, a collection of Erasmus Grey's novels in her arms, and turned slowly on her heel to see Betony standing in the corridor behind her with arms crossed and a wide grin on her face.

Best to pretend ignorance. "I beg your pardon, Betony. What was that you said?"

"You *like* him."

"Who do I like?"

Her younger sister wasn't one to take a hint, apparently. "You are nursing feelings of tenderness for the former guardsman. You admire him, you think of him often, you *like* Mr. John Sterling. It took me all week to think it through, but now that I have, it is the only thing that makes sense with regards to how odd you acted during dinner and in the days afterward. Even now—" She pointed to the stack of books Juniper held. "You have gathered those up from all over the house and have reorganized the shelves in your room at least three times. You are attempting to distract yourself from something. It isn't working."

Juniper swallowed. "Perhaps I wish to distract myself from the mortification that lingers from you showing my less-than-perfect portrait of Mr. Sterling to his entire family."

"They all loved that painting and you know it," Betony said with mock severity. "You are not unhappy about that, even though you blushed all evening. No, I think you like him."

Unfortunately, Betony saw far too much and knew too much about Juniper. Denying her supposition more would do nothing but goad Betony into stubbornly proving her theory.

There was nothing for it.

"How did you know?" Juniper asked instead, voice soft as she hugged her stack of books to herself.

Betony's eyebrows raised and her focus narrowed on Juniper's. "I suspected it at dinner. Every time I looked to see what you thought of something our guests said, you were glancing at Mr. John Sterling from the corner of your eye, if not outright staring. But I knew it for a fact when I brought out that portrait."

Her stomach swooped. "I have had that portrait for ages. How did that give anything away?"

"Juniper, my darling sister, you blushed like a rose. I have never seen you react that way to sharing your art. You are delightfully confident in your artistic abilities, usually. I knew something was amiss at once." Betony grinned broadly. "And, as I said before, you have been distracted ever since that evening. Too distracted."

Juniper went to her bedchamber door and opened it, beckoning Betony with a little movement of her chin. Once they were both inside, Juniper nudged the door shut with her hip before hurrying to put her books on the shelves.

"You haven't told anyone about this, have you?" she demanded, turning again toward her sister. "Not Ivy? Or anyone else?"

"Of course not. I might ask you about your feelings, and

have my own thoughts on them, but I am not the sort to run off and tell anyone else your private thoughts or emotions." Betony clasped her hands beneath her chin, her eyes bright with interest. "This is adorable, Juniper. I cannot think of a time, besides that summer we first met Fanny's family, that you looked at a boy with anything other than polite indifference."

Her words brought up a memory of Juniper, all of fourteen years of age, following about their sister-in-law's younger brother, trying to imagine him as a hero from one of her books. The boy turned out to be rather full of himself, and Juniper had swiftly realized she liked fictional gentlemen better than the reality.

Her present-day cheeks flushed. "I am not certain I wish to be called adorable. I feel rather foolish, in fact." Juniper sank into one of two matching chairs in front of her fireplace. "Because Sterling—Mr. Sterling said almost nothing to me. He barely looked at me. Understandably, of course, he is in the midst of an enormous change. His family needs him."

Betony sat in the other chair, her expression one of pure delight. "How long have you liked him? Since the summer? Or only after his family rose in rank?"

"It...it would have been inappropriate to look at a servant with any sort of feeling beyond general human decency." Juniper hadn't ever allowed herself to look at servants, at employees in the households she'd lived in or visited, with any degree of personal interest. The indecency of the suggestion made her frown, even if she had rather liked watching the former guardsman as he moved about the castle, or stood stoically in place until called upon. "And you had better not ever entertain such a thing, Betony Amberton."

"Never." Betony put her hand to her chest. "I am well aware of the imbalance between ourselves and those who are in service."

Juniper sighed, her gaze drifting momentarily towards the

neatly arranged novels before meeting her sister's eyes. "A lady of our position must never entertain such thoughts toward a servant. It's not merely frowned upon; it's a breach of decorum which could lead to scandal, ruining the lives of all involved."

Betony nodded solemnly, her earlier excitement dimming in the face of the reminder. "I know. The lines between us and those who serve us are not just lines of employment but of entire worlds apart. To cross them..." She paused, searching for the right words. "To cross them is to risk everything—our reputation, our social standing, even our family's name."

Juniper's expression grew stern, reflecting the seriousness of their conversation. "Exactly, and it's not just about us. A moment's folly could ruin lives."

"I follow all the rules, Juniper, you know I do," Betony murmured. "But we are not speaking of the things that have ruled us since birth. We are speaking of something entirely different." Her earlier levity didn't return, though a more reflective expression appeared on her face, her smile slight and her eyes thoughtful. "Is this why you are struggling, Juniper? It's a lot to carry, knowing you could feel something for someone who was once a servant. But now, with Mr. Sterling's rise in fortune..."

Juniper's lips curved in a small, thoughtful smile. "Yes. I know it's different now. His father's elevation changes things." She glanced at her books and her heart sank. In novels a heroine would catch the eye of a man such as him, likely by doing nothing more than standing in a perfect beam of sunlight through a canopy of leaves. Unfortunately, Juniper doubted her ability to orchestrate such a scenario in her favor at all let alone in midwinter, as much as she doubted the moment's ability to be as effective in life as in fiction. "But it hardly matters if he isn't paying me any attention."

"You have met him but once since his rise in station,"

Betony pointed out. "And as you said, he is absolutely consumed with his family's entrance into Society."

"Yes." But Juniper shook her head as her thoughts caught up with her. "No. That is—I cannot blame his lack of notice on his family's situation. It is as likely that he does not find me of interest. Perhaps he remembers too well what it was like to follow us about, making certain we stayed out of trouble. Perhaps I remind him of a time he'd rather forget, in service to another."

"That is a great deal of supposition." Betony pointed to the books on Juniper's shelves. "What would your heroines do if confronted with such a thing?"

"Oh, them." Juniper wrinkled her nose and sank deeper into her chair. "They have never had such a practical problem. None of them, in any of those books. It's all treasure maps and mad uncles and thunderstorms." For the first time, her books had failed her. In truth, the heroines of her favorite stories tended to swoon when things became interesting—or get kidnapped. She didn't foresee herself having either of those issues in the near future. "I am afraid I am left to my own devices when it comes to my interest in a gentleman. Any gentleman."

"But we are discussing a particular gentleman." The glitter of mischief in Betony's eyes made it quite clear that she would not allow the subject to drop until she had solved the problem Juniper faced. "We should go visit the Sterlings. Today." She rose from the chair. "Get dressed, properly I mean. At once."

"Wait. What?" Juniper remained sitting, mind whirling. "Why are we going to visit? And without knowing if it is their at home day?"

"It hardly matters. We already promised we would help the Sterling ladies to acclimate to London society. We can begin today. Come, I can be ready in a quarter of an hour."

Startled by her sister's enthusiasm, Juniper had barely risen from her seat before Betony opened the door. "No, Betony—

wait! We cannot barge into their home, uninvited, merely because you want to tease me about a gentleman!"

"Teasing you is an unlooked-for bit of fun." Betony wriggled her eyebrows up and down. "Yet I am also helping you. You will sit about for the rest of the Season, reading your books and doing nothing if I do not prod you at least a little. And we *did* offer our friendship and help to Lady Emily. We must make good on that promise." She tossed her head and raised her nose in the air. "We will teach her exactly how to behave as a proper lady, and then tell her all the ways she can break the rules, too."

Juniper's startled expression made Betony giggle before she darted out the door. Nothing about the situation made her want to laugh as she scurried through her room, readying herself for a visit to the Sterling home. Chances were excellent she wouldn't even see him there, if they went primarily to see Lady Emily or the other women in the household. Yes, she was unlikely to see him—and they had promised to help Lady Emily.

"Right," Juniper murmured to herself as she put her bonnet on her head, looking in her mirror. "I likely will not even see him. Which is good. I need to focus on the sister."

That little touch of self-reassurance steadied her enough that she had regained her composure by the time she met Betony in the foyer for their walk to the Sterling home, a maid ready to accompany them.

Of course, the somewhat alarming gleam in Betony's eyes brought back a touch of worry. Though the older of the two, Juniper knew Betony's ability to promote a touch of chaos and possessed a healthy respect for her sister's abilities in that regard.

Oh dear.

CHAPTER 6

N othing caused an anxious spirit so much as unexpected visitors. At least, that was Juniper's feeling on the topic of sitting about, enjoying her day—most often deeply engrossed in a book—when someone appeared in her sitting room expecting her to drop everything to chat with them. Such was her feelings that being on the opposite side of the scenario, that arriving at the house of another without giving prior warning or receiving a pointed invitation made her feel somewhat sick to her stomach as she and Betony approached the Sterlings' townhouse.

"We ought to come back tomorrow," she said, slowing her steps as they neared the door. "After we send a note. Turning up without even sending a note is rather rude."

"It isn't when we are all friends," Betony insisted. "And we are going to be good friends before long. Lady Emily is charming, and we both wished to see her. Think on that, if considering the *other reason* for our visit twists you in knots."

A good piece of advice, that. Juniper pulled in a deep breath and held it as she knocked on the door with the large brass ring. The door opened instantly, a fresh-faced footman standing at the ready.

"We have come to pay a call on Lady Emily." Betony gestured to Juniper to hand him one of her cards. They both had them, thanks to their brother-in-law, but generally agreed to use Juniper's as the elder sister when they went visiting together. "Will you let us know if she is at home?"

The footman stepped aside to allow them to wait in the foyer, as was proper given their obvious status as ladies. He disappeared quickly, and Juniper finally released a relieved sigh. "How did I let you talk me in to this?"

"The same way I talk you in to everything. You know I am right." Betony's subtle lift of her chin made her opinion of herself clear. "As often as you and Ivy think you are protecting me, I am in truth driving the two of you to action."

Rather than respond to that pointed remark, Juniper let her eyes take in the foyer and what little she could see beyond it. The floors were marble, the columns here and there painted bright white, and the walls a bright blue that made her think of summer skies. The house was elegant, in an older—though still fashionable—neighborhood. It couldn't say much about the occupants, though, given how short a time they'd had possession of the house.

It made her wonder what their home looked like—the place where Sterling came from. How different had his life been prior to the family's change in status?

The footman returned at the top of the stairs, and he was not alone.

"Lady Juniper and Lady Betony," a deep voice greeted them, and Juniper's heart gave an inconvenient little kick to her ribs. John Sterling came down the steps toward them. "You are both most welcome."

Today he wore tan trousers, a dark blue coat, and a silver-blue waistcoat. Tall boots, too, as though he meant to go riding. The cut of his clothing was excellent, setting off his broad shoulders and otherwise slim build quite well.

Juniper nearly forgot how to speak, but words were not necessary as she remembered to sink into a polite curtsy. She ought to have taken the lead, as the older of the two sisters. Betony, most unlike herself, didn't say a word...which meant Mr. Sterling remained still, looking at them with his usual solemn expression. Juniper couldn't find her tongue, until he finally raised his eyebrows.

Words, Juniper, words! "We came to see your sister," she finally blurted, her chest tightening. "Lady Emily. Is she at home to visitors? I know it may not be her morning to take formal visits, but we hoped she would not mind if we came. To see her. As friends." She plastered on what she hoped was an amiable smile.

He studied her closely, his gaze assessing. Then his lips tilted the barest amount upward. "Emily will be pleased to see you both. I was sent ahead to give her time to make herself presentable." He gestured to the stairs. "Please, follow me."

Juniper glanced at Betony and immediately regretted it. Her sister wore a wide grin and her eyebrows had arched nearly to the brim of her bonnet. There was nothing subtle in Betony's expression, the younger woman far too delighted in that moment.

After narrowing her eyes in warning, Juniper followed Mr. Sterling up the steps. "I hope we are not interrupting anything important," she said, trying to cover the somewhat awkward silence.

It seemed a change in station truly hadn't made Mr. Sterling any more talkative than he'd been before. Perhaps that was merely habit, though, given that he hadn't much opportunity for open conversation yet.

"Not at all," he said, tone formal. "She was assisting with the children in the nursery and merely wished to change." He paused on the landing and turned, making Juniper and Betony hesitate. His brow was drawn down. "Given our conversation at dinner the other evening, you both know that my family is still adjusting to our position. In truth, Emily would have come straight down to see you both and I doubt you would have minded the state of her gown. She had paste and paper stuck to it, along with a few splatters of paint. It was an older gown, from...before." His shoulders were stiff as he explained, his hands curled into fists at his side.

He sounded rather protective of Emily, even as he described her state of attire as less than ideal for even an informal visit.

As it seemed he expected her to say something, Juniper glanced briefly at Betony before speaking. "You are right, Mr. Sterling. We would not have minded."

"But it is best to practice the expected behavior as often as possible," he said, not sounding defensive. Not exactly, anyway.

Juniper eyed him with raised eyebrows. "Were you the one who told her to change?" she asked, tilting her head to the side. Taking his measure.

"Yes." His jaw tightened. "She was not pleased."

His response tugged a smile from her. "I imagine not. My impression of your sister is that she is a determined, independent-minded lady. A woman like that does not enjoy being told what to do. Even by a well-meaning brother."

His eyebrows drew together. "Should I have done differently?"

Juniper wanted to place a reassuring hand on his arm, a gesture wholly inappropriate given the nature of their acquaintance. To prevent the temptation, she clasped her hands in front of her. "As you knew it was us, a gentle suggestion would have been all she needed, most likely. I will be certain to speak with her, though."

He gave a silent nod of thanks and released a deep sigh, yet looked no more relaxed than before. He glanced from Juniper to Betony, and back again. "I hope you will have better luck than I have, Lady Juniper. My sister's 'independent-minded' nature, as you call it, often expresses itself as sheer stubbornness."

The break in his usual stoic silence made her heart flutter and inspired her to speak more freely. "I do not see that as a negative quality. In fact, I quite like that about her."

Betony made a soft sound of amusement. "We both do."

Mr. Sterling did not soften, precisely, but he did offer them a sharp nod before he turned and continued to lead them through the corridor to a sitting room with a window overlooking the street. He allowed them to enter ahead of him, and this room immediately caught Juniper's attention. Everything in it was new. New wallpaper, new furnishings, new carpet—and it was comfortable. Not overly fashionable, but timeless. Soft colors, furniture with elegant lines, and floral patterns which did not overwhelm the senses.

"This is lovely," she said, looking about with interest. "Did your mother decorate this room?" She looked up at him, and her heart skipped a beat when she realized he stood directly behind her.

"Indeed." Mr. Sterling gave another of his brief nods, his gaze flickering briefly around the room.

Hope surged through Juniper as she surveyed the decor. Had it been filled with garish, expensive yet tasteless decorations, she would have been concerned about the family's prospects. The sensibilities of a matriarch often dictated a family's place within the intricate hierarchies of London society and one's décor was a statement of intent. Thankfully, Lady Benwaith's preference for subtle, timeless pieces suggested a discerning eye which would serve them all well in their social endeavors.

"The whole of it is most welcoming." Betony stood at the window, looking about with interest. "Lady Benwaith has excellent taste."

His expression lightened, his eyes on hers. "It is one of the first in this house she made her own." The slight crack in Mr. Sterling's usual stoic mask prompted Juniper to speak, hoping to see more.

"Beyond what it says of her taste, I quite like it. I think anyone who visits will feel at ease here. It's comforting, reminiscent of a home meant to be lived in, not merely displayed."

Mr. Sterling's expression softened and a hint of a gentler emotion flickered across his face. "It reminds me of the cottage where I grew up. It is nothing as grand as this, of course, but my mother always had a way of making even those smaller rooms feel inviting. She believes a home should embrace those who enter, not intimidate them."

Juniper stepped toward him, intrigued. "A cottage?" she asked, curiosity dancing along her thoughts. "That must have been a lovely place to live, if it felt like this."

"It was...humble," Mr. Sterling acknowledged, his gaze drifting as if he could see through the walls of the townhouse to the simpler, presumably smaller home of his childhood. "Nestled on the edge of a meadow, with ivy creeping up the walls and wildflowers always pushing their way through the garden paths. There wasn't much room, especially for a family of our size. But it was ours, and it was home."

Juniper could well imagine the looks of such a place thanks to the heartfelt way that he spoke of it. She had grown up in a large house which had been rather devoid of life after her father's death. Her sisters kept it from feeling too empty, yet it had never really felt like home again once William and Fanny moved in.

"It sounds charming. I imagine it was a wonderful place to grow up." She took in his stance, the way his hands had relaxed as he spoke. It was difficult to drag her eyes away.

"For me it was," he confirmed, a trace of a smile playing at the corners of his lips as he returned his attention to her. "It's those aspects of our past that I hope guide how we, as a family, approach this new chapter in our lives. If we strive to maintain that sense of home, perhaps we will not lose ourselves entirely to this new way of things."

"That's a beautiful way to think of it." Juniper's admiration for him could not help but deepen. She'd felt drawn to him the first time she'd spoken to him when he was merely Sterling, a guard instructed to look after her and Betony. Sterling—Mr. Sterling now—had a presence to him that set her at ease; made her feel safe. Despite his formality, there was something comforting about him.

Perhaps she had sensed more than his steadiness of character. A man who had grown up in a cottage filled with familial love had to have more to him than a stern frown and a commanding presence, did he not?

Here, at last, she saw evidence of the warmth and authenticity she'd guessed at existing before.

Betony, who had been quietly observing from the window, spoke with a somewhat playful tone. "It's lovely to hear about your beginnings, Mr. Sterling. It explains the warmth both you and your family exude."

Mr. Sterling nodded his thanks for the compliment, his posture stiffening again. "Thank you, Lady Betony. I can only hope we are fortunate to find such acceptance of our origin among our other new acquaintances."

The moment lingered, a comfortable silence settling among them as Juniper took in the room anew, seeing within the walls the layers of Mr. Sterling's past and his family's values. Juniper's initial apprehension about the visit was replaced by a hope that this house—and its inhabitants—might one day become a regular part of her life.

No sabers to rattle, no uniform to hide his feelings behind, Jack hated how bereft he felt doing nothing other than standing there in the middle of a sitting room. Two ladies watched him, expecting him to make conversation.

Posted at attention in a corner, unobtrusive and waiting to be of use in the livery of his master, that had been much easier than what he did now...especially when he saw Lady Betony's slight smirk directed at him while Lady Juniper's expression turned thoughtful.

She looked undeniably lovely all over again. Kindness softened her smile as he spoke about the cottage where he'd felt much more at home than he did presently. Or was it sympathy he saw? Did she find his background quaint? Saying it sounded *charming,* well, that could have any number of meanings. Yet he sensed nothing in her bearing or tone to hint at anything less than her sincere appreciation of his past.

When she and her sister continued to stare at him, it took calling upon his training to stand at attention for hours to keep from shifting with discomfort.

Heat crept up the back of his neck as the silence stretched. Did it fall to him to fill it? As the host until his sister arrived, it must. Jack cleared his throat and considered them both. Perhaps a comment on the weather might suffice? Or a query about their family's health? Or any number of inane things he couldn't bring himself to say aloud, though he'd grown uncomfortably warm in the seconds ticking past.

Thankfully, his ears picked up the faint creak of floorboards from the corridor, signaling the arrival of his sister to his rescue.

Emily entered the room at the next moment, somewhat breathless but with a cheeriness that immediately drew all attention to her. "I am terribly sorry I kept everyone waiting. It is too good of you to come visit, Lady Juniper, Lady Betony." She curtsied, her form perfect, then gestured to the couches. "Please, ladies, do make yourselves comfortable."

Jack wanted to curse aloud. Blast—he'd kept them standing all this time, hadn't once thought they kept on their feet because of him. The simplest of etiquette, and he'd stood about like a fool, speaking of his past, while they listened with politeness.

Lady Betony sat at once and immediately launched into raptures about Emily's lovely gown. Lady Juniper drifted toward him, letting her sister explain the reason behind the unexpected visit.

In a low voice, Lady Juniper spoke to him. "Do not look so stricken, Mr. Sterling." Her gaze met his, and that familiar smile of hers felt like a soothing brush of a hand. "You did nothing wrong."

He raised his eyebrows. Had she read him that easily? "I am sorry I kept you both standing."

"We could have sat without a direct invitation, too," she said, giving a slight shake of her head. Then she sat in a chair across from the couch occupied by her sister and his.

He hesitated, looking at another empty seat. "I will take my leave of you ladies now, if you have no further need of me, Emily?"

"Hold, one moment," Emily said, raising her hand to stop him before Jack could make a move toward the door. "I want to hear what they think of your instruction to me this morning." She lifted her chin and looked from one Amberton sister to the other. "Did he tell you he made me change before coming to greet you? Is that the done thing? It's not as though I wore rags or was covered in filth."

Jack sighed deeply. Why did every member of his family insist on trying his patience? "Emily, things are different now. Even in the privacy of your home, you're expected to look the part of an earl's daughter." He sent a look of appeal to Lady Juniper.

Her head tilted, and she turned to Emily with a friendly demeanor as she spoke. "Given that we performed a minor breech in etiquette by not sending word ahead of our visit, it would not have been the worst thing for you to either send us away or appear in whatever manner you were dressed, so long as it was modest. Of course, had we been visitors you were less acquainted with, or were welcoming us by appointment, changing first would be the most appropriate course of action. Often the manner in which you dress is seen as a reflection of the level of respect you have for your visitors as well as yourself. Betony and I would not mind a less formal appearance in the least. Other ladies would take offense."

The simple explanation seemed to appease Emily, but she looked at Sterling with narrowed eyes. "You see. They would not have minded."

He gave a slight shrug. "I didn't think *they* would. However, best foot forward is never a bad thing to adhere to in social situations."

"It is best you changed, though," Lady Betony added, "because we want to take you out for a walk. Mr. Sterling, you must come, too. Even though it is nippy outside, with the sun shining the elite of London will want to take a little exercise. Taking a turn out of doors in the closest park will allow for your neighbors to see you with others who match you in rank."

"Thus strengthening your prominence and reputation in Society," Lady Juniper added with her usual softer tone and smile. She blinked up at him, and a disconcerting desire to please her made Jack wish to immediately agree.

"That is an excellent idea," Emily said before he could. "Go get your hat and coat, Jack—and gloves too, perhaps, it looks frightfully cold. I will do that same."

A quarter of an hour later, they were walking through the nearest patch of greenery. He'd tried to walk behind all three ladies, the better to keep an eye on them, but Lady Betony had looped her arm with Emily's and walked ahead. Leaving Lady Juniper a few paces behind on the narrow path. As he was, in fact, a gentleman, Jack moved to keep pace next to the singular woman. His gaze swept from one side of the park to the other, noting the number of couples present, how many gentlemen, where carriages parked along the edges of the road, which children appeared to be with which nursemaids or governesses—

"Do you ever get tired of it?" Lady Juniper's soft inquiry pulled his attention back to her.

"Tired? Of what?"

He had the feeling she'd been staring at him for a while, given the amusement in her eyes. "Always being on alert for danger. Forever acting as a sentinel."

That gave him pause. He'd never considered that his ability to maintain awareness of his surroundings might tire him—or others. "It is simply something I do. I cannot recall a time before I kept watch over the people under my care. My family often calls me a shepherd dog."

Her eyes glittered and a breath that sounded akin to a laugh escaped her. "Do they? I suppose there are worse things to be compared to than a loyal creature, tasked with keeping others safe. Goodness. That is quite the image, though, isn't it?"

His lips twitched. "Still. A *dog*."

"I wonder what domesticated creature I might be compared to? Perhaps a faithful spaniel, the sort that stays curled up on a rug next to the fire."

He raised his eyebrows. "You sound as though you like the idea."

"Who wouldn't?" Lady Juniper's grin grew brighter. "Especially if it were a hearth in a library. I can think of nothing more cozy."

"The books would be of little use to a spaniel, though. As far as I am aware, dogs of all varieties cannot read." That drew a laugh from her, and Jack immediately wanted to hear the cheerful sound again.

Immediately, however, he censured himself. He shouldn't

tease or jest with her, or...no. He could, now. As a servant, it would have been the height of rudeness. An offense beyond reckoning. But as a gentleman? The bounds changed.

"Then perhaps I would not enjoy the life of a spaniel, or any animal, as it would mean a distinct lack of novels," she said, a merry smile still twitching her lips upward.

"And novels are one of your life's greatest joys," he remarked without first thinking the comment through.

Lady Juniper's head turned sharply, her eyes widened in surprise. "How do you know that?"

It was a pertinent question—how? He had paid attention to her during her stay at the duke's castle the previous summer. He had followed her about, of course, but then the guards talked about all the guests, too. They spoke of where they spent their time, how they behaved, and so on.

From both his own observations and the words of others, Jack knew that Lady Juniper Amberton enjoyed reading as much as her elder sister, though what they read differed widely. Lady Juniper went about the castle with gothic novels tucked beneath her arm. The former Lady Ivy had borrowed titles more related to intellectual pursuits than entertainment.

He cleared his throat. "An observation made in the past and a touch of assumption. Nothing more."

Rather than seem offended, Lady Juniper appeared amused. Perhaps, even, pleased by this piece of information. "Indeed. The shepherd dog sees everything, it would seem."

"Not everything," he said, trying to reassure her. "But I try to notice the things that count."

"And what I read last summer counted?"

It had. To him. Though it likely shouldn't have been a thing he noticed. Why did he even remember what she read? "It was an interesting detail to note."

Lady Juniper adjusted the reticule on her wrist, glancing away from him. She looked ahead where Betony and Emily walked, speaking animatedly with their hands. They pointed at plants and nodded toward people walking along the other side of the path. "I imagine your attention to detail will be invaluable to your family."

"They seem more annoyed by it than anything," he said, then winced. "I apologize. I should not have said that."

She glanced at him from the corner of her eyes. "I will not repeat what you say. In truth, it was not difficult to guess at such a thing, given how your sister reacted to your guidance on the matter of her gown. If they do see you as their shepherd dog, they must have felt you nipping at their heels a time or two since your arrival in London."

Jack tried to keep his expression steady and let his gaze sweep across the park again. "They have accused me of that very thing. On multiple occasions."

"Perhaps a gentler approach is warranted?"

That brought his attention to her. "Perhaps. I find it difficult to envision anything other than what I have attempted. I tell them the truth of things, of exactly what they need to know to succeed."

"With the succinctness and tone of a military commander, I would venture to guess."

He liked her smile that seemed made of half amusement and half smugness. "A good guess." He did not mind rewarding it in the slightest with a grin of his own.

"Your family are neither sheep nor soldiers, Mr. Sterling."

"Are they not?" Jack feigned surprise, raising his eyebrows at her, watching for another smirk, hoping for another laugh.

Instead, the lady merely shook her head and sighed as though exasperated by him. "They are ladies and gentlemen—they are your family. As I said, a gentle word will likely help far more than a commanding one. Especially if it is as I imagine, that everyone is overwhelmed. The changes they have been through, this new way of living, likely overcomes the senses. I know that when I face a complex array of thoughts and emotions, someone barking orders at me would make matters worse. Not better."

"I do not *bark*." Jack protested quietly, though he turned her words over in his thoughts. "I need to be heard over everything else taking their attention, Lady Juniper."

"Do you? Or do you need to be the calmest voice in a sea of confusion?" She turned more fully toward him as she asked that question and his steps slowed.

Goodness. He had not considered that tactic even once. Instead, he had let his frustration dictate his tone. And his sense of urgency. "I will think on your advice, Lady Juniper."

"I hope it proves helpful, Mr. Sterling. I speak from my own experience as one who needed guidance and support, and was instead commanded and governed. It was...not a pleasant experience."

He could remember her sister-in-law's sharp tongue all too well. He had caught many of the woman's diatribes and censures against the Amberton ladies. Being compared to her, even indirectly, smote his pride.

He winced. "Guidance instead of governance is a good way to think on it," he said at last, the admission still difficult to make.

Navigating his family's transition into nobility required vigilance, yes, but also sensitivity. Lady Juniper hinted at using a subtler strength, one which could instruct and inform without overwhelming. Most interesting.

As they continued their walk, the park's scenery faded somewhat as he focused on Emily's laughter ahead of them. Emily, and her change of gown. The way the sisters had spoken to Emily about her manner of dress had been far gentler than his own conversation with her. Emily had listened intently to them. Would she listen to her own brother if he softened his tone?

"Thank you, Lady Juniper. Your perspective is invaluable.

Perhaps..." Jack hesitated, choosing his words with care. "Perhaps you might allow me to seek your advice again, if necessary? It seems I have much to learn about guiding without governing."

Her smile broadened, touched with a hint of surprise. "I—I would be delighted to help, Mr. Sterling. And who knows? Perhaps in teaching you the finer points of subtlety, I might learn a thing or two about cultivating a more commanding presence from you."

"Have you need of a commanding presence?" Jack had to ask, glancing at her slim form and height. She wasn't short, necessarily, but the top of her head did not even reach his chin. "Hmm. Never mind. I can see why you would wish to possess one."

The ridiculous remark drew another laugh from her, a startled laugh that she immediately stifled with a hand over her mouth. "Mr. Sterling, that is too horrid of you to poke fun at my stature."

"Merely making another observation, my lady."

"That I am small?"

"That you are not the least bit intimidating."

"Could you teach me to be as fierce in appearance as you are?"

"That is a tall order, Lady Juniper, for a short woman. And you haven't my natural forbidding expression."

"*Short* woman? I believe I am of average height, sir."

"Still. Not forbidding enough."

"Ought I to scowl more?" She drew her eyebrows down sharply and stuck out her bottom lip. "Would that make up for the lack of stature?"

"My lady, that is a pout. Not a scowl." Jack laughed softly, and her cheeks turned a soft pink. A rather pretty shade on her, and a thing he should not take such delight in seeing.

"I shall have to practice my scowls, then." She sounded oddly pleased by the idea.

Ahead of them, Betony turned and put one hand on her hip. "Juniper? We need to confer with you about the Ladies Aid Society meeting tomorrow."

Lady Juniper glanced at him, a curious light in her eyes, before hurrying forward at a faster pace. He remained walking behind the ladies, watching over them and their surroundings.

His family's path to adapting to their new roles might be fraught with missteps and difficulties, but with allies like Lady Juniper, things seemed less daunting. Over the course of their brief conversation, his earlier discomfort had transformed into a cautious optimism. Perhaps he could bridge the gap between his family's past and their future, between his own duty and affection for them.

"Guidance over governance," he muttered to himself.

It was worth a try.

CHAPTER 7

"You hate balls."

Normally, Juniper would completely agree with Betony—but that evening, meeting her sister's gaze in the mirror, she shook her head. "Hate is a strong word. I dislike balls on most occasions. They are stuffy, overcrowded, loud, and take away from time I could better spend in occupation with books, art, or music." She considered a moment. "Or the theater. Or the outdoors. But if we wished to be exact, I should say that I find the crowds of people the most uncomfortable part of a ball."

"I truly do not understand why you dislike crowds." Betony handed Hettie another ivory colored ribbon so the maid had no need to lift her hands from Juniper's dark hair. "People are interesting. I enjoy watching them and listening to them. No two are alike, you know, for all they try to mimic one another."

"People are rude, forever in each other's way, laugh obnoxiously, and at times smell horrid." Juniper wrinkled her nose, her reflection doing the same in the looking glass. "No amount of perfume can cover some things, either. In fact, most of the time, strong colognes make matters worse."

"Which is why you so often come home with a headache."

Betony winced in sympathy. "And then spend the next day like a hermit, hidden away from everyone."

"It is more so the people than the headache that I must recover from over the course of the next day." Juniper tilted her head to ease Hettie's work. "People exhaust me."

Hettie smiled a little. "You seem a friendly sort of lady, for all that you don't like other folk."

"Oh, I like individuals well enough." Juniper released a weary sigh. "It is large groups that I am not fond of."

"Then why go tonight?" Betony's eyes sparkled with mischief.

"You know precisely why. I promised Lady Emily I would be there."

"And Lady's Emily's brother will be present."

Juniper gave her sister a warning glance in the reflection of the looking glass. "The whole family will be present, and we promised we would help them. That is why I am going to the ball."

"A kind reason, my lady," Hettie said, tucking a final curl in place. "And you are ready to dazzle, should you wish it."

Juniper rose and stood before the longer mirror in her room, turning about only once to ensure she liked the look of things. She wore a pale blue gown with ivory lace at the hem and ivory gloves on her hands, the light colors making her dark eyes and hair stand out all the more. She picked up her matching reticule.

"Your fan." Hettie handed her the lace fan and stepped back to admire her handiwork. Then she looked at Betony, who wore a gown of similar style but in a rose pink. "You are both lovely. I hope you enjoy your evening, my ladies—crowds or no."

They thanked her and left the room. They were in the carriage moments later, with Teague and Ivy seated across from them. Teague was wearing a dark green coat and gold waistcoat, and Ivy a gown of shimmering gold. They looked like a matched set, in truth, and made a handsome couple.

"Have you not a book in your reticule, Juniper?" Teague asked with a knowing raise of his brows. "It doesn't look large enough for such a thing."

"Oh." She had slipped a thin volume into the bag from mere habit. "Well, I do have something, yes."

No one censured her for it. They all merely seemed amused, which she supposed was better than any other reaction she could hope for.

Teague gave a small shake of his head. "Sometimes I think I ought to adopt your propensity for carrying around reading material. There are days in parliament when I should infinitely prefer a book to listening to my colleagues."

It was only minutes later that they arrived at the ball, hosted by Lord and Lady Jersey. The event would be as near to a crush as someone of their standing wished, without going into the vulgarity of having too many guests and not enough room. Of course, given their wealth and size of their house in Town, Juniper seriously doubted the Jerseys would have any trouble should they wish to invite every titled person in Britain.

It was an excellent event for the Sterling family to attend. There would be so many people present, it was most unlikely anyone would notice any minor social *faux pas*. Juniper had high hopes for Lady Emily to make a good impression this evening: she and Betony would see to it.

"Before you wander off," Teague said, once they were safely in the corridor outside the ballroom, "there are introductions I would like to make."

It was Ivy, his wife, who huffed. "Really, Teague. Must you?"

"I am not truly playing at matchmaking," he said quickly, which made Juniper and Betony exchange a glance. Their brother-in-law chuckled and raised both hands. "I promise you both, I am not. Old Farleigh asked that I introduce myself, and my family, to an old friend of his. It never hurts to know more trustworthy gentlemen, does it?"

"We promised Lady Emily we would meet her right away," Betony said, narrowing her eyes at Teague.

"Excellent. After you meet my new friends, you can bring them along to introduce them to Lady Emily and her family." Teague seemed entirely too confident in himself at times.

Juniper adjusted the ribbon of her reticule and resigned herself to a widening acquaintance. "All right. Who are we meeting?"

Teague took his wife's arm again and led them into the ballroom as he said, "Roman Eastwood, titled Baron Hartwell and his brother, Lyness Eastwood. They tend to keep themselves in York, though I cannot think why."

"They likely feel about Yorkshire the way you do about Ireland," Betony teased as she and Juniper followed.

"Perhaps." Teague led them along the wall, to an obviously pre-determined meeting place.

Two men stood together, so alike in appearance they could only be brothers, though the older of the two was a touch shorter than the other. Teague bowed and first introduced Ivy, then his sisters-in-law, to them both.

Juniper considered them. The men were both handsome. Tall, light brown hair, blue eyes and narrow builds. It was something of a surprise they were not surrounded by matchmaking mothers or swooning misses.

Lord Hartwell's smile was tight, but polite, as he addressed them. "It is a pleasure to meet the ladies of Dunmore's family at last—and your connection as cousins to my close friend, Lord Farleigh, came as a pleasant surprise."

It always fell to Juniper, as the elder of the two single sisters, to speak before Betony could do so. At least, with new acquaintances. "It is likely if we look back far enough in our family trees, we are all related to half the room at this very moment.

But we are grateful to have a good friendship with our cousins, the Dinards."

"All of whom are absent," Lord Hartwell said, his smile unmoving. "No news on that front yet, I trust?" He spoke, delicately of course, of the impending birth of Lord and Lady Farleigh's first child.

"We do not expect anything for another month or so." Juniper glanced at his younger brother, who had a more genial expression than the baron but seemed content to remain silent. "I wonder that we have not met before, Lord Hartwell."

"Ah, that is easy enough to explain." His lips twitched upward, though again his eyes did not seem to share in any pleasant humor. "I am across the aisle from your brother, the earl. We do not see eye-to-eye on nearly anything."

Neither Juniper nor Betony had anything they wished to say about their half-brother. After he'd ceded guardianship of them both to their brother-in-law, they'd rarely seen him. Much to their relief.

Betony had apparently finished with the small talk. "Lord Hartwell, Mr. Eastwood, we are to meet a friend of ours, quite new to London's social world. We would be honored if you would come and allow us to make introductions, assuming you have not yet met the new Earl of Benwaith and his family?"

"Ah, I have had the pleasure of meeting Lord Benwaith." Lord Hartwell glanced around, as though looking for the older man. "Farleigh sent a letter requesting I make the acquaintance."

"Of course he did," Teague murmured with the slightest of improper grins. "His Grace's family intends to rally support for the Sterling family."

"Ah, that is how you became acquainted as well?" Lord Hartwell asked politely. "At times, I think I am good at social and political maneuverings, and then someone like the Duke of

Montfort shows that he is winning at chess while I have been amusing myself with draughts."

"W-We haven't met the rest of the f-family," Mr. Eastwood said at his brother's elbow, his stutter somewhat surprising Juniper, yet she maintained her polite expression. "Lord Benwaith's f-family."

That made his older brother heave a sigh. "No. We ought to do so, and a ball is an excellent place for that. And then we will have more ladies to dance with." He sounded mightily unenthusiastic about that prospect, giving Juniper and Betony another reason to exchange a look of amusement.

"I must introduce my wife to another acquaintance at present. I trust you can look after my sisters-in-law long enough for introductions?" Teague said, giving the Englishmen a nod of his head.

Lord Hartwell bowed to Juniper and offered his arm. "Lady Juniper, I will deliver you safely to your friends."

"W-With p-pleasure." Mr. Eastwood offered his escort to Betony, who accepted with a friendly grin.

It didn't take them long to find the knot of Sterlings. Lord Benwaith and his countess stood at the center, his married sons and their wives on either side, with Lady Emily and the youngest son standing slightly apart from the rest.

It took a great deal of self-control for Juniper to keep her gaze from lingering on John Sterling, but it was he who came forward and introduced his entire family to Lord Hartwell and his brother. *Poor man.* Knowing as she did how much responsibility he took upon himself, for his family's sake, she wondered if he ever took a moment for his own sake.

Drifting from her escort, Juniper came to Emily's side and took in her new friend's gown. "Oh, you look lovely—your gown, your hair, everything."

Emily's cheeks pinked and she laughed, somewhat shakily. It was only then that Juniper noticed the slight tremble in her new friend's hand as she touched the necklace at her throat. "Thank you. I admit that choosing a gown for this evening was daunting. Lady Jersey, as a patroness of Almack's, is someone I have been informed I ought to impress."

"Oh, Almack's," Betony muttered, nose wrinkled as she stood on Emily's other side. "It isn't at all as important as some would have you think—certainly not as enjoyable. You can tell that none of the eligible men want to be there, but they have been dragged by their mamas. The refreshments are hardly worthwhile. There are far better places to meet people."

Mr. Eastwood remained close enough to turn to them, over-hearing their conversation. His bright blue eyes sparkled with humor. "I have n-never heard a lady d-dis-disparage Almack's."

Betony appeared unrepentant, but Emily looked down as though she was the one caught speaking of the institution's lack of interest, her cheeks flushing, which made Juniper bite her lip with sympathy. She had often found herself feeling accountable for Betony's more candid opinions by mere association.

Mr. Eastwood bowed to them. "Lady B-Betony, might I have the p-pleasure of the next d-dance?"

"Of course," Betony said, sounding as delighted as she always did to accept a partner. She accepted his hand and he led her into place, preparing to step into the next formation of couples.

After a moment of quiet, Emily leaned toward Juniper. "Mr. Eastwood is rather handsome."

The word made her eyes dart inexorably to where the former-guardsman stood, conversing with Lord Hartwell. It was difficult to think on other men at a moment when she was quite aware of him, and somewhat mournful that Mr. Sterling had yet to speak to her directly.

As though her thoughts were spoken aloud, however, he turned toward her with his usual stoic expression. "Lady Juniper. Would you care to dance with me?"

"Yes." The word slipped from her at such speed that she immediately berated herself for letting her eagerness show. Yet he did not even react, except to offer his hand to guide her to the floor. She was only vaguely aware of Lord Hartwell asking Emily the same question, for which he received a pleased acceptance.

Mr. Sterling leaned closer to her as he led her through the crowd. "Thank you for setting Emily at ease. My sister is rather nervous this evening."

"I haven't done much as of yet," Juniper protested.

"Merely having a friend smile and converse naturally makes all the difference." Mr. Sterling's expression changed the barest amount, his eyes lightening somewhat as he looked down at her. "Many times this evening she has expressed relief that you and your sister would be present."

"It is a pleasure to be considered her friend." Juniper meant it quite honestly—the fact the pair were siblings was a charming bonus.

"I hope my sister is not the only one to claim such a thing." The words, murmured close to her ear as they came to the edge of the crowd, surprised her with their boldness.

It was bold, wasn't it, for him to say such a thing?

But then, he only meant he wished to be her friend, too, did he not?

Juniper's mind tumbled about, shocked and questioning whether it ought to be shocked, while she looked at his profile with eyes she knew had opened far too wide for politeness.

They took their places across from one another in the row of dancers. Mr. Sterling looked down the column to where his sister stood, then back to where he had left his family. With a satisfied nod to himself, as though pleased all members of his flock were present and accounted for, he then turned his full attention to Juniper. Those deep brown eyes of his immediately making her heart skip forward in her chest.

She needed to say something when he stepped near. She had to. It was part of dancing together—yet his last words to her left Juniper struggling to put a thought together.

Thus a rather truthful thing, rather than an interesting one, slipped out. "Ballrooms are far too crowded for my liking."

His head tilted ever-so-slightly to one side. "Are they? I have never been fond of them either, though I imagine our reasons for our shared feeling differ."

A glance around them made her wonder what, precisely, he could dislike. "My reasons are the noise, the scents, the exhaustion that comes from speaking to dozens of people in one evening. What are yours?"

He waited until they joined hands again to murmur, "The difficulty of keeping one's eye on a charge, to keep watch."

Ah yes. That would have proven a challenge for his former employment. She looked to where Betony partnered with Mr. Eastwood. Keeping an eye on only her younger sister in rooms full to bursting often proved challenging. "I think I can understand that, Mr. Sterling."

"Your sympathy to my plight is appreciated."

That teased a smile from her, and when their eyes met she saw a glimmer of amusement in his. "I would offer my assistance, though I am but a humble library spaniel."

An actual smile escaped him. Getting him to smile was as rewarding as it had been at the park. The man had a smile that pulled an answering warmth into her chest every time she caught a glimpse of it.

"Lady Juniper, I will always accept any gesture of kindness you see fit to extend to me or my kin." Did she imagine the softness in his gaze as he spoke? His words did not sound as though he jested. Not in the least. No, he certainly meant them.

"We should take Lady Emily on an outing," she blurted, her cheeks blazing with heat again. "Day-after-tomorrow."

His eyebrows rose, and he passed her through another

movement of the dance, parting them for several beats of the music. When they came together at last, his hand took hers. "What have you in mind?"

It was still frightfully cold out, most days—a long walk had the disadvantage of increasing the likelihood of a cold...and red noses all round. Her mind sorted through appropriate activities quickly, thinking through places she had visited in the past. "The Tower of London."

That brought a sharp look from him. "The Tower?"

"Lots of people go," she said, then had to wait to speak more. Dash it all. Why were there so few dances that would let them keep still long enough to have a full conversation? If ever she spoke to someone who arranged such things, she would request it specifically.

"What will we do at the Tower?" he asked. "Visit the animal enclosures?"

"No, no. The Line of Kings," she said. "You have never been?"

He would only have visited if the duke's family had gone and taken him as a guard. It wasn't inconceivable to think he had lacked the opportunity to go inside the old castle fortress. Not everyone enjoyed such things.

"It sounds intriguing." He was at her side again. "I will ask my sister, and secure us transportation."

Juniper had done the unthinkable—at least, her sister-in-law Fanny would have been mightily displeased with Juniper's achievement. In mere moments, she managed to secure an outing with the man she most wanted to spend time, issuing an informal invitation under the guise of spending time with his sister. It was scandalous!

She couldn't help feeling triumphant. "I am certain we will have a marvelous time. I will tell her of the scheme myself," she promised.

Mr. Sterling took her in with a smile. "First we must make it through this evening in one piece."

"I am certain we will manage." She looked to where Lady Emily danced with Lord Hartwell. They appeared pleasant enough. Neither of them frowned, at least. "Has your sister had many callers yet?"

He blinked at the change in subject, then shook his head. "Not yet. But perhaps tomorrow." His brow furrowed. "I should not be dancing overmuch."

That sent a stab of disappointment into her otherwise warm bubble of enjoyment. "Really? Why?"

"Then I will have to make calls, and I would prefer to be at home while she receives hers."

Given his protective nature, it made perfect sense. "Send flowers instead," she suggested. "Flowers are an acceptable substitute for the gentleman's company, should he merely wish to thank a lady for giving him the time of a dance. You ought to know that."

Her gaze met his. "I had momentarily forgotten. Still...I have no desire to spend my night dancing with strangers who are only interested in the novelty of a family raised up from nothing."

"I doubt that would be the only reason for their interest," Juniper said in a dry tone, then pressed her fingers over her mouth and missed a step in the dance. *Heavens.* What was wrong with her? If things like this continued happening, he certainly would not trust her to help his sister in the least way!

Instead of appearing scandalized, or uncomfortable, or any other horrible thing she felt must follow her utterance, John Sterling laughed. Not loud or boisterous; indeed, only one head turned in their direction to see the source of the sound—and it was his sister's. But he laughed, and she truly enjoyed it.

When the dance came to an end and he lead her back to the company of his family, Juniper felt rather hopeful. She had made Mr. John Sterling smile and laugh, and he wanted—at the very least—to be her friend.

Mr. Eastwood brought Betony back, then whisked Emily away, while his brother then asked for Juniper's hand, and Mr. Sterling took Betony as his next partner. To have such attention paid to all three of them brought the notice of other gentlemen and Juniper, Betony, and Emily were not without partners for the rest of the evening.

CHAPTER 8

J ack looked impatiently at the clock, then back to his sister's room full of admirers. Since they started taking callers at eleven o'clock, gentlemen had flowed in and out of the house continuously...for over an hour. He knew Emily had danced a great many times, but he hadn't realized half the men of the *ton* had stood up with her, or wanted to stand up with her —and when they couldn't, decided to pay their respects the following day.

Flowers covered the tables in the sitting room where Emily held court, trying her best to show genteel courtesy to everyone who called upon her. His mother and sisters-in-law sat in the room with her but were somewhat less than helpful.

No one quite knew what to do.

It fell therefore to Jack to watch his sister's reaction to each gentleman, and if she seemed less than comfortable with their attention, he found reason to step in and extricate her or thank them for coming and show them the door.

At one point, his sister whispered to him, "Can we not send for Juniper and Betony? They would know how to help."

He had thought of that himself, but had also quickly realized it would be of no use. "They will have their own sitting room full of men, I imagine."

Emily grimaced and then put her polite smile on once more and returned to her next guest.

Not for the first time, Jack's mind wandered to Juniper—Lady Juniper. Was she truly flooded with callers, too? How many gentlemen had visited her that morning, and how many had sent flowers as he had done? Though it was of course for the best that he remained home with Emily, for the best that he not pay a specific call to the Amberton sisters, his mind unendingly flitted across London streets to their home.

One of Emily's more persistent callers, a Mr. Waldegrave, had brought her a stunningly large bouquet of red roses—a somewhat presumptuous offering, considering he barely knew her. Mr. Waldegrave had danced with her toward the end of the evening, after introducing himself to their father. He lingered in the sitting room past the quarter-hour most of the men had allowed themselves, and Jack's irritation prickled.

Footmen brought two more flower deliveries into the room, and Jack took the opportunity to step between Mr. Waldegrave and his sister. "Emily, these two seem especially grand. What do the cards say?" He cut the gentleman at his elbow a quick glance. "Mr. Waldegrave, I must thank you for coming to see my sister. It has been a pleasure." He spoke calmly, but with the unmistakable air of someone bidding farewell.

Mr. Waldegrave drew himself up, but was not quite eye-level with Jack, the man not striking him as someone particularly comfortable with conflict. His eyes flickered from Jack to Emily, then he bowed. "The pleasure was all mine. I look forward to seeing you again soon, Lady Emily."

Emily, who held the many cards from the flowers in her hands, gave him a somewhat distracted curtsy. "Indeed, Mr. Waldegrave. Thank you. And thank you for the flowers."

He had not even made it out of the room before Emily

sighed with what sounded like disappointment. "They are from Lord Hartwell and Mr. Eastwood."

"Nice of them to send something," Jack said, watching until the door closed on the irritating gentleman. "Mr. Waldegrave was not my favorite of your callers today, Emily."

"Nor one of mine." She shook her head and her expression at last relaxed. "This is overwhelming. Must this always be the way after a ball? Every gentleman I danced with or spoke to coming to call, it feels excessive."

"Lady Dunmore assured me it was likely," their mother said with a sigh, fanning herself. "Dear me. Our kitchen staff will be worked to pieces, making an unending supply of tea and cakes and sandwiches for everyone who visits."

"That is their purpose, Mother," Jack reassured her. "And they are well compensated for it, never you fear."

"What would we do without you, Jack?" his mother asked softly.

That was the question. The whole household and everyone in it would fall apart. He looked forward to the day Richard found himself comfortable enough in his role as heir and viscount to stand as leader. Their father had no intention of doing more than the minimum of fitting into their new life, claiming he was too old to pretend he belonged in a room full of fancy nobles.

Jack looked over the flowers Emily had received with interest. One was full of a variety of bright flowers, looking rather expensive. The other was not nearly so large, and the flowers were a mix of more common blooms, such as daisies and chrysanthemums. It was the simpler bouquet that his sister held in her arms. "Eastwood sent the smaller of the two arrangements?"

Emily glanced up. "Yes. How did you know?" She looked at the flowers. "Do you think it means something?"

"All flowers mean something," Susan, their brother George's

wife, said from her place near the fire. "And after speaking with Lord Hartwell last evening about his mother's passion for gardening, I would wager a guess both he and his brother are somewhat versed in at least the common meanings behind each bloom. Bring them here."

Katherine shook her head. "Men rarely pay attention to such things as the meanings of flowers. Examine at the jumble around us and you can know that at once."

"Let her have her fun, dear," Jack's mother said genially. "The large bouquet first, Susan."

"Simple. Pink roses are for grace, wisteria for welcome, and laurel wishes you success." Susan pointed to the smaller gathering of flowers. "Those are what interest me. Daisies are innocence, white carnations are sweet and lovely, and the greenery..." She put her nose in the flowers and laughed. "Oh, it's peppermint."

"Useful, but is it meaningful?" the new viscountess asked, eyebrows arched.

"Of course. It indicates warmth of feeling. This is from which brother, Emily?" Susan handed the flowers back with a teasing grin.

Jack watched his sister with interest as she took the flowers carefully, a light pink stealing into her cheeks. *Interesting.*

"Mr. Eastwood," she said.

"Oh, the man with the stutter." Katherine shook her head. "He only danced with you once. Was it difficult to make conversation with him?"

Cradling the flowers close, Emily shook her head. "I did not find it so."

That had Jack raising his eyebrows. His sister's soft smile unmistakably hinted at her own warm feelings about the baron's younger brother. He would need to keep an eye on that. He liked what he knew of Hartwell and Mr. Eastwood, but it was precious little. He could not permit—

With a wave of her hand, Susan dismissed Katherine's remark. "If he can speak with flowers, has he need of greater eloquence?" Then she pointed at Jack. "Did *you* take my advice on what sort of flowers to send to your dancing partners?"

All the women in the room looked at him, Susan with expectancy and the other three with curiosity.

Jack's stomach twisted as he kept his voice calm. "I did. Small bouquets of violets, sweat peas, and white clover."

Now they all looked at Susan. "All innocent—and respectable—ways of saying thank you," she said, lifting an eyebrow. "What about the one you said was special?"

His mother, his sister, and both sisters-in-law stared at him.

"Jack," his mother said, a slow smile appearing on her gentle face. "A special bouquet? For a special woman?" She had a look in her eyes that he had seen many a mother wear before, usually when they were introducing their children to the duke's children in hopes of a match. His mother hadn't shown much interest in the idea of him marrying before, when he would visit home on rare occasions.

Of course, he hadn't entertained the idea himself, given that his work for the duke had consumed all his time and energies. He hadn't even thought he would ever have the luxury of marriage, not until he retired from service.

He felt his ears grow warm. Not that he was thinking of such things now, either. He cleared his throat. "I merely wished to show my appreciation to Lady Juniper, for her kindness and friendship—to us all. That was the only reason I thought to send her something other than what I gave to the rest of my dancing partners."

"What was in the bouquet, Susan?" Emily asked with a wide smile. "Tell us, please."

Before Jack could say a word, Susan answered. "Primrose, forget-me-not, and lily of the valley. Affection, remembrance, and happiness. In that order." She tapped her chin thoughtfully.

"Of course, my interpretation of such flowers would normally be that the one sending that medley is indicating he holds the person receiving them in high esteem, with the first stirrings of something other than friendship."

"Oh, Jack," his sister said, expression bright with excitement. "Do you really like Lady Juniper?"

"Of course he does, look at his blush." Katherine folded her arms and laughed. "Jack is smitten."

His mother, to his alarm, appeared ready to cry. "Oh, she is such a lovely girl—"

"Enough," Jack said, raising both hands and trying to sound stern. He heard the amusement in his tone, though, and he had to shake his head somewhat ruefully. "I have not said anything to make any of you believe such things. Lady Juniper is a fine person, and she is proving a good friend to Emily as well as to me. That is all."

"Why?" Susan asked, standing up and putting her hands on her hips. "Why not more than that, Jack?" She gestured to the other women. "We all saw the painting she made of you. We all saw how the two of you interacted first at dinner and then at Lady Jersey's ball."

"When she and her sister paid their visit to me, Juniper spent a long time speaking directly to Jack. Especially whilst on our walk." As Emily made her pronouncement, Jack sent her a playful glare.

"Traitor."

She stuck her tongue out at him. "It's the truth. She even made him laugh."

Katherine put a hand to her throat dramatically. "The man laughed? It is a miracle. Jack, you must wed her at once."

They all giggled and laughed like school girls rather than the adults and fine ladies they were, and he looked to his mother for some support, feeling suddenly helpless in the face of his female relatives. His mother was the worst of the lot, however, smiling at him with a gentle fondness that made him think she was already planning his wedding.

"This is nonsense," Jack said, trying to return to a more even tone even as his lungs tightened. "I have absolutely no thoughts toward more than cordial friendship with Lady Juniper."

"But *why*?" Susan asked again.

There were reasons. Several of them...a primary reason being that he had spent most of the last summer following her about a castle, dressed in the garb of a servant, watching over her and her sisters. He had spent hours of his day ignoring—or trying to ignore—the fact that she was a beautiful woman, because she had been so far above him in rank and dignity.

He had resisted the urge to smile every time he saw her make a book appear, seemingly from nowhere, to snatch moments reading while no one else saw. He had forced himself not to laugh when she and her sisters teased and jested with one another. Then he had spent months dismissing her from his mind after she went to Ireland upon her eldest sister's marriage.

Juniper's kindness at present did not surprise him. But the question remained: would she ever see him as more than the guard who had stood in the corner while she enjoyed the benefits of her close kinship to a duchess?

Jack cleared his throat. He had thought too long. "I ask that you do not speculate about more than friendship between myself and Lady Juniper—or any lady, for that matter. If there comes a time to discuss such things, I will let our family know. I promise."

The ladies did not return to complete sobriety, but the giggles diminished and they merely exchanged knowing looks.

A footman brought in another gentleman, and everyone's attention returned to Emily. Despite the busy morning, Jack counted the number of his sister's callers as a success for their family. Whether men came specifically to know her better or to satisfy their curiosity about the new Earl of Benwaith's family,

London Society was coming to know the family. So long as Jack could keep them behaving respectably, everything would be fine.

As tempted as he was to wonder what Lady Juniper's sitting room looked like at that moment, he contended himself with knowing that he'd be in her company again soon enough. They had confirmed their plans to visit the Tower of London, with Lady Betony and Emily, in a few days' time. While walking through a medieval relic might not be everyone's idea of entertainment, he suspected Juniper would show particular delight in every old stone and story the place held.

He could hardly wait.

CHAPTER 9

The last day of February experienced a creeping dawn, yet the winter-gloomed skies did nothing to dampen Juniper's spirits. She was going to the Tower of London today, with Mr. Sterling. And his sister. And her sister.

"Are you certain you do not need me to accompany you?" Teague asked as he sat in the front room with Juniper and Betony, watching for the Benwaith carriage to arrive. "It seems a tall order, having Sterling shepherd three unmarried ladies around all on his own."

"We will be perfectly behaved," Betony said with a toss of her head. "You really needn't worry so much about us, Teague."

"I am afraid that is what brothers do," he said, amusement in his tone. "Fiona is a handful, true, but I worry about all of you. I would gladly forgo my time in Lords today to escort you both. The items on the docket are of little interest to anyone but the people discussing them."

"You would shirk your duty for us?" Juniper asked, feigning a gasp. "You are indeed a splendid brother. We will be certain to bring you home a gift—but Betony is correct. We will do well enough without you today."

"Mm. Well. When they come to the part in the tour where they show off the weapons taken from the Irish, remember that there are two sides to every story, and the Irish side is quite different than what you will hear at the Tower."

Betony gave him a serious nod. "We will forever be more partial to the Irish side, you have our word."

He chuckled and looked out the window. "Here they are at last. Do not rush with your bonnets, I must have a word with Sterling before you go."

"Oh, Teague," Betony protested. "Must you, really? He has to be the most trustworthy man in the realm, given his former post."

"Most trusted man in the realm?" Teague's tone danced with amusement. "Yet here I am, declared the best of brothers. I think it my duty to ensure you are well looked after. Juniper? What think you?"

She shook her head at him, but took his arm so he could escort them both outside. "If you must, you must. Though do remember that he has copious experience of being overly protective of those in his charge, more than most gentlemen."

Jack—surely, there was no harm in thinking of him thus in her own thoughts—stood outside of the carriage, ready to assist them into the vehicle, and his sister looked out the window at them with a wide smile. Teague stopped before the carriage, and Juniper met Jack's quizzical look with a little shrug.

Teague adorned his brow with a frown. "Here are two people who mean the world to me, Sterling. Can you assure me they will be safe in your care today?"

"As safe as my own kin, Dunmore," Jack said with a slight bow.

Juniper immediately frowned. Own kin? Oh. That did not sit well with her. Sadly it seemed to satisfy Teague, who—after a few more friendly remarks—handed both Juniper and Betony into the carriage...depriving Juniper of the chance of even touching her gloved hands to Jack's. Which was a rather silly thing to feel disappointed about, and yet here she was, disappointed.

Perhaps she had finally read too many novels with ridiculous heroines.

"Have you been to the Tower of London before?" Emily asked, eyes bright with excitement. "Of course, every child knows the stories of the ghosts, the horrible things that happened there, the histories—but to actually go, I admit I never entertained the idea."

"Why are children always so interested in the bleak parts of history?" Betony asked, her tone musing. "We told Fiona—our brother-in-law's youngest sister—that we planned to visit the Tower today, and she begged and pleaded to come too."

"You make her sound bloodthirsty." Juniper had to laugh as she thought on Fiona's wide-eyed begging. "I think she is simply eager to leave the house."

Emily picked up a small pamphlet from the carriage bench with an illustration of the Tower on its front. "Visiting a medieval castle sounds adventurous. What child wouldn't wish to go on an adventure?"

Mr. Sterling chuckled. "Miss Fiona Dunmore's opinions on castles are well known to any who have spent a few moments in her company. She has visited many in Ireland and Scotland, and she will happily tell you how superior both are to those on English soil."

Juniper looked at him in some surprise. "You remember that about Fiona?" Was there anything this man hadn't noticed in his days as an employee of the duke?

"Repetition of her opinions within my hearing ensured I would never forget them." Though he did not smile, there was a pleasantness to his expression that made her relax. "Miss Dunmore was always an entertaining guest at Castle Clairvoir."

"Oh, do let's not talk too much about that," Emily said with a shake of her head. "I cannot think it is a good thing to bring up your time in service so often. Of course Juniper and Betony do not mind, but what if I should slip and say something in company? People will surely look down on us."

"Emily, people already know—and if they do not, the gossip and rumors will eventually reach them," Jack said, his tone gentle. "It is less shameful for it to be in my past than it would be for us to humiliate ourselves by misbehaving in the present."

"Which will not happen," Betony assured them. She bounced a little in her seat. "We are going to show everyone what lovely people you are. Today, anyone else visiting the Tower will see you both and remark on how mannerly you are, and how sophisticated it is to take an interest in our nation's great history."

"Staring at the executioner's ax which took the life of Anne Boleyn is 'sophisticated'?" Jack asked, plucking the pamphlet from his sister and opening to the page dedicated to that particular entry in the booklet. He cleared his throat and read aloud, "'The ax with which Queen Anne Boleyn was beheaded, on the 19th of May, 1536. She was wife to Henry VIII and mother to Queen Elizabeth; and at the age of nine-and-twenty fell sacrifice to the mutable temper and the impetuous violence of a jealous Prince, and to the malicious calumnies of the enemies of the reformed religion.'" He turned the page. "And then, after another several sentences about her 'protestations of her innocence,' it says, 'The Earl of Essex was afterwards beheaded with the same ax.' Yes. Absolute sophistication."

Biting her lip to keep from laughing, Juniper turned her attention to the strings of her reticule.

Emily gaped at her brother. "Jack, are you—teasing us? You never tease!"

Behind her hand, Betony snickered.

"I am merely saying that our touring a place that puts such

things on display hardly seems something which should be universally approved of by the same people who insist on entering a dining room in a specific rigid order. I understand the need for all of it, of course, but there are moments when even I tire of the shallow show." He handed her the pamphlet again. "My apologies, ladies. I am looking forward to our outing—I simply find certain aspects of it more telling of human nature than actual history."

"I suppose there is something of that childhood interest in such things in all of us," Juniper ventured with a little smile. He didn't truly seem upset, and his pointing out the ridiculousness of it all charmed her. "Fiona loves ghost stories and tales of Irish fairies. I am quite partial to Gothic novels with their mysteries and shadows. All of England knows the stories of the worst moments in our history, and we retell the tales in our warm houses tucked up next to our hearths with arguably far too much gusto—and relish."

Jack met her gaze with the slightest upturn of his lips. "As I said, human nature."

"You both strike me as somewhat morbid today," Betony ventured. "Emily, we must ignore them. Let them be grim if they wish, but I choose to focus on the enjoyment of seeing Queen Elizabeth's suit of armor. Oh, and we ought to look at the Regalia."

"Oh, the Crown Jewels?" Emily opened her pamphlet. "I do wish to see everything, especially given how recently it was used for our king's coronation. I read all about it in the newspapers last year."

It did not take long to arrive at the Tower of London, the name now given to everything within its sturdy outer walls. The castle itself was at the center, but there was a veritable little village within, consisting of offices, homes, a church, and barracks.

As they left the carriage and approached the tower entrance on foot, Emily looked upward at the structure. "Jack, would the Tower be of any use if London were attacked today?"

"None whatsoever," he said immediately. "It would not hold out even an hour, is my guess. Our modern cannons would tear through the stone. Its walls could be scaled easily." He shook his head. "Though I am certain it was formidable on the day it was completed. William the Conqueror knew what he was doing, building towers and fortresses along the coast and in principal cities like London."

Juniper shuddered when they passed through the portcullis, and it was on the other side that they were greeted by a Yeoman of the Guard, wearing the same uniform they had in the time of Henry VIII.

"I feel suddenly as though we have stepped back in time," Emily murmured to Juniper. "What funny clothing."

"Welcome," the Yeoman said, his bearing soldier-straight-and-stiff. "If you have come to view the Tower, I will happily provide you with a tour of the grounds."

"It's an honor to be chosen for this position," Jack murmured to the ladies, bending down near Juniper's ear. "One must be a decorated officer to even be considered."

Soon they were collected, along with a few other ladies and gentlemen who stood near the gated entrance, and shown about the Tower grounds. The Yeoman seemed to take his job quite seriously, and as it had been several years since Juniper's last visit, she paid intense attention to all he said. He spoke of the history, showed them where it was believed Anne Boleyn and others were executed, spoke of the church, the guards, and Traitor's Gate.

"There are twelve acres of land that comprise the inside of the tower, and the circuit wall is more than three-thousand feet in length," he continued. "All who live on site are the officers and servants of the public, and their families." He marched them along a small rise and pointed out the ravens hopping along the grass. "Who here knows the legend of the Tower Ravens?"

A woman on the arm of her husband delicately raised a gloved hand, and the Yeoman bowed slightly to her as she offered, "Isn't it said that London Tower, and with it the Crown, will fall if the ravens ever leave the Tower?"

"Indeed. We know that ravens have been bred and kept at the Tower since the time of Charles II. Imagine, if you will, the number of historical events that have occurred here with ravens in attendance." He cleared his throat. "From the deaths of queens and traitors to the best moments of our nation."

There were murmurs of interest, then the tour continued on. The woman who had spoken of the legend, walking before Juniper and Emily at the moment, said quietly to her husband, "I do think ravens rather supernatural creatures, as it was one such bird that brought me to you."

The gentleman chuckled and gave her a look of such fondness that Juniper nearly sighed aloud.

When he spoke, though his voice was soft, she heard every word. "I am f-f-forever grateful to that bird and everything else that f-f-followed, my dear."

Emily's head jerked toward the man, her eyebrows raised with sudden interest as she glanced at Juniper, though she could not think why her friend would appear so intrigued.

As they slowed their steps, she leaned closer. "Is something the matter, Emily?"

"Did you hear that man's speech?" she asked in a whisper. "He reminded me of Mr. Eastwood." Emily glanced forward again. "He and his wife seem rather fond of each other, do they not?"

Betony stood ahead of them, speaking with another young lady in the group between the Yeoman's explanations for the things around them. They were nearly to the stairs that led up into the fortress, so the outdoor tour was nearly spent.

Jack came along Juniper's other side. "The outdoors are as grimly connected to death as what we will find inside, it would seem."

She gave him a glance from the corner of her eye. "Should I not admit to enjoying myself? As you are so troubled by the gruesome history of the White Tower, perhaps it would diminish your opinion of me if I did so."

His eyes flicked from her down to the cobblestoned ground. When he spoke his voice was soft, and did not carry far or disturb the others around them. "I do not think anything would accomplish that, Lady Juniper. My high opinion of you is rather fixed."

Her heart fluttered and her cheeks warmed, despite the cold February air. "And here it was that my sister-in-law, Fanny, was so certain my Gothic fixation would be the end of my respectability."

The woman in front of them, the same who had credited a raven with meeting her husband, glanced over her shoulder at that moment. Her eyes met Juniper's, and a quick look of interest showed in her eyes.

"As I am yet new to Society, I'm not certain my opinion matters one way or the other," Jack said.

It was then she ought to have said that all his opinions mattered, to her at least, but the Yeoman urged them to climb the stairs in front of them, offering his services as guide inside the Tower, too, if they were desired—but their group was given leave, when they entered the fortress, to wander about in the public areas as they wished. There were signs here and there which gave more information about each display.

Betony and Emily had linked arms and gone forward at once, looking over suits of armor that shone as though they had been polished that very morning.

The lady with her husband turned to Juniper, though, before she and Jack could join the other two. "I beg your pardon, but did you say you enjoy reading Gothic novels?"

Her husband winced. "Louisa," he said softly. "You c-c-cannot do this to every reader we meet." He turned an apologetic smile to Juniper and Jack.

His wife did not seem to give him any heed, aside from her smile growing wider. Instead she waited with an expectant gaze on Juniper.

Juniper stepped a little closer to Jack, her cheeks burning, and he looked down at her with raised eyebrows. She prepared herself for censure as she answered, "I did say that, yes. I am an avid reader of the genre."

"Oh, as am I," the woman said, face shining with delight. Before Juniper could find relief in this revelation, the woman asked, "Have you read the new book by Mr. E. Grey?"

"Indeed, I have. It so delighted me, I immediately found my copy of his first novel to read it again. I quite enjoy how he depicts his heroines—I never feel as though they come into trouble due to stupidity, as so often is the case in other novels." Juniper bit her lip and then offered an apologetic, "Excuse my enthusiasm. He is one of the few masculine writers I enjoy, and for that very reason."

The woman beamed as though Juniper had praised her directly, then prodded her husband's side. "You see? What I've told you is true. Intelligent young ladies need you to keep writing your novels precisely in the manner you do, my darling." Then she looked proudly at Juniper. "I am Mrs. Erasmus Grey, and this is my husband, the author himself."

It was interesting to see a grown man blush, but Mr. Grey did exactly that. He bowed to Juniper and then to Jack. "How do you do. P-P-Please, excuse my wife's enthusiasm. She is p-proud of me, I am afraid, and must let everyone else know of it."

Jack took over their introductions at once, quite properly. "I am Mr. John Sterling. Please, allow me to introduce Lady Juniper Amberton, sister to the Earl of Haverford, currently residing in London with her brother-in-law, Lord Dunmore of Ireland."

Jack struck her as highly amused, if Juniper read the twinkle in his eye rightly, but she had nearly lost the ability to speak. She stared at Mr. Grey with wide-eyed wonder, a thousand questions rushing to her lips, and she finally had to give her head a slight shake to find any words at all. "Mr. Grey...it is an honor to meet you. I have read and enjoyed all your books, several times each. Thank you for writing such thrilling stories. They have made me laugh, cry, and wish dearly for one-page-more every time."

His blush if possible darkened, and he bowed. "You are m-most welcome, Lady Juniper. I am gratified to hear that you enjoy my endeavors."

She looked from him to his wife, and then up at Jack. It would be the height of rudeness to interrupt their outing to appease her curiosity and release her enthusiasm, she knew that. But the idea of simply ending the conversation at that moment, without any further opportunity for discussion, made her feel ill. In the moment reason failed her, and she knew not what to do.

But Jack gave her a reassuring smile—a real one this time—and gracefully withdrew a card from his pocket. "I do not wish to distract from your enjoyment of the Tower, Mr. Grey. But I would be honored if you would call upon me at my father's home while you are in Town."

Oh, her card. Of course! Juniper withdrew her own and handed it to Mrs. Grey. "And I should dearly love to have you for tea, Mrs. Grey. I think my sister, Lady Dunmore, would be pleased to meet you."

The couple graciously accepted the cards and exchanged them for their own, then continued onward.

Juniper looked up at Jack and grinned. "I am so glad you were with me, I felt like a ninny for a moment."

"You were merely a touch overwhelmed, as one would expect when unexpectedly meeting someone you admire. You recovered well." He held his arm out to her. "Now, our sisters are about to leave this room for the next, and I must keep them in my sight, so we had better pick up our feet."

She laid her hand on his arm and allowed him to whisk her into the next room.

THE ABSOLUTE DELIGHT JACK HAD SEEN ON JUNIPER'S FACE when she met Mr. and Mrs. Grey had done a considerable job toward making the day brighter for him in turn. Her genuine compliments, delivered with enthusiasm, had made him wish to read the books by the gentleman—if only to better understand a thing that pleased her.

Truly, a foolish notion, and an impulse that his sisters-in-law would declare to be absolute proof of his interest in her...something which, he admitted to himself as he observed her studying a suit of armor said to belong to Queen Elizabeth, he couldn't well deny to himself any longer.

Lady Juniper Amberton, a lady born and bred, had captured his curiosity the moment he'd first heard her speaking with her sisters at Clairvoir. She'd eagerly called the castle itself a perfect homage to Gothic architecture and wondered aloud if the duchess had hidden secret passageways throughout to better assist in that endeavor.

Curiosity had turned to admiration, and now admiration turned from interest to something more.

Affection.

An affection he had to tamp down upon severely, as he had

absolutely no business in having any such feelings toward a lady befriending his sister as a favor to his former employer who undoubtedly saw him still in the role of servant. Juniper, delightful as she was, was still several rungs above him—at least, in his own mind. Out of his reach. Even if they both now existed as children to English lords, he'd been thrust unwillingly into the position; she embodied it quite beautifully.

"She was a tall woman, wasn't she?" he heard Juniper remark as she examined the armor on its mannequin, with a face painted to resemble the most popular of the former queen's portraits.

"I find it interesting that most of the suits of armor seem the size of an average man, rather than tall men," Emily said in reply. "One thinks of knights as larger than life—or at least strapping enough to accomplish great heroic feats or look fearsome in battle." She looked back at Jack. "My brother is rather tall, and he's a former lieutenant."

Jack approached and eyed the armor behind the chain-rope, looking it over with a critical eye. "Her Majesty certainly wasn't meant to fight in this, merely make an appearance to rally her troops."

"Encouraging them to rout Spain," Juniper said with a quick nod. "Which the weather ended up doing on England's behalf."

"Ah, here you are," a voice said, far too loud in the quiet rooms of historical armor.

Jack and the ladies turned, wondering who was being addressed thus, and his eyes landed on the man quickly approaching their party as his heart sank.

Mr. Waldegrave. How had that ridiculous man found them at the Tower?

Emily made a somewhat choked sound as she whispered to Juniper, "One of my callers yesterday. Do you know him?"

"Not in the slightest."

That spoke further against the man's favor. If Juniper had

never been introduced to him, by either her brother or brother-in-law, he likely wasn't worth knowing. Jack's stomach twisted; the thought was perhaps a bit harsh—after all, he himself had only recently joined Society—until the man opened his mouth.

"Lady Emily, Mr. Sterling, a true pleasure to finally join you both on this most prodigious outing. Ah, the history of our country on full display, in all its might. Wonderful, do you not think, Lady Emily?"

Presumptuous man, to come upon them and then attempt to join them without an invitation! Jack cleared his throat. "Lady Juniper, may I present to you Mr. Waldegrave. Mr. Waldegrave, this is Lady Juniper Amberton, and her sister Lady Betony, sisters to the Earl of Haverford. We are escorting them on their outing this afternoon."

There. That was a clear, precise, polite boundary to offer. The party belonged to the sisters Amberton, and the gentleman could not simply invite himself along.

Except after making brief bows to them, the fool ignored them completely and turned his sights fully on Emily again. Making no move to excuse himself, Mr. Waldegrave continued loudly, "A dark-weather day like this makes it a fine time to stay indoors. I had no notion anyone, least of all a fine lady such as yourself, would venture out when the sky could open up at any moment in winter torrents. Lady Emily, I am pleased I could make haste to see you here when I found you not at home."

Who the devil had told this man where they had gone? Jack had every intention of taking them to task at the first opportunity; no one in the duke's home would have dared give the location of family away to someone not already an intimate acquaintance. Were servants of earls less competent than those of dukes?

Lady Juniper bent her head to receive a genteelly whispered remark from her sister, nodded sharply, and stepped forward with a graceful raise of her hand. "Oh, Mr. Waldegrave, have you visited the Tower before? You sound like you are well informed of its history."

He blinked at her as his chest puffed out. "Oh, indeed! I have not been here since boyhood, but every man in England knows all about the Tower and its magnificent history. Have you not a pamphlet?" He held his hand out, and Betony slid her thin booklet into his hand, stepping slightly in front of Emily as she did so.

"Ah, yes. Here we are." He opened it, and began to read loudly about Elizabeth, adding none of his own thoughts or conversation, merely posturing with one hand raised as though he delivered a sermon rather than read aloud from a common guidebook.

Jack took his sister's arm and led her a few steps away, blocking her from Waldegrave's sight. "You look decidedly uncomfortable. Shall I dismiss him?"

"Wouldn't that be terribly rude?" Her cheeks were red and her eyes lowered as she looked around at the other people milling about the room, several of them sending confused glances toward Waldegrave. "We cannot give offense. He has important relatives, and he has mentioned them several times."

"You have important friends, and it was rude of him to show himself here, uninvited."

"Who do you think told him—?"

"Whoever it is will be sacked."

"Jack! You cannot!" She gaped at him. "Correct the behavior, but do not punish anyone for it. You needn't be a tyrant."

He glowered at her as a voice he recognized whispered *guidance, not governance.*

"What exactly was it like to work for the duke? Was he prone to throwing out good servants for small mistakes?"

"This would not be a small mistake in his household," he said, voice lowered. "It is a matter of security—and your safety."

Emily winced. "I sincerely doubt whoever told Mr. Waldegrave where we were thought it would lead to any harm." She lifted her chin. "I can put up with him for a short time. We are nearly finished in the Tower anyway. After we see the Regalia, we can leave him behind and go home."

Annoyed by both Waldegrave and his sister's determination to let the man follow them about, Jack ensured to offer her his arm to keep the other man from doing so. He was therefore forced to grit his teeth when Juniper politely accepted Waldegrave's escort through the rest of the Line of Kings.

The idiot kept reading aloud from the pamphlet every time they came upon a new display, and both Amberton sisters continued to listen to him as though fascinated by the words they had every ability to read for themselves. Every time he looked over his shoulder for Emily, either Betony or Juniper would claim his attention by asking him another question.

They acted as though they had distracted annoying suitors before, and such was their success that they had Mr. Waldegrave walking ten feet ahead of Jack and Emily on their way across the courtyard to where the Regalia was displayed in a dark room, called the jewel office.

Strong iron bars divided the room, stretching from ceiling to floor. There were no windows, no light, and the room walls were made of stone. An elderly woman on the other side of the bars stood from a chair, holding a candle as she gestured to each piece within. The display was splendid, the jewels set in gold, the crowns, diadems, scepters, and such glittering in the soft light.

"The imperial crown," the woman said, holding her light to the crown itself. "It has been used for more than seven-hundred years, adorning the heads of the kings and queens of England upon their coronations."

The crown consisted of a purple velvet cap, lined with ermine, richly adorned with pearls, emeralds, sapphires, rubies, and diamonds. It was a dazzling sight.

"To think, so many of our kings and queens have worn those fine jewels," Mr. Waldegrave said loudly as they stepped again into the gray light of day. "It makes one rather proud to be English, does it not?"

Lady Juniper casually took her hand from his arm. "Of course—excepting when one considers how horrid some of the things that happened here were. Did you not have a Yeoman's tour? You simply must, Mr. Waldegrave. Look there—one is just beginning. Surely, someone as interested in English history as yourself would not pass up such an opportunity."

Though Jack sensed that Juniper laid a trap for Mr. Waldegrave, the other gentleman seemed to have no idea the precariousness of his situation and blithely took her bait.

"Oh, of course, absolutely. One simply must take in the tour by the Yeomen. I had no notion of forgoing the pleasure today, in fact I am quite looking forward to it," Waldegrave insisted with a grin.

Lady Betony put her hands behind her back and looked upward at the sky, and Jack caught a twitch at her lips.

His sister had caught on, too, and lent her voice to their efforts. "It is such a good thing, I think, when a gentleman shows interest in intellectual pursuits, expanding his knowledge of history and our culture. Truly, an admirable thing." Emily's modest smile was as much directed to Juniper as to Waldegrave, but the pompous man puffed up like a peacock on display.

"I would not dream of missing such a thing. Indeed, one must seize the moment at hand. This tour is exactly what we need, I think, to further shore up our minds for the day's events."

Jack had to cover his laugh by turning it into a cough, putting his gloved first to his mouth and turning away slightly.

"And we would not dream of depriving you of that pleasure," Lady Juniper said as she took a step away. "I hope you enjoy yourself immensely. Until we meet again, Mr. Walde-grave." She curtsied and Betony did the same beside her.

Watching the man come to understand Juniper's maneu-vering gave Jack more pleasure than it ought to have, and indeed it was the same sensation he had felt on the battlefield when a particularly clever plan came to fruition and routed the enemy.

First Waldegrave appeared confused, then surprised, and finally irritated. "You—you are not to take the tour yourselves? Lady Emily?" he asked, looking at all of them.

"We enjoyed the tour of the grounds before we entered the Tower," Juniper said in a most controlled voice that sounded far too innocent to Jack's ears.

"You will enjoy it, Mr. Waldegrave," Betony said, linking arms with Juniper. "I am certain it will provide much to think upon. Good day."

With the sisters having taken their leave, all Jack and Emily had to do was bow and follow them. A few steps ahead of them, Betony's shoulders were shaking terribly. He heard Juniper whisper to her sister, "Do *not* laugh until we are over the bridge!"

He snorted, and Juniper cast him a disapproving look over her shoulder...or she tried to. Her own eyes twinkled far too merrily for him to take the correction seriously. When they finally crossed the little bridge that had once stretched over a moat, Jack allowed himself a chuckle, Betony burst into giggles, Emily heaved a huge sigh of relief, and Juniper shook her head at all of them—then had to cover her mouth when she snorted aloud.

It was an adorable little sound.

Jack cleared his throat as he led them to the waiting carriage. "Ladies, I believe this particular battle victory calls for a celebra-tion. Is it too cold to get ices at Gunter's?"

"It is never too cold for ices," Betony said decidedly, and the other two swiftly agreed.

As Jack settled himself in the carriage, directly across from Juniper, he met her gaze, trying to show his full approval and gratitude with no more than a smile and his eyes.

Given the slight pinkening of her cheek and the way she nodded at him, once with deliberate slowness, he was quite certain she understood him. It was an exceedingly good feeling, to be understood by one as lovely as she.

CHAPTER 10

Rain pattered at the window where Jack stood looking out on the street below. He counted the number of carriages out on the day, noted someone in the house across the street looking out the window, and wondered briefly if anyone other than him thought having a drainpipe so near the window could tempt particularly adept burglars.

The large, square snout of a dog landed upon the windowsill next to him, and Jack looked down at the impressively sized animal just as it huffed, breath fogging up the glass near its nose.

The German-bred boar hound was massive; Jack could easily pet the beast's shoulder without bending to do so. Perhaps one needn't concern themselves with drainpipe-climbing thieves with dogs as large as Apollo and Athena.

Apollo gazed up at him with large soppy eyes and a slight wag of his tail.

"Look." It was his brother George's voice, stage-whispering. "Now we have two guard dogs at the window."

"Aye, but Apollo is the handsomer of the two," Richard added, somewhat gruffly.

Jack smirked, despite himself, and scratched behind the boar hound's ears.

"Ah, I see he hasn't given up his habits then, scowling out windows at the least provocation," Lord Hartwell said from across the room, where he held a cue stick at the perfect angle to knock another's ball into a hazard.

The men in the room, Jack's brothers Richard and George, and Hartwell's brother Lyness Eastwood, all turned toward Jack at the exact instant Hartwell struck the ball. All looked back at the table and groaned. Hartwell was a rather deft hand at the game, trouncing all of them.

"We need a table at our house," George said, looking at Richard. "Playing once a week at the club will never improve our abilities in this *gentlemanly* game."

Richard, eldest of them and rather bright, continued staring at Jack. "Lord Hartwell, do you mean to say you remember our youngest brother's role prior to our family's elevation?"

"Indeed. I cannot claim to know the servants of every nobleman in England, but one pays attention to the people the Duke of Montfort employs. Your brother was assigned to Lady Josephine for a time, which marked him as a trusted servant. That is when I met him." Hartwell stepped back so his brother could take a turn at the table. "I was always rather struck by his stoicism."

Jack smiled to himself and raised his eyebrows at Hartwell. The baron was clever enough to have realized Jack hadn't been a mere footman, even if he'd never been directly told what the duke's servants were prepared to do on behalf of His Grace's kin. He'd spoken directly to Jack about his duties at that time. Good of him to not bring it up in that moment.

"I count it a compliment that you noticed me at all, Lord Hartwell."

"Drop the 'lord' business, please. Saves so much time.

Hartwell is good enough." He nodded to George. "Your turn, Mr. Sterling."

"May as well trim down the confusion and time, as myself and my brothers are all accustomed to being the only Sterling in the room. Call me George."

"Tenby does well enough for me, though I am still learning to answer to it." His oldest brother, the freshly minted Viscount Tenby, looked at Jack. "What is it you prefer these days, Jack?"

"Jack is well enough for friends and foes alike," he said, coming to the table as Apollo trotted off to sit by the hearth with the female boar hound. "And your preference, Mr. Eastwood?" He looked to the baron's younger brother.

"Eastwood is fine." Lyness Eastwood didn't stutter often, Jack knew. He hadn't heard him stumble over his words once in his own home. Perhaps it was a matter of comfortability. "It has been rather entertaining to watch your family's adjustment." He cut a glance at Richard. "I think half the *ton* knows the duke is invested in your family. The speculation on that account is...interesting."

"Interesting how?" George asked after missing his shot, the ball clattering harmlessly against the side and gaining him no points. "I have had a few dolts make sly remarks to me speculating on the connection, but most know it is Jack who connects us to His Grace's family."

"Through honorable employment," Richard added gruffly. As the eldest, he'd never left home to seek any sort of employment. He'd stayed and managed the family holdings, modest as they were, with full expectation of taking them over one day—which, in a way, was still true. Sharpness entered his tones. "Though I suppose there are those who will never forgive him for being in service, or George and Arthur for being in trade, or me for knowing how to plow a field."

Hartwell and his brother exchanged a glance, and Jack

cleared his throat as his heart sank. "Have a care, brother," he said quietly. "We are in friendly company."

The baron folded his arms, cue still in one hand. "We cannot help from whence we came, and those who matter will not judge for it. You are to be commended for doing so well that the gossips have little they can say to amuse themselves at your expense."

"That is a relief to hear," Richard said with a tight nod. "And I...apologize. For my outburst. I had a conversation with my wife this morning, and I believe the ladies are feeling a greater amount of pressure than we are."

"Are they?" Lyness Eastwood struck his ball perfectly before straightening, his brows drawn together. "One would hope that ladies would be granted more grace."

"Not by other ladies," Richard muttered. "It is greatly to our benefit that our sister Emily has been taken under the wings of the Amberton sisters. She has become almost popular."

"We ought to call on your sister," Lord Hartwell announced with a sudden grin. "Though I doubt she needs help filling her at-home hours. She is the very picture of an English lady in form and grace, she does your family credit."

While the baron spoke, Jack kept his gaze on Lyness, sensing a sudden tension in the younger man's bearing. He twisted the cue in his hands, looking down at the floor. "We ought to have c-called after the ball when we met all of you, but we had other obligations."

"The flowers you both sent gave all the ladies in the house great pleasure," Jack volunteered, still watching Lyness—whose ears had reddened somewhat. "Though your company would certainly have been preferred compared to some of the gentlemen we entertained that afternoon."

"Is there anyone you need more information about?" Hartwell chalked the tip of his cue. "We might have insight into them if you have yet to look into their backgrounds and finances.

Every man has his failings, of course, but I doubt you wish your sister to end up with a gambler, rake, or debtor."

"Waldegrave," Jack said without hesitation. "Mr. Edgar Waldegrave."

The Eastwood brothers exchanged a glance, Lyness frowning and the baron raising his eyebrows.

"He is well connected," Hartwell admitted. "Grandson to an earl, his mother is Lady Helen Waldegrave. His father is a wealthy gentleman with property in Shropshire."

Lyness snorted and put his cue into the rack. "Waldegrave has nothing to r-r-recommend him. He is a snob."

"Really? Then I am surprised he doesn't see our Emily as beneath him," George remarked. He totaled up the scores in the notebook they'd used for the length of the game. "Hartwell wins. Of course. Then Jack, Eastwood, myself, and Richard."

Richard grumbled as he pulled his coat on again. "We most definitely need a table of our own."

Far more interested in the subject of Waldegrave than the game, Jack kept his eyes on Lyness. "Why would a snob be interested in a woman not raised to reflect her current station? Even if she technically outranks him—daughter to an earl has to be higher than a grandson, is that not correct? George is right, his persistence with Emily seems out of keeping with such a character."

"Money is always a p-powerful motivator." Lyness's stutter returning said more about his feelings on the subject than the frown did. "And as we said, Lady Emily c-c-conducts herself with d-decorum."

The baron put each stick back where it belonged, speaking over his shoulder. "One who did not know her circumstances would be hard-pressed to suspect she wasn't born into her position, or at least in a higher climb of the gentry than a gentleman farmer's daughter."

"Good thing better men than Waldegrave are interested in

our Emily, then," Richard muttered. He looked at Jack with his brows drawn together. "You are keeping her safe in that way, are you not, brother? As we agreed?" Richard's anxiety likely came from the knowledge that Jack filled the role Richard ought to, as eldest brother. Someday, Jack hoped his brother would have the confidence to manage the family's affairs. Until then, it fell to Jack.

Delivering a tight nod of affirmation, he said, "She has my whole attention at present." Still, guilt settled in his stomach at the partial falsehood.

Yes, he was keeping an eye on Emily and her prospects, but he'd grown somewhat distracted during their outing with Juniper and her sister. He'd spent more time admiring Juniper's cleverness and fair face than focusing on Emily. Waldegrave's routing hadn't even been his doing.

A servant entered the room bearing a silver tray with a letter on it. "My lord, this letter has just come from York via special messenger. As it is from the baroness, I thought it best to bring it to you at once."

Lord Hartwell took the paper and broke the seal at once, and his brother stiffened and stared at him with concern. The brothers lived in York most of the year, only coming to London for the most crucial parts of the parliamentary season. It had become something of a joke for the men of Lords, from what Jack understood, that if they saw Roman Eastwood, Lord Hartwell, on the streets of London that one knew important votes were on the docket.

Whatever was in the letter wasn't a laughing matter, evidently. Hartwell looked up at his younger brother. "I cannot leave until day-after-tomorrow. The bill for the canals..."

Lyness nodded once. "I will leave immediately." He held his hand out for the letter, and he seemed to relax a little as he read, then he shook his head ruefully. "It d-does not s-s-sound like an emergency. More a re-request."

Hartwell looked up at the rest of them. "Gentlemen, I apologize, but I must cut our afternoon short to attend to this family matter with my brother. I will make it up to all of you in the near future, I am certain."

They bowed and began to take their leave, with Jack the last to go to the door—but Lyness stopped him. "A moment, Jack, if you p-please."

He hesitated, waited for the man to continue.

With a somewhat subdued smile, Lyness said quietly, "P-Please give my regards to your sister. And d-do warn her about Waldegrave. The man isn't a devil, but he's a nuisance. The sort to make a lady's day unpleasant rather than something of merit."

At that moment, Jack realized that Lyness Eastwood might have more than a passing interest in Emily, and after only one meeting between them. He kept his gaze steady on the other man, measuring what he knew of Lyness and the family for a moment. Then nodded. "I will make certain she is aware of your concern for her, sir."

The other man cleared his throat as the tips of his ears pinked. "It n-needn't come from me."

That merely made Jack chuckle. "I think it ought to." If there was a man he trusted near his sister, it would be this one. Lyness Eastwood had always conducted himself modestly, respectfully, and showed himself fair-minded. There was a reason he and his brother were often welcome at the Duke of Montfort's castle. "It is a shame you must leave Town so immediately. Tomorrow my family is to visit the Burlington Arcade with Lord Dunmore and the Amberton sisters. I should have liked your help in escorting the ladies."

A pained expression briefly touched the man's features, then he smiled somewhat ruefully. "I hope there will be another time when I m-may assist you in such a noble endeavor. Until then, give my best to...to all of them."

Lyness bowed slightly, Jack returned the gesture, then

followed after his brothers—both of whom teased him about moving too slowly for their liking. He endured their jests with no more than a slight roll of his eyes as he climbed into the family carriage.

CHAPTER 11

"Absolutely under no circumstances may you enter the bookshop."

Juniper looked from the Hatchard's window display of beautiful leather tomes to her younger sister. "I am quite certain I do not understand your vehemence on the matter." Which was a falsehood. She knew precisely why Betony appeared somewhat cross. The last time Juniper had stepped into the bookshop with Betony in tow, they had lingered for nearly two hours—or at least, she had lingered, and her sister had loitered.

Their eldest sister and her husband came closer, Ivy on Teague's arm, and it was she who said with an air of indulgence, "If there is something in particular you want, you may go in and find it, Juniper."

"She will find a dozen things she particularly wants," Betony moaned. "And you only give her permission so you may wander in behind her and collect at least as many new books for yourself."

"Absolute slander!" Ivy's aghast protest, complete with her hand going to her heart, did absolutely nothing to make Betony's frown relent. "I will have you know that the last time I visited

Hatchard's I departed with but three books ordered. One was even a gift."

"A gift to me," put in Teague with an amused twist to his smile. "Which you then promptly informed me you also wished to read, and I have not seen it since."

Unable to resist further teasing, Juniper tapped her bottom lip and peered more intently at the window display. "Do look at the new copies of poetry, at the very least. Such slim little books can hardly be any trouble to examine and purchase."

Betony groaned and turned her back on the window, looking across the road where they were supposed to walk to meet with the Sterling family. The Burlington Arcade was the main draw of the day, at least in terms of destination.

As none of her favorite authors had a new work available, and Juniper had a twist of excitement in her own belly that refused to loosen, she really had no interest in going into the bookshop. Or at least, much less interest than normal. She turned slightly, looking at the window of the next shop over: Fortnum & Mason, an established part of Piccadilly and London's social culture.

"I wish the weather were finer," she said to no one in particular. "I should like to get a hamper from Fortnum's for a picnic."

A deep voice spoke from behind her, soft amusement in the undertones of the familiar gentleman. "I will have to remember that when we no longer require winter coats to step out of doors."

Juniper looked up, catching the reflection of herself in the window briefly before her eyes darted upward to find Jack's reflection, too. She turned around, finding him alarmingly close. How had she missed his approach? He ought to have his entire flock of family with him. And where had her sisters gone?

Movement on the other side of the glass made her look again, and she saw both Betony and Ivy inside Hatchard's. She shook her head at their betrayal and turned her attention to Jack. "Good afternoon, Mr. Sterling."

"Good afternoon to you, Lady Juniper, though I think it had better be Jack today," he said, bowing slightly. "My brothers are in tow, and we ought not confuse them."

"You know better than that," she chided, her heart skipping a beat. He'd given her leave to use a familiar name, which was even better than using his given name. "If anything, I must call you Mr. John Sterling."

"But why use five syllables when a single one will do?" he asked, his brown eyes glittering down at her. "Did I startle you?"

"You must know you did. I saw my reflection leap at least two feet in the air."

"Not at all. It was barely an inch." He nodded to the window. "Does your family often abandon you outside your favorite haunts?"

"Favorite—?" She looked back at him again. "Because it is a bookshop, you think it must be my favorite?"

"Isn't it?"

"Truthfully, at times. But Hatchard's doesn't always carry as wide a supply of my favorite genre as I wish it would."

"Hm. Perhaps their Reader considers himself above the Gothic." Every large bookshop had a Reader, someone designated to choose the titles which would form part of the inventory. Jack's eyebrows tilted upward. "Speaking of which, Mr. Grey visited my family yesterday. My father invited both the Greys to come to dinner day-after-next."

"Overmorrow," she said, tucking her hands deeper into her muff. Juniper bit her lip. "Forgive me. My brother-in-law taught us the word and I have adored using it ever since."

"An apt word." His lips quirked upward, and Juniper rather wished he'd let himself fully smile again. She did so adore his smile. "Very well. The Greys are to dine with us overmorrow, and I should like to extend the invitation to your family, too. I thought to ask you before speaking to Lord Dunmore, in case you would prefer to do without an evening at table with an author?"

Her lips parted as she gasped, less surprised by the threat than the playfulness behind it. "Mr. Sterling—Jack, are you teasing me?"

Something in his eyes sparked, and at last his mouth curved like a bow, the edges going upward revealing a charming smile. "I have never been accused of teasing a lady before. That does not sound like me in the least."

That gave Juniper's heart the perfect reason to flip forward and backward behind her ribs. "You *are* teasing! I did not truly think you capable of such a thing."

"Truly? I thought one who has such a love of novels as you do, my lady, would be capable of imagining all sorts of feats. Even in one as dull as myself."

The banter absolutely shocked her, but in a most delightful way. She had to laugh, and she found herself wishing very much to reach out and take his arm. "Do you think yourself dull?"

"I am told by my brothers that very thing often enough—at least, they say I am less than interesting company."

"How unfortunate for them." Juniper could not stop the words spilling from her mouth in that moment, as her tongue seemed most determined to run away from her. "I find you absolutely fascinating company."

His eyes softened. "A high compliment, Lady Juniper."

Bells jingled, and Juniper turned to see her family exiting the bookshop, though with nothing in hand.

"Did you not find something to suit you, Betony?" she asked, her tone changed to one more suitable to public conversations. She had spoken in such a low voice to Jack it was incredible he had heard her over the sounds of the street—which she'd also somehow completely ignored as they exchanged pleasantries.

"You know very well that I am not so much a reader as you or Ivy." Betony curtsied to Jack. "Good afternoon, Mr. Sterling."

"Sterling." Teague bowed while Ivy curtsied. "But where is the rest of your kin? I thought our adventure today included a large number of Sterlings."

"Six of us," Jack said with a tilt of his head across the street. "My sister Emily waits in the carriage with my sisters-in-law, and my brothers are most regrettably late. They had business to attend to, so I thought to keep the ladies out of the cold until we had all gathered in front of the Arcade."

"Wise of you," Ivy said. "The moment my husband turned us loose upon the street, we began shopping."

"*You* began shopping, and for books," Betony corrected with a huff. "Some of us are waiting to spend our pin money at the proper shops in the Arcade."

"I think it high time we cross the road then." Teague looked at the busy thoroughfare. "A simple enough matter if we time it right. Betony, with me and your sister. Sterling, I can trust you to keep Juniper safe from being trampled?"

Jack extended his arm to her, his eyes already on hers again. "It would be an honor to protect her from the horses' hooves, Dunmore."

Heavens. That sounded as though Teague was encouraging an attachment to her—which simply could not be. No one knew Juniper harbored feelings for him, no one but Betony—and she would not have revealed such a thing after promising to keep mum on the subject.

Juniper took a hand from her muff and tucked it into the crook of his arm, trying not to notice the shiver of delight that rushed through her own.

They crossed the smaller Duke Street with little problem, but did not attempt to cross Piccadilly proper until they drew even with the Arcade's entrance. The men attached to the shopping area, paid for from the Earl of Burlington's own pocket, frequently halted traffic to help patrons of the Arcade to cross the busy street. They did so the moment Teague signaled them with a lift of his hand.

Crossing without incident, Juniper marveled at her good fortune to be in company with the people she liked most. Even if the weather was less than cheery, and the clouds above looked as though they might break open in a deluge at any moment, they would be well protected from rain in the Arcade, a lovely row of shops that connected Piccadilly and Burlington Gardens. With over seventy shops selling all sorts of lovely items, from stationery to jewelry, it was an ideal spot for a genteel group to pass an afternoon—and be seen in company with all the right sorts of people.

"Have you visited the Arcade before, Lady Juniper?" Jack's eyes were not on her, but they swept from one side of the street to the other, taking in the guardsmen standing on either side of the long shop corridor's entrance.

"Many times, though I confess I do not take as much pleasure in purchasing goods as my younger sister does." She looked ahead to where Betony already stood so near a window that her breath fogged up the glass. She glanced up at Jack to see if he had seen the same, and found him looking over his shoulder instead.

She had to shake her head at him. "Do you never rest from your observances, Jack? We are quite safe here—and none of us are so important as the Duke of Montfort to need such a high level of protection upon as at all times."

Jack's eyes settled on her, his gaze unexpectedly heavy. "I think of you at least equally as important, my lady."

Her breath caught in her throat. Surely he did not mean it? Yet she could not remember a single time that Jack had engaged in idle compliments or flattery.

He turned his attention away again. "My family ought to join us at any moment."

"Do you need to assist them?"

Shaking his head, Jack turned his attention to her again. "As much as I should like it, I cannot do everything for them. As we discussed before, gentle governance is not nipping at their heels like a sheepdog."

They stood still, a few feet away from the Arcade's entrance, while ladies in fine clothing streamed in and out of the archway, and gentlemen—fewer in number—tried not to look bored as they escorted their wives, sisters, and daughters.

"Have you found that you have more time to yourself now?" Juniper asked, eyes on his. For a man, he possessed such lovely eyes. Dark brown, with thick black lashes, even if his brows were drawn tightly together more often than not.

"It is time I spend worrying, I am afraid."

That answer did not satisfy her in the least. "Worrying? That will not do at all. You will make yourself ill, I am certain, if you do not learn to enjoy time to yourself."

Something about that statement made his lips quirk upward again, and Jack sounded amused as he spoke. "I have never had such a thing before, so I am not certain it is required for one to live a healthy life."

"Never had time to yourself?" Juniper was forced to step a little closer to avoid collision with an elderly gentleman's elbow. "But what will you do when they do not need your guidance so often? The day will come when they can manage themselves. How will you get on after that without anyone to care for?"

His gaze left hers and the line between his eyebrows deepened as he gave a sharp nod. "Here they are at last."

His brothers, their wives, and Emily approached, bundled up against the cold and wearing cheerful expressions.

Jack did not answer her question, instead calling to his brothers about their tardiness. The three of them exchanged teasing, and the ladies left their husbands to move into the Arcade ahead of them. Emily's smile invited Juniper to join her so she did, the two of them linking arms, and she tried not to worry about Jack...who was doubtlessly at that moment worrying about everyone else.

How did a grown man admit that he did not possess the slightest idea for his future life? Had anyone asked Jack a few short months ago where he saw himself in future, his answer would have been simple. He would take over as captain of the duke's guard from Rockwell when the man entered his well-deserved retirement, then eventually retire with a lovely pension in a cottage somewhere near his kin. Perhaps, between the present and that distant ending, he would find someone to share his life with; likely a woman from the serving class, like himself, who understood the requirements and duties of his position.

But now, walking along behind several ladies dressed in fine cloth and wearing soft furs and finely made woolen capes, he hadn't the slightest idea what he ought to plan for...or where he would go when his family no longer needed his guidance.

No one had asked him about it, either, until Juniper extended the question. It wasn't really something he could think on yet, was it? Not when the immediate needs of the family outweighed any of his own desires.

"You look put-out," George said, adjusting the way his tall black beaver sat upon his head. "Not keen on following the ladies about the market?"

Richard, ever the practical eldest, snorted and stared point-edly into the windows of a jeweler's shop. "This is not a market, 'tis a luxury bazar."

"I heard a chap at our club recommend a tobacconist in the Arcade." George tilted his hat again. "Is this thing meant to sit so low on the forehead or am I wearing the wrong hat? Is it yours, Richard?"

"What makes you think it is mine?"

"Your head is a great deal larger than my own, for one."

Richard narrowed his eyes at George. "Because my brain requires a larger box than yours. Obviously."

"Not public conversation," Jack muttered, barely loud enough for them to hear him.

"Ah, at last. He speaks, and—as usual—it is to correct us." George bumped Jack's elbow with his own. "You do seem rather dour. More dour than normal, I mean."

"There is much on my mind. George, what will you and Susan do at the end of the Season?"

"I intend to go back to the farm," George said at once. "Make improvements upon it, now it is my inheritance and Richard will be earl. Hire more hands and staff. Send the boys to school so they can become whatever it is that most appeals to them. Father and Richard have no use for the farm, Emily will marry well, and Arthur and our other sisters are happily in the lives they prefer. Where else would I go?"

Richard had paused in front of a stationery shop, looking into the window. He shook his head at the mention of their brother, the sailor. "By the time Arthur ever finds out our family's fortunes have changed, we will all be well settled. I doubt we will see him change much. He'd rather be blown about at sea than sit before a quiet hearth fire."

Though Jack had his doubts about that, he gave a slight nod of concession. "You will have estates to manage. A title. A future earl to raise, along with your other children. Are you at all anxious for the future?"

Richard shook his head. "I am anxious for Father, trying to learn everything afresh at his age. But then, what are land and estate agents, stewards, butlers for if not to assist in these matters? Running the farm all these years has given me some basic understanding for prices and procedure. I think everything will work itself out, so long as I find the right advisors to listen to."

The ladies ahead of them were entering a shop with a store-front full of elegant hats. Juniper was the last to go in, and when she looked over her shoulder their eyes met, a mere moment before the door closed behind her, and Jack's heart stuttered in his chest. He leaned as though to take a step toward that door, but stopped himself.

George cleared his throat and Jack turned his head, finding both his brothers staring at him.

"What is it *you* intend to do after the Season ends, Jack?" Richard asked him, crooked smile growing larger by the moment.

Lord Dunmore joined them at that moment, saving Jack from having to answer the same question Juniper herself had posed to him.

Why hadn't he given the matter any thought until now?

"We have managed," Dunmore said, voice low, "to attract a fair bit of attention today, from people whose opinions matter. I'm not entirely certain being in my company is a feather in your cap, but my wife's presence will certainly be noted as a positive."

"I cannot say I mind your company, Dunmore." Richard inclined his head as he spoke. "Your advice has already been of great help to us."

While his brothers spoke to Dunmore, Jack moved to set his back to the shop window, allowing him a clearer view of the long Arcade's corridor in both directions. Not long ago, in his other life, he had witnessed angry men storm through the area to discomfit the ladies present—a cowardly thing, in his opinion—but the situation had dissolved peacefully thanks to another gentleman, and Jack hadn't had to involve himself.

It didn't matter how pretty the surroundings; there were

always those willing to thrust their ugliness into any situation. He couldn't simply pretend that his family's new station meant they were safe from harm.

The ladies spilled out into daylight again, laughing with one another as they continued down the row of shops, all six of them in walking gowns and coats of different hues, like song-birds flitting about. Emily's eyes were wide and her expression happy, Katherine and Susan seemed equally pleased though perhaps more subdued, and Lady Dunmore with her two sisters struck out ahead of them, confident in their place in the world.

Juniper lingered before one window longer than the others, who had stepped ahead to the next glass. Moving to stand behind her, Jack peered inside over her shoulder. "Do you wish to go in?"

"Oh." Juniper seemed to realize the other ladies were not with her as her cheeks pinked. "I suppose no one else is inter-ested in beads or art at present."

"But if you wish to go inside, you ought to," he said, motioning to the door.

"Go ahead, Juniper," her brother-in-law said blithely, walking by them. "I will make certain we don't leave you too far behind."

"There, you see?" Jack cupped her elbow in his hand, using subtle pressure to guide her. "I will come with you."

A slight huff escaped her lips. "Must you always look after everyone?" When her gaze met his, however, Jack saw the plea-sure in them. "A few moments inside, no more."

"Of course, my lady." He opened the door and let her precede him inside, then closed it behind them.

Glass jars and colorful tins stood on shelves, labeled with names of colors and ingredients for color-making. He looked around with interest. None of the duke's female kin had set foot in this shop before. He'd seen them work on all manner of artistic projects, but they obtained most of their supplies by ordering from London or their own local apothecary.

Juniper went directly to the proprietor behind the counter. After an initial exchange of pleasantries, she asked a series of questions. "I'm looking for a ground pigment that would give a soft glow to skin tones—what would you suggest for painting fair complexions?" And then, "Could you tell me more about the quality of your linseed oil? I've found it affects how smoothly I can blend my colors." Followed by, "What do you recommend for achieving the most delicate shades of green? The shades I have seem too harsh for the ivy I am currently working on."

Standing at the counter with her, listening to her exchange with the man sorting through powders and showing them to her one by one, Jack found himself smiling. His whole focus was attuned to the way she spoke, the gestures she made with her hand, the loveliness of her profile as she listened intently to the answers given. He felt content, absorbed as he was in enjoying Juniper, and everything else fell into the background.

What if something like *this* was in his future? What if being near her was the whole of his plans? Or—no. What if being with her was his reason for making plans in the first place?

The idea set Jack's mind to work like a general on a hilltop, looking for possible paths to gain the best advantage.

He could see his destination. He need only march in the right direction.

Juniper turned toward him, her smile soft and warm as ever. "I think that will do for now. Shall we find the others?"

His landscape had shifted, putting her squarely in the middle. It made him slow to nod and offer his arm, but she did not seem to notice. They stepped out of the shop, the bell jingling merrily behind them, and Jack lifted his gaze from her smile most reluctantly—and immediately saw his sister standing several yards off, delicate brows drawn together as she spoke with an earnest expression to—Mr. Waldegrave.

A curse slipped through his lips, and when he lunged forward, Juniper stayed with him.

None of the others were in sight. How had that fool Waldegrave found them on an outing *again* and managed to get Emily on her own?

"Do not make a scene," Juniper said quietly.

He gave her a quick glance. "What?"

"You are a gentleman, not a guard," she said, her voice soft.

He didn't have time to respond as he'd arrived at Emily's side who looked up at him with wide eyes. "Jack."

Giving his attention entirely to Waldegrave, Jack's smile grew as he bowed stiffly. "Mr. Waldegrave. Good afternoon."

Waldegrave's expression was however somewhat sour. "Mr. John Sterling. Here I had hoped to have the pleasure of your sister's company whilst admiring the Arcade's delights, but she inexplicably assures me this is quite impossible."

"I have assured him our party is already quite full," Emily said hastily.

Juniper winced, a movement Jack barely noticed from the side of his eye, before she spoke with measured politeness. "I am afraid we have a large party with a rather restrictive schedule, Mr. Waldegrave."

He tilted his head. "One would hope such large parties could accommodate a gentleman of modest company. Surely one more rambler would not weigh too heavily on a joyous outing such as this?"

"Indeed, Mr. Waldegrave." Juniper kept her hand on Jack's arm and gave it a gentle squeeze when his muscles stiffened. "We truly regret the timing, Mr. Waldegrave, but I fear we've left a number of our party scattered as it is. We must regroup and leave quite soon."

"Ah, I see." He cut his gaze first to Jack and then to Emily. "The demands of chaperoning such a...a newly prominent family must be taxing indeed. I daresay some might find it difficult to manage the nuances of social outings when there is so much that is not yet understood."

Jack stiffened. A dozen retorts sprung to his lips, but none were all that diplomatic.

Thankfully Juniper came to his rescue yet again, her voice warm and seemingly unflapped. "On the contrary, I believe they are managing quite well, thanks to their kind friends."

"Of course." Waldegrave offered a slight bow, but his words were colder than frost. "Well, I shall take my leave. It would seem my presence here is unnecessary. But rest assured, Lady Emily, Mr. Sterling, I shall remember to mention to all my friends how *delightful* your family is to all they deign to entertain." He didn't speak quietly, and people walking along the shops glanced in their direction with interest.

The entire situation rankled Jack, raising his hackles. It was effort to prevent his hands from becoming fists.

His sister frowned as the man withdrew, her lips twisted with puzzlement. "I did not mean to offend him but he seemed rather upset."

Unable to let the matter rest, Jack took his sister's arm and whispered more harshly than he intended. "Why were you out here in company with him? Where are our brothers? The other ladies?"

Emily shook her head and pointed vaguely across the small walkway. "In the shops. I saw Mr. Waldegrave looking at me through the window and thought I had better speak to him. He seems quite determined to—"

"This isn't the time for this conversation," Juniper said lightly, looking for all the world as though she found the window of pipes near them worthy of her attention. "Nor the place. I suggest we rejoin the others and find something else to do with our time. A gallery, perhaps."

Jack nodded tightly. "Of course."

"I will go. You two stay here." She slipped away from them,

walking without rushing, and entering the shop Emily had gestured to a moment ago.

His sister wore a contrite frown. "Did I do everything wrong?"

He shook his head. "I wasn't there to help, that is all. And Waldegrave is clearly determined to secure your attention." He repressed a sigh. "His pride was hurt. That is all."

He hoped his words would prove true, though he knew enough about the pettiness of the upper class to doubt Waldegrave would take the perceived offense in stride.

Hopefully, this error would not prove detrimental to their family's position in Society, shaky as it was. And it had happened because he had allowed himself to be distracted by the beautiful Lady Juiper.

CHAPTER 12

One unfortunate circumstance to being an unwed lady related to a baroness was the numerous social obligations that came with that connection. As Juniper lived in the same household as Lady Ivy Frost, Baroness Dunmore, she often found herself a companion to her sister. Betony, though only slightly younger, avoided many of Ivy's outings by pointing out it was really Juniper who ought to get out into Society more.

Thus Juniper found herself once again in a grand drawing room, where Lady Roswell hosted the monthly meeting for the Ladies Charitable Aid to the Unfortunate Women and Children of London Society. It was one of Ivy's preferred groups because, despite their ridiculously long name, they did a great deal of good for impoverished widows and their children.

The furnishings in Lady Roswell's townhome were elegant, well-made, and rather modest for a countess of her standing. The woman herself, nearing seventy years of age, had greeted each arriving member of the Committee for Literacy with warmth. The entirety of the committee sat in a dozen chairs arranged in a semi-circle before the fireplace, discussing their efforts to procure funding for a school that educated both grown women and their children.

Juniper, not truly an official member of the committee, had excused herself to sit in a chair near the window, where she could listen to the going's on without feeling on display. Several daughters and companions of the ladies present were scattered about the room, some in their own conversational corners, others seeking a thoughtful solitude like Juniper.

The gentle murmur of voices with only the occasional clink of teacup meeting saucer, lulled her into thoughts unrelated to the worthy cause under discussion.

Staring out the window at the dismal gray sky, wishing March had brought with it brighter weather, Juniper closed the book she'd brought with her and held it to her chest. It was another of Mr. Grey's books, one in which the heroine's grandmother appeared as a ghost to lead her to a family diary. It was a favorite of hers, read more than a handful of times before. Perhaps the familiarity was what made it difficult for her to keep her attention today on its pages.

Instead, she found herself thinking of Jack Sterling. Their last two interactions had been far friendlier than she had thought herself likely to experience. He was kind, as always; conscientious, mindful of the comfort and safety of others, and ever the gentleman. But he'd been a touch *more* than that, too.

He'd complimented her. Laughed with her—even bantered, somewhat, and allowed her glimpses of his far too infrequent smile. Perhaps she was, like the heroine in an overly dramatic book devoid of common sense, reading too much into things.

A stirring behind her alerted her to the ladies' usual break when they reached the halfway point of their agenda. That meant she could either leave her cozy chair and risk conversation, or remain in place and pretend absorption in her book. As she'd spent the whole of the day before in company with people, she did not find herself prepared to take on yet more interaction. Best to sit quietly, then.

Juniper tried to concentrate on the pages of her book, ignoring the laughter and conversations behind her, yet her mind drifted away again to thoughts of Jack. What would he say when next they spoke? They were to take dinner together, their two families with Mr. and Mrs. Grey. Jack's invitation had thrilled her, for more than one reason. The thought of sitting at a table both with him and her favorite author made her head spin.

Truly, though...it was Jack she looked forward to seeing again the most.

It was then that a softly-spoken phrase caught her ear, pulling her from her flights of fancy.

"No, the *Sterling* family—the new Earl of Benwaith. I had heard they were in trade before, but I have come to learn that they were little better than farmers."

Another female voice answered, "Oh, *them*. Yes. The first word I had of them was that they hung their washing out the windows. I could not believe it."

"That is hardly as disruptive as the other things they have been about. Do you know, they have had several important families call upon them, and be seen with them in Society, to the point that they believe themselves above the rest of us?"

"Truly? I had heard that they were making appropriate house calls."

"Oh yes, to Lord Hartwell, the ambassador Lord Atella, Lord Dunmore, and others—but now they parade about as though they are equal to their company due to more than an accident of rank." The voice lowered its volume, though her words still carried across the room. "The unmarried daughter, Lady Emily, has apparently been seen gadding about alone and in public with all manner of gentlemen, only to spurn them when they show any sort of genuine interest."

SALLY BRITTON

"Surely not."

"Rumor also has it that part of the reason for their rapid rise in popularity is because of the Duke of Montfort."

At this point, Juniper realized she frowned so fiercely that her head ached. Who were these women, saying such horrid things about the Sterling family? Ought she to do something about it?

"Why would His Grace care a whit about them?" the lesser-informed of the two voices asked.

"The youngest Mr. Sterling used to hold a position on the duke's household staff...as a footman."

"No!"

"Yes. Why would a duke waste even a moment's thought on such a man? I think he must fear that the former footman knows something, perhaps scandalous, about the family."

Juniper clutched at the arms of the chair, clenching her jaw shut to keep from bursting out in fury at them. How could they —where was Ivy, she had to say something!

"Do you truly think he would blackmail a duke?"

The haughty voice's owner sniffed. "A footman one moment, a gentleman the next? Of course it is a reasonable supposition. The man—indeed, the whole family—has no concept of what it truly means to be noble. They are playing at it, and they are getting away with it."

"I sincerely doubt they will, not for long. The people who matter most in Society will never truly accept them."

Would saying something make matters worse? Juniper squeezed her eyes shut. She'd heard naught but unfounded rumor and the truth, mixed up together. Jack had been a foot-man. The Duke of Montfort had indeed put the family forward, despite his absence from London. The Sterling family had lived on a farm, content to tend to their land and naught else...yet everything had sounded so horrid coming from that woman's mouth.

"Ah, Lady Dunmore," the haughty-voiced woman said. "We were just discussing some acquaintances of yours. Your family has been in company with the Sterlings of late, yes?"

"Oh, indeed," came her sister's voice. "The Sterlings have been quite busy this Season, have they not? It seems everyone is talking about them and their foray into Society."

Juniper winced. Nothing her sister said was damning, but in light of all she had heard, her sister's words almost felt like confirmation of what the other ladies had said.

"Indeed. It seems they are seen everywhere, and always in the best company," the other gossiping woman said.

"Perhaps we ought to see if the countess would care to join our society?" Ivy's suggestion was not exactly ignored, but instead met with a quick change in topic.

"I do believe we ought to rejoin the others—oh goodness, look at the time, we will never accomplish anything if we continue to enjoy the refreshments and company rather than pay attention to our agenda."

The ladies' voices withdrew, and soon the murmuring quieted again as the chair of the committee called everyone back to order.

Juniper remained where she was, staring blankly at the window rather than through it. Guilt smote her heart. She should have risen, should have said something to the women to discredit their unkind suppositions.

Was it her place to shield Jack and his family, though? For an unmarried woman to do so, openly, while contradicting women of higher standing than herself with whom she was not acquainted...that was likely to have the opposite effect of what she hoped. What had been the alternative, though? Sitting in silence as she had felt wrong, too.

After a vain attempt to swallow back her discomfort, Juniper rehearsed all she had heard in her mind. She could see no point when she might have stood and said a word. The situation continued to vex her when Ivy collected her, after the meeting, to take her home again.

After they climbed into the carriage, Ivy gave her a concerned look. "Are you all right, dear? You look rather somber."

"I am fine. Merely a bit tired, that is all." The lie didn't settle well, and Ivy seemed prepared to press more, but Juniper hastily shook her head. "I need to rest. I will be well after a nap, I am certain."

"All right," her sister said softly. "Do tell me if there is anything I might do to give you greater comfort."

"Thank you, Ivy." She fell silent for the brief ride back to their townhouse, and went directly to her room to pretend to rest. But one of the final things those horrid ladies had said—that the Sterlings would never be accepted by those who mattered—swirled about to the forefront of her mind again.

"What if they're right?" she said to herself in a low voice as she sat on the edge of her bed. What if the Sterlings were not accepted? Even with their title and funds? It would be a rather bleak future for all of them if Society suspected them of ill deeds, accused them of poor manners, and dwelt upon their humble beginnings. It was all such a mess.

And what could Juniper do about any of it?

AT DINNER WITH A TABLE FULL OF GUESTS, JACK KEPT HIS attention on his plate; or at least, he tried to. The Earl of Benwaith's dining room was a stuffy, formal room that any English nobleman would be proud of—elegant chandeliers bathed the table in softly flickering light, the portraits on the walls looked on with grim satisfaction, and the dishes themselves were delicious. Best of all, across from him Lady Juniper

Amberton sat, and though he knew better than to stare, his eyes strayed far too often in her direction.

Her head was tilted slightly toward Mr. Grey, who Jack had managed to convince his mother to sit beside her. The writer—whose novels Juniper was clearly fond of—continued to speak with a slight stutter but seemed more than pleased to engage in her discussion. Jack couldn't hear every word of what they were saying, but snippets floated across the table.

"Your last novel," Juniper said, her familiar voice warm, "kept me up late into the night to finish. That final visitation at the end—the grandmother's ghost guiding the heroine—it was so unexpected. How do you think of such things?"

Mr. Grey flushed slightly at her praise, his fingers gripping his wine glass. "It c-c-came to me," he began, then paused, collecting himself, "w-when I was visiting my f-f-family home, up north, in Harbottle. A dash of inspiration, I s-suppose." He glanced at his wife, seated beside Jack, and Mrs. Grey bestowed a delighted smile upon him.

The two were clearly besotted with each other, an encouraging thing to see for a gentleman and gentlewoman of the middle class.

Jack pretended to focus on the conversation Lord Dunmore was having with Mrs. Grey to his left, but his attention drifted back to Juniper. She was lively in her conversation, but never in an overly distracting way. Her smile was soft, her gestures graceful, yet somehow she commanded Jack's attention even when she wasn't looking his way.

How was it that she could be so engaging, so effortlessly lovely? He'd always known her to be kind, a lover of books and art, but lately, something had shifted...or perhaps it was he who had changed, noticing more than just the quiet beauty she carried within her. What was it that drew him to her? Was it the way she leaned in when speaking, her sincerity clear in every word? Or the spark of wit she'd shown the few times they'd exchanged banter? There was a joyful cleverness to her that he enjoyed seeing every time they interacted.

Juniper laughed softly at something Mr. Grey said, and Jack's heart skipped a beat. He'd seen her smile so many times before and thought her an attractive woman, but now it felt somehow...different. She was no longer just Lady Juniper, someone so far removed from his reach that he could admire her from afar without consequence. Now she sat here, across from him, close enough to touch.

And he found himself wanting—more than anything—to be the reason for that smile.

"I am glad you enjoy the Gothic novels," Mr. Grey was saying. "W-Writing them is an e-e-escape of sorts. Though," he gave her a sheepish grin, "I hope I haven't given you too much anxiety as you read them."

Juniper's eyes sparkled. "Only the enjoyable kind, Mr. Grey. You do have a habit of crafting such excellent suspense, leaving me guessing until the very last page."

Jack smiled to himself, listening to her warmly tease the author. She had that way about her, didn't she? A way of making people feel at ease, drawing them in with her cordiality.

Could this—being near her, seeing her every day, sharing the small moments of life—could this be his future? The thought had struck Jack before when he wasn't paying attention, but now it landed with full force.

He could imagine it, even if it felt impossible. Sitting across the dinner table from Juniper every evening, with or without guests, seeing her smile and hearing all her thoughts on books, the theater, what she had seen and done that day...he was sorely tempted by the idea of making it a permanent arrangement. Was there any chance at all she would be interested in such a future?

But even as he asked himself the question, he discovered what he desired. He respected her, admired her mind, her kindness. And if she could ever look at him as something more than the former footman or a family friend, if she could see him as he saw her...

His pulse quickened at the mere thought.

"Perhaps I will have to convince you, Mr. Grey, to write a gentler novel to put all your readers at ease, just the once," Juniper was saying, her smile soft, eyes glancing briefly in Jack's direction. She met his gaze, and for a moment, he thought she held it longer than she needed to.

Perhaps there was a reason for him to hope.

The ladies departed before Jack had taken in that dessert had even been served, and he sat dazedly through the port and cigars without being able to contribute much to the conversation. As the gentlemen entered the drawing room to join the ladies, the low hum of conversation filling the room that had his mother's touch on each article within, making it far more comfortable an atmosphere for his family. The fire crackled gently in the hearth, and the candlelight made even the shadows seem soft.

He stood near the window, looking out over the back garden, alert for any movement that did not belong—as he ever would be, he supposed, for the rest of his life. He could not make his watchfulness leave him. It had become part of his nature.

Juniper appeared at his side, glancing up at him, one of her engaging smiles in place. "Mr. Sterling, you have been very quiet this evening," she said, eyebrows lifted, her voice low enough for only him to hear. "I hope you have not grown tired of our company."

He smiled, shaking his head. "Not at all, Lady Juniper. I find myself enjoying the evening and the conversation."

"Even when you are not part of it?" she asked, her tone curious. Her fingers brushed along the edge of the windowpane.

"Especially then," he admitted quietly. "I am rather used to listening and observing. It is as much preference as habit now, it would seem."

For a moment, they simply stood there saying nothing, but something unspoken passed in that glance. Her eyes softened and she lowered her gaze, but Jack had felt that moment of connection as surely as he would the heat of a fire on his skin. Although the room was full of people, full of laughter and conversation, for that brief moment it felt as though it was empty except for the two of them, standing alone near the night-darkened window.

Then he saw a slight crease form between her brows.

Juniper cast a quick glance around the room before speaking softly. "Mr. Sterling, may I ask you something?"

Jack turned to face her fully, still held aloft by the feel of what had passed between them. "Of course, my lady. What is on your mind?"

She hesitated, fingers lightly brushing at a curl of her hair. "I...I overheard something the other day. At a charity meeting I attended with my sister."

Her words drew his attention but he smiled easily, unable to imagine more than a minor concern prompted such a tone from her. His own emotions were too bright, too warm in her company, and could not immediately shift to worry. "What was it?"

Juniper took a breath, clearly collecting her thoughts. "They...they were remarks about your family. About your rise in Society. I did not wish to trouble you with it, but I thought perhaps you should know."

Jack blinked, the shift in tone not fully settling within him. His mood was still light and he found himself almost chuckling at the thought of it. "Remarks? About my family?" He shook his head slightly. "I imagine there is plenty of gossip about us, as we expected. We are yet a novelty in the *ton*, after all. People are curious. Something new will catch their attention soon enough."

Juniper frowned, as though not satisfied with his response. "It was not mere curiosity I heard," she continued quietly. "They questioned your family's propriety. Your right to be among them."

Jack's smile faltered for a brief moment. He glanced around the room, still feeling the warmth of the evening. What harm could anonymous people's words do to him, standing here in the glow of Juniper's company? "People will always question things they do not understand. But we have been welcomed by those who matter—thanks to His Grace the Duke. We will have to continue to prove ourselves to the rest."

Juniper's brow furrowed further, frustration evidently starting to seep in. "They were so unkind. It was not fair in the least."

Jack's gaze softened as he looked at her, still not fully grasping the weight of her distress. He reached out to lightly touch her arm, offering reassurance. "I know it bothers you, Juniper, but trust me—it is nothing. Let them talk. All will improve with time."

"They mentioned Emily in particular," she said, voice a mere whisper. "By name."

Jack's eyes met hers, and for a moment, he could see the depth of her worry. He frowned, his good mood dampened but not entirely dismissed. "And what would you have me do, Lady Juniper? Chase after every whisper and set it straight?"

"I don't know," she replied softly, "but I don't want to see you or your family hurt by such untruths."

"So did you say anything to refute those who spoke?"

At that, her skin turned pale. She pressed her lips together and shook her head, and a prick of disappointment touched his heart. Yet she had well proved his point.

"At times, it is best to say nothing." He softened his tone. "It means a great deal to me that you care so much." He paused, his tone softening. "But I promise you, we will be well enough. The people who delight in such gossip do not know us and they do not matter, so long as our friends continue to stand by our side."

Juniper stared at him, the lingering look of unease still upon her lovely face, but Jack's calm, steady confidence remained. He had no wish for her to worry; he certainly did enough of that on his own. He would examine her words later. In the moment, he wanted to enjoy her company and nothing more.

She offered him a reluctant smile. "I suppose you are right. I just... I wish people could know you—your family, I meant to say, the way I do."

Jack's breath hitched at her words and his eyes searched hers. The unspoken connection between them flickered again, warmer and brighter.

"If they did," he said quietly, his voice thick with meaning, "then I'd consider myself very fortunate indeed."

For a moment, the room seemed to fade around them, the crackle of the fire and the soft murmurs of conversation blending into the background. Juniper held his gaze, her earlier worries still obviously present, but softened by the feeling growing between them.

And then the moment passed, and Jack straightened, returning to his usual self with a slight smile. "Now," he said, his voice lighter, "shall we return to our guests? I believe Lord Dunmore is trying to convince Mr. Grey to share the inspiration for his next novel."

Juniper let out a quiet laugh, the tension easing from her shoulders, though not entirely disappearing. "Yes, we should."

She took his offered arm, and as they moved back into the center of the room, he wondered if the rumors would prove worth her worry. But he was simply too happy that night to let it ruin the moment.

CHAPTER 13

The ballroom shone with light and was alive with the motion of hundreds of people, chandeliers and lamps blazing over the sea of gowns and glittering jewels of the *ton*. Music swirled in the air, punctuated by the sound of laughter and murmured conversations. Jack stood near the edge of the dance floor, keeping a watchful eye on his sister Emily who sat on a chair a few feet away with her back straight, her gloved hands folded neatly in her lap. The very picture of a proper English lady.

Jack had watched her dance twice that evening—fewer times than usual, given how long they had been present. The novelty of their arrival in Society, it seemed, had begun to wear thin. The week before when they attended a ball, many of Emily's dances had been claimed before the first note of the orchestra played. But tonight, fewer gentlemen had approached to even pay their respects and her card remained empty.

"It is a shame Lord Hartwell and Mr. Eastwood have left Town," Emily remarked lightly, her eyes drifting across the crowd. The lack of partners had done nothing to her outward

SALLY BRITTON

calm, at least. "I enjoyed dancing with them both. They were excellent conversationalists and very polite, the pair of them."

Jack tucked his hands behind his back, trying to keep his expression neutral. "Yes, a pity," he agreed, though his mind was elsewhere, sorting through the minor things he had noticed in their interactions with others over the past few days.

Now he was looking for it, he had noticed the change in their reception when he and his brothers went to their club, and some strange glances when they were out in public—a subtle shift in the way people regarded them. At first they had been a curiosity: the Sterlings, the family who had risen from nothing. But something had changed... Could it only be that the interest was fading, and that judgment now took its place?

Susan drifted near them, her eyebrows drawn together in concern as she waved a fan softly before her face. "No new partners yet, Emily?"

Emily shook her head. "No, but I do not mind."

"What is keeping them away?" their sister-in-law asked quietly, looking to Jack for an answer.

He hated that he did not have a clear cause to give them. "I cannot guess. Nothing in our status has changed. Nothing about Emily has changed."

"I suppose it is quieter this way," Emily said, giving first him and then Susan a small smile. "Calmer. I do not mind too much."

Jack returned her smile, though his attention was caught by a pair of women whispering behind their fans, their eyes flicking toward his sister before quickly turning away. His jaw tightened, but he kept his tone light. "Then I will not mind either. There is nothing wrong with a quiet evening, Emily. Besides, you will have more time to enjoy the refreshments."

She laughed, the sound bright but a little tight to his ears. "That is true enough."

He cast a quick glance at Susan, who nodded and held her

gloved hand out to Emily. "Perhaps we ought to fetch some punch now. I declare myself quite parched."

As the three of them made their way toward the refreshment table, Jack noticed yet more glances. People's narrowed-eyed gazes followed after them, along with their whispers. It wasn't blatant, but it was there—an undercurrent of something displeasing running through the room like a thread pulled tight.

He could tell by the stiffening of his sister-in-law's shoulders that she had picked up on the attention, and she stepped closer to Emily. For her part, his sister was busily speaking about the music and did not appear to notice anything amiss.

As they passed a small group of well-dressed aristocrats, a snatch of conversation in French caught his ear.

"...une telle famille de parvenus... un pied-dans-l'plat à chaque occasion..."

Jack's spine stiffened at the words, his French fluent enough to catch the meaning: a family of upstarts...blundering into every opportunity...

He had learned the language as a soldier, along with German. He'd spent all his free time speaking with officers to sharpen his understanding of the languages of the continent. It had served him well in both the military and in the Duke of Montfort's household.

He glanced at Emily, but she was busy accepting a glass of lemonade from Susan at the refreshment table, blissfully unaware of the slight.

Jack, on the other hand, felt his blood heat.

Turning on his heel, he approached the group who were still chatting in French, likely assuming their words went unnoticed by an uneducated *upstart* such as him. He tucked his hands behind his back to avoid clenching his fists, frustration simmering beneath his skin, and cleared his throat loud enough to draw their attention. Their conversation faltered, eyes turning toward him in surprise.

He bowed elegantly toward the group, wearing a smile he had seen occasionally on the duke's face when the man was dangerously displeased. The small group paused, eyes shifting toward him in surprise and irritation. They had to acknowledge him—or at least, one of them did.

"Mr. John Sterling, is it not?" one of the gentlemen asked eventually.

"It is." He stood to his full height, which was above that of those who now looked at him with open contempt. When he started speaking again, their expressions changed slowly to shock. "*Je ne peux imaginer de qui vous parlez, bien que je ne trouve pas cela poli de critiquer les gens dans un lieu public,*" Jack said, his French smooth and confident. Then, with a pointedly pleasant smile, he continued in German. "*Aber lassen Sie uns diesen unangenehmen Moment vergessen. Ich hoffe, Sie genießen Ihren Abend.*"

What he said was not accusatory in the slightest. If anything, it was too polite. *I cannot imagine who you are speaking of, though I do not think it polite to critique people in a public place,* and then in German, *But let us forget this uncomfortable moment. I hope you enjoy your evening.*

A stunned silence fell over the formerly chortling men. One of the gentlemen flushed, his mouth opening as if to apologize, but no words came out. Another looked down, clearly embarrassed, while a third gave a nervous laugh as though that would somehow soothe away the discomfort.

Jack raised an eyebrow, letting the moment hang in the air a second longer than necessary. "Now, if you will excuse me, gentlemen."

He turned back toward the refreshment table and his sister, who had missed the entire exchange. Susan nibbled at a small sandwich and appeared to fight back a smile.

Jack offered both of them his arms, maintaining his composure as best he could. As they moved along the wall of the room, he glanced back, noting with satisfaction the still-flustered expressions on the faces of the gossipers.

"What was that all about, Jack?" Susan asked softly.

"They were conversing in French about something they did not understand, so I offered enlightenment," he said, as calm as he could manage. "It was nothing serious." He hoped he spoke the truth.

"Nothing serious?" she repeated with a lift of her eyebrows. "My, I wonder what you *would* consider serious. Perhaps a hurricane?" Her eyes brightened with amusement, and he could not help but return her smile, as though she knew full well what he had stepped in to correct.

They rejoined the other members of their family present that evening, his two brothers and his other sister-in-law, in a room where people played cards. Jack left both ladies there and went to the window to take up a watchful post over all of them. The peripheries of rooms still impressed him as the most comfortable from which to observe the others, even if he was trying to give them more room to learn for themselves.

As he stood beside the wall, watching over his family as Emily sipped her lemonade and the others played cards, Jack could not help but wonder what had changed. Why were they now the subject of whispered conversations and critical stares?

Was this the gossip Juniper had attempted to warn him of, spreading like wildfire through the ranks of the *ton*? He frowned, and what remained of his good mood slipped completely away. What could people possibly say about his family that would shift the general perspective on them so completely? There were no scandals attached to them. They had done nothing in public to warrant even a humorous obser-vation. Those who spoke had called them *upstarts*. But why? What did this mean for them?

Gossip could destroy reputations, if it was cruel enough or

found to hold truth. If misinformation was spreading about them, who was spreading it? And how best could he counter it?

Jack's jaw tightened. He needed to know his enemy in order to put a battle plan in place. He needed to know exactly what was being said.

Whatever it was, he would not allow his family's happiness to be sullied by petty remarks and thinly veiled insults.

Not while he was standing.

CHAPTER 14

J uniper sat at her dressing table, watching through the
mirror as Hettie fussed over the last section of her hair,
gently securing it with a ribbon. Her dark hair looked quite
elegant, thanks to the maid's deft hands. She tugged lightly on a
curl that spiraled above her ear, watching it impressively bounce
back into place.

"Hettie, you always work such wonders with my hair. I only
wish I had been able to show your handiwork off last evening."
Juniper wrinkled her nose at her reflection. She still sounded as
though her nose needed clearing.

Catching cold two days earlier had been awful timing, no
matter how mild her symptoms felt at present. The cold had
robbed her of a chance to see Jack, and those opportunities were
fewer in number than she wished. The late morning light
filtering through the window did little to lift her spirits. She
pressed a handkerchief to her nose, sniffling softly.

"I'm sorry you missed the ball, my lady," Hettie said sympa-
thetically, placing the last pin in her hair. "Everyone is sayin' it
was quite the affair."

Juniper sighed. "I suppose it was for the best. I would hardly want to spend the evening sneezing into a fan and dabbing at a red nose."

"As you say, my lady. Your rest was important, and you seem much better today." With that cheerful announcement, Hettie put a stack of clean, folded handkerchiefs on the table. "Best tuck a few of these about your person, my lady."

Juniper tucked one in her sleeve, another in her reticule, but left the others. She likely wouldn't stir far from her room today even if she was feeling somewhat better. Still, the ache of disappointment for last evening lingered. She hadn't wanted to miss the ball, not when Jack would be there. She wondered if he'd noticed her absence. He was likely busy dancing with others. How silly of her, to wish him disappointed when she ought to wish he enjoyed himself, she thought with a pang.

Juniper rose and moved to the little chair beside the fire, where she had left her book. It was a delicious novella from America; her brother-in-law had gifted it to her, promising it had elements of romance, suspense, and the supernatural. A perfect little volume for her stuffy head to enjoy. Yet she had barely sat down in the chair, shawl around her shoulders, when there was a knock at the door. Without waiting for permission, the door swung open to reveal Fiona Frost, her eyes bright with excitement.

"Juniper!" the girl exclaimed, her eyes wide as she hurtled inside the room with the same exuberance she had for everything. "There's someone here to see you, the man who used to follow us about at the duke's castle, Mr. Sterling." Her grin widened. "I said I'd fetch you quick as a wink, but I warned him you were sneezing like a cat with the pepper pot."

Juniper's heart leapt in her chest, and for a moment, she forgot the sniffles entirely. "Mr. Sterling is here?" she asked, voice a little faint as her mind raced ahead, wondering what could have brought him to call upon her.

"Yes." Fiona bounced on her heels. "You know, the guard

who didn't make cross faces at us. The one who was always there, looking after everyone. He's come to pay a call on *you*."

Juniper stood quickly, nearly upsetting the small tray of tea her maid had set on the table by her chair. "Thank you, Fiona," she said, her pulse quickening. "Hettie, please keep the tea warm. I doubt Mr. Sterling will stay long."

Hettie raised an amused brow but stepped back with the tea. "As you say, Lady Juniper."

The heat rising in Juniper's cheeks had little to do with her cold, and everything to do with the man waiting downstairs. What must she look like?

As she hurried toward the door Fiona followed at her heels, her curious eyes shining. "You look happy," the girl observed. "Why are you smiling?"

Juniper stifled a nervous laugh, her hand smoothing over the front of her gown. "Why not smile when someone pays a call? It is always a compliment, is it not?"

"I suppose so." Fiona raised her eyebrows as she followed Juniper out of the room. "It's odd, though. He used to be just a guard, a footman. Now Teague pays calls on him and you rush out to meet him. I think he must be someone very important now."

"He was always rather important," Juniper said, unable to stop the small smile tugging at her lips as they made their way through the house. Her heart raced in anticipation, thoughts swirling through her mind. *Why had Jack come? Perhaps he missed me at the ball?* Her feet quickened their pace, matching her pulse.

By the time she reached the drawing room her cheeks felt flushed, and she took a moment to collect herself. Juniper's hand hovered over the door handle for a moment. She smoothed the front of her gown, took one deep breath, and prayed her voice wouldn't betray the nerves bubbling inside her. With a final glance at Fiona, who was still grinning and skipping along behind her, she opened the door.

Juniper stepped inside the drawing room, leaving the door open behind her, her pulse quickening the moment her gaze settled on Jack. He stood near the window, looking out at the street below, the morning light casting his dark hair with a soft, amber hue and highlighting the sharp angles of his face. He looked handsome—as he always did—and the sight of him made her breath catch in her throat.

And he was here to see her.

Heat filled her heart and spread through her chest as their eyes met, rising up her neck and spreading across her cheeks. Though she had admitted to herself her affection for him had grown every time they met, this was a feeling Juniper hadn't expected, so sudden and intense, and it left her momentarily rooted to the spot. Her hands gripped the folds of her gown, fingers tightening briefly on the fabric as she tried to calm the flurry of emotions inside her.

This is foolish, she told herself, *he's surely only here as a friend, to ask my opinion on some matter regarding Emily*—but her body ignored her rational thoughts, heart thudding in time with her growing feelings.

Jack's gaze softened when he saw her, the faintest hint of a smile tugging at the corners of his lips. The intensity of their silent exchange, lasting a moment but feeling like much longer, stirred something deep inside her.

Fiona bounced into the room with a grin, her bright eyes darting between them, clearly curious about the unspoken energy between her elder companion and Mr. Sterling.

"I told you I could find her quickly, didn't I?" she chirped.

"That you did, Miss Frost," Jack said, nodding deeply to the girl, amusement in his eyes.

Juniper blinked, snapping out of her trance when he looked away, and turned to the girl with a composed smile though her heart still raced. "Thank you, Fiona, for bringing him to my attention so quickly," she said kindly. "Perhaps you ought to tell your brother that Mr. Sterling is here. I am certain Lord Dunmore would like to see our guest, too."

Fiona's eyes widened, and she nodded enthusiastically. "Oh! Of course. I'll find him straightaway." She spun around and darted back out the door, her footfalls light and hurried.

She left the door open behind her leaving Juniper alone with Jack, the quiet of the room suddenly far more intimate. She took a breath, pulse still racing, and gave him a soft, but controlled smile. Something...friendly. Nothing that would give away how her thoughts had changed. Yes, she had entertained romantic notions of him in the past because he was handsome and kind, because she admired him, but today it was as though a final barrier had fallen. A barrier that had surrounded her heart, and let her put her thoughts of him purely in the realm of fantasy. The moment it fell, Juniper woke to the reality of her situation.

Juniper was falling in love with Jack Sterling.

Jack took a step forward as though he meant to close the remaining distance between them, but she instinctively raised a hand, suddenly overcome by nerves.

"Please," she said quickly, gesturing toward a nearby chair. "Sit. I—I've kept you standing long enough."

Jack hesitated briefly before nodding and taking the seat she indicated. He moved with that same unhurried steadiness she had come to expect from him, but for some reason, today, it made her heart quicken all over again. She turned away slightly, walking to her own chair near the hearth, her movements less assured than usual.

Why am I so nervous? she wondered, though the answer was all too clear.

Her feelings for him had crept up on her slowly, like a tide rising. She'd told herself she was aware of the coming water, that it wasn't anything she need concern herself with. But now, faced with the reality of him sitting there, mere feet away, the depth of those feelings hit her all at once and she was cut off from the shore, from sanity, surrounded by nothing but the waters of affection. She couldn't stop the flutter in her stomach or the way her hands trembled slightly as she adjusted her shawl.

This is absurd, she told herself. *He only sees me as a friend.*

But then she sneezed. It was not a quick, delicate sound either. The noise rushed from her and she barely had time to cover her face with her shawl and turn away from him. The fearful, crashing sneeze broke the silence and startled her out of her racing thoughts.

"Bless you," Jack said, his voice warm and low. He leaned forward slightly in his chair, watching her with that steady gaze of his. To his credit, he neither seemed repelled nor amused by the outburst. "You are still feeling unwell?"

Juniper sniffled softly and pulled a handkerchief from her sleeve with what she hoped was a graceful flourish. "Oh, truly it is nothing," she said lightly, dabbing at her nose as though she frequently sneezed violently before gentleman callers. "Merely the remnants of a cold that refuses to leave me. I am determined to outlast it."

Jack's lips curved slightly, but the concern in his eyes remained. "Are you certain you should be out of bed?"

She laughed softly, waving a dismissive hand. "If I stayed in bed every time I sneezed, I would never see daylight. Besides, I would much rather be up and about than missing any more balls. Or visitors, for that matter." She gave him a pointed look, trying to deflect the conversation with a bit of humor.

"My family missed yours at the ball last evening. Emily and my sisters-in-law send their wishes for your good health."

"That is kind. I truly was sorry to miss seeing them." That they missed her was immensely gratifying. That he had come to speak to her in person, however, left her wanting to ask if *he* had missed her in particular.

Of course, no lady would ever ask such a bold question of a gentleman.

"You look somewhat puzzled, my lady," Jack said, pulling her out of her thoughts.

"Oh—forgive me. I am merely ruing that I had to miss the ball at all. I hope you will return my good wishes to your family. Was it an enjoyable evening? Did everything go well for Emily?"

"I believe Emily enjoyed herself." His expression grew more serious, his brows drawing together. "However, there is a reason I came to see you today."

Juniper's heart skipped a beat at his change in tone. She sat up a little straighter, her fingers tightening around the handkerchief in her lap. A reason?

For a fleeting, ridiculous moment, her mind raced ahead to impossibilities, conjuring daring hopes. Could he—? No. Surely not. But what if he was here to speak to her about something more personal? What if—what if he was going to—

"I wanted to talk to you about something that happened at the ball last night," Jack said, his voice pulling her back to reality with an unpleasant jolt.

The foolish, irrational hope which had briefly bloomed in her chest wilted instantly. He wasn't going to ask about courtship; of course he wanted to speak about the ball.

Juniper forced a smile, trying to hide her disappointment, and nodded for him to continue.

"There were...rumors," Jack said, his tone careful. "Unpleasant ones. People were speaking about my family and not kindly. It felt as though half the room stared at us, weighing us in a way they have not since our arrival in Town."

Juniper frowned, the lightness in the air vanishing completely with her concern. "What do you mean?"

"They were calling us upstarts, gossiping about how we don't belong in Society," Jack explained, his voice low but steady. "Gossiping openly. Questioning why we are being welcomed by certain families."

Juniper felt her chest tighten with a mix of anger and frustration. She had overheard some of this gossip herself, and she had even tried to warn him of it. But Jack being confronted with it—hearing how deeply it affected him—made her heart ache for him.

"Jack, that is awful," she whispered, her earlier nerves forgotten as her concern for him took over. "I trust it was not worse than what I overheard."

JACK RAN A HAND THROUGH HIS HAIR, FINGERS CATCHING briefly in the strands as he looked across at Juniper. She was so lovely, sitting there with her hands delicately folded, her expression a mix of sympathy and concern. That soft warmth in her eyes—a tenderness which never seemed to waver, no matter the situation—made his heart twist painfully in his chest. She was everything gentle and kind, and he ached with the desire to reach out to her, to take comfort in the simple act of holding her hand.

What would she think of me if I told her how much this gossip is weighing on me?

Jack wasn't supposed to be the type of man who let idle whispers shake him; yet here he was, feeling the weight of every cruel gaze and unkind word spoken the night before...words he hadn't realized would burrow so deep. His family had come so far—farther than they ever imagined—but it seemed Society would never approve of or forget how they began.

His gaze flickered to Juniper's hands, so small and delicate in her lap, and before he could stop himself he reached out, gently taking her hand in his. Her skin was warm against his, and for a brief moment, the connection between them chased away the shadows of doubt gnawing at him.

"Juniper." He spoke quietly, voice low. "The gossip at the charity meeting. I need to know—what was it that you over-heard? Perhaps if I know exactly what others are saying, I can find the root of the problem. Perhaps there is something I can do to alleviate the worst of it."

Her lips parted slightly, the hesitation tangible in her eyes. She didn't want to hurt him, he knew that. But he needed the truth, however jarring.

"It was nothing worth repeating," she said softly, her free hand clutching at the handkerchief in her lap. "I did not think... I did not want to bring it up in the first place, but—"

"Please," Jack urged gently, his thumb brushing over her knuckles as he held her hand, so small and delicate compared to his own. "I need to know."

Juniper looked down at their joined hands for a moment, as though gathering her thoughts. When she spoke again, her voice was soft, almost hesitant. "They said you, all of you, were playing at being noble. That you and your family don't belong. Some of them suggested that you only hold your place in Society because the Duke of Montfort put you there. And..." Her gentle voice faltered.

Jack's heart grew heavier with each word. His grip on her hand tightened ever so slightly, and he felt her return his grip. *Playing at being noble.* He had heard that before but hearing it now, from Juniper's lips, stung in a way he had not expected.

"And?" he asked, his voice lower than before.

Her voice was so soft, he could barely catch it. "They implied you might know something scandalous about the Duke, and that is why he helped you. That as his former servant, you had seen something or learned something to give you power over him. That you were perhaps using his influence to rise higher than the sudden change of rank would allow."

Jack sat back in his chair, releasing her hand with reluctance as a cold wave of self-doubt washed over him. His pulse pounded in his ears. He'd known there would be whispers about his family, but *this*? Did people truly think so little of him? That he would betray the man who had given him so much?

He rubbed the back of his neck, frowning deeply. "Of course people would think that," he muttered, more to himself than to Juniper. "My family knows no one in London, yet we are invited everywhere. I have no title, no land of my own yet here I am, in the middle of the *ton*, trying to pretend I belong." His hands fell to his lap, his fingers curling into fists. Juniper started to say something, but Jack shook his head. "It is not just the gossip, Juniper. I look at everything we have been given, and I wonder...did we really earn it? Would we have been welcomed anywhere at all without His Grace's generosity?"

His eyes met hers again, and the pain within must have been clear in his expression, given the sudden sympathy in her own.

Jack sighed heavily. "Sometimes I wonder if they are right. We may have inherited a family title, but it is not one any of us were prepared for. Perhaps...perhaps we ought to have remained quietly tucked in the countryside until we could raise ourselves to the expectations that come with my father becoming an earl. We are only here because of His Grace. Without his name attached to ours, we would not be worth a second glance."

"That is not the least bit true." The adamant tone of Juniper's voice caught him by surprise. "Jack, all of you are so lovely—I like your family. Your parents are warm and kind, your brothers are polite and obviously care for the rest of you a great deal, your sisters-in-law are clever, Emily is an absolute angel, and you—"

Juniper's fingers twitched, as though she wanted to reach for him, but she appeared to fight the instinct.

Jack's heart ached in response. "Me?" That he dared ask her to continue was a mark of his severe lapse in decorum.

Her cheeks flushed a lovely shade of pink that put him in mind of the soft sunlight at dawn. How many mornings during his life had he risen before the sun and watched a cloudy sky turn that rosy shade, and counted himself lucky to be alive to see it?

"You," she repeated the single word, meeting his gaze a moment before lowering her own to her lap, where she twisted the handkerchief in her hands. "You are a good man, Jack. One of the best I have ever met."

She drew him to her as a fresh spring would draw in a man dying of thirst. How many things could he liken to her presence? He was not a poet, but a soldier at heart yet being near her, he thought of springs and sunrises.

At the moment of his doubt came the revelation: that he did not want to build his future plans around her merely because he *liked* her, nor because she was so lovely and kind. He wanted to set her at the center of his future because his heart belonged more to her now than it did to him.

And yet....

How could he ever be worthy of her? Someone so bright, so lovely, deserved a man of true standing—one who didn't owe his position to a happenstance of birth and the charity of others.

He wanted to say more, to ask her if she thought the same, but the words caught in his throat. Instead he shook his head slightly, forcing a smile to his stiff lips. "I apologize, I should not burden you with this. You have already been kind enough to take my sister under your wing."

As Jack looked at her the need for comfort returned, stronger now. He wanted nothing more than to take Juniper's hand again, to feel the warmth of her touch and know, merely for a moment, that she did not think less of him. But he could not bring himself to reach out. Not again. He had already pushed beyond the boundaries of politeness by taking her hand the first time.

Her expression had changed, falling into something rather somber, as he struggled against his wants and the rules of appropriate behavior.

"You wanted to know all I heard," she said, still looking at her lap. "As I said before...there was mention of Emily."

He sat straighter, pushing away his own selfish thoughts. He was here for his family; for Emily. He needed to concentrate on that, not his fruitless longing for the woman seated so near him.

"What was said about my sister?" he breathed.

Juniper's gaze met his, her brow furrowed. "They said she was seen 'with all manner of gentlemen,' but that she spurned them when they grew serious in their attentions. Obviously you and I know this is not at all true. But where would such a rumor come from?"

It was an ugly rumor which would make gentlemen hesitate to be seen with Emily; if such a thing circulated widely, it would explain why Emily had not gained many dance partners the evening before. No man would wish to be seen with her and counted the next victim of a fickle nature or a woman on the hunt for an advantageous match.

Before he could ask for her opinion on the matter, the Irish lilt of Lord Dunmore broke through the tension of the room. "Ah, Sterling. Welcome to our home, as always. I apologize for the delay in greeting you properly, but I had to see my sister back to her governess in person else she may have slipped away again. But then, you know all about her skills at escaping the schoolroom." He grinned broadly as Jack rose and bowed to him.

"Miss Frost and Lord James were quite the challenge when it came to keeping them under the watchful eye of their attendants," he said with a solemn nod. Though he doubted Dunmore meant for his words to remind Jack of his former place, he felt the mark of his past position keenly. A guard disguised as a footman, he had watched and protected people of rank—he had not been one of them.

He may never truly fit in among them, either, and such a man as he had no claim on Lady Juniper's heart.

"To what do we owe the pleasure of your visit?" Dunmore asked, sitting near his sister-in-law with a crooked smile. "Fiona said you asked for Juniper and me. Is anything amiss? Or perhaps you come with a particular request to put to both of us?"

A jolt of surprise coursed through Jack. He knew instantly what Dunmore meant. Juniper, her mind sharp, obviously took in his meaning too given the widening of her eyes.

Dunmore thought Jack had come to ask for a courtship.

Perhaps he had not been as subtle in his wants as he wished. Jack would have been amused had he not felt a prick of regret in his heart at that moment.

Juniper on the other hand sneezed again, then fixed her brother-in-law with a glare.

Jack hastily put that line of thought aside. "I have no requests to make, I merely wished to pay my family's respects to yours and wish Lady Juniper on her way to full health." He kept his posture soldier-stiff. Control, that was what was needed, and until he had control over the situation with Emily, self-control would have to suffice. "I have been tasked with asking if your family will be attending the Italian ball at Bell's Hotel."

"We would not miss it for anything," the Irish baron said with a wide grin. "Atella himself would not think a thing of it, but his contessa would rain terror upon us if we were absent that evening."

"Oh, Teague." Juniper huffed and a small smile returned to her lips. "Emma would never."

"She would," Dunmore insisted. "So we dare not miss it, and we look forward to seeing your family there, Sterling. It will be an enjoyable evening."

Hopefully Jack's family would experience such a thing. With unkind rumors and gossip circulating about them, his uncertainty over the idea lingered. He changed the subject, keeping his tone all politeness. "Is there any word on the health of your sister? Lady Farleigh and the entirety of His Grace's family remain at Clairvoir, do they not?"

"They do, but we expect to have word of a safe delivery quite soon," the proud Irishman said, though Jack did not miss the flash of worry in his eyes. Dunmore's sister had wed Lord Farleigh, the Duke of Montfort's heir, and was to deliver the next member of the ducal family this month. His Grace had not come to Parliament, a thing unheard of since the births of his own children, and most of the immediate family remained near the castle in support of the expectant mother.

"I look forward to offering my congratulations after the happy event comes to pass," Jack said, the words formal even if his tone was quite sincere. As far as he was concerned, the Duke of Montfort and all connected to him were worthy of the best of things. With the lightness returned to the room, he rose to take his leave. "For now, I must be on my way and allow you to continue about your day."

Dunmore and Juniper both rose, and Jack tried not to believe the look of disappointment he saw on both their faces. He had imagined it, surely.

"You are always welcome here," Dunmore said as he bowed. "And we look forward to seeing you and your family at the ball."

"Thank you. Good day to you both, Lady Juniper. Lord Dunmore." After his final bow he left quickly, resisting the urge to look over his shoulder as he exited through the doorway.

He needed to put aside his feelings for Lady Juniper Amberton, a lady whose heart he was not worthy to hold. Her family, connected as they were to the best of the land, would surely not wish for a match with the youngest son of an upstart family. He had much better turn his attention back to his own kin, and their situation. They needed him. And he had rumors to sort out and dispel, if at all possible. Thinking of Lady Juniper, a woman above his touch, would distract him from that purpose which he could not allow...no matter how pleasant thoughts of her had become.

CHAPTER 15

U pon her usual chair in the sitting room, her hands holding a book in her lap, Juniper couldn't stop her fingers from toying with the edge of the pages. She wasn't reading it, of course. She couldn't. Her thoughts were far from the shadows of the old estate in the story, nearly as far from the quiet room where her sisters and the Dowager Baroness Dunmore sat, each absorbed in their own pursuits. Instead, her mind was tangled in knots of worry—worry for the Sterling family and for Jack.

She glanced up at Ivy, sitting nearby with a volume of sonnets in her lap, her lips moving slightly as she read to herself. Betony, ever the industrious one, was absorbed in her beadwork, her needle moving with practiced precision as she embellished the hem of a gown with beautiful embroidery. Across the room Ivy's mother-in-law sat by the fire, the soft rustle of the pamphlet she read the only sound breaking the silence. They had all taken to calling her Máthair, as her children did. The Irish honorific for 'mother' suited her, even though the Amberton sisters were related by Ivy's marriage only.

Everything was in the room itself was calm, peaceful—yet Juniper's heart fluttered anxiously in her chest, and she had to tug her thoughts out of the snarl of concern and confusion in her mind.

What is wrong with me? she wondered, her fingers brushing absently over the smooth fabric of her gown. She had tried to push thoughts of Jack—she could no longer consider him Mr. Sterling—from her mind, but it was impossible. Every time she closed her eyes, she saw him: sitting before her, his hand warm in hers, his voice low and filled with doubt. He had been so vulnerable when he visited three days before, so unsure of his family's welcome in the world. It had broken something in her to see him like that.

How could anyone think him or his family unworthy of notice and honor?

"You are very quiet, Juniper," Ivy's voice broke through her thoughts, light and teasing. "Your cold is long gone. What is troubling you?"

Juniper blinked at her older sister, startled by the question. "Oh, nothing," she lied quickly, offering her sister a weak smile. "I am merely thinking."

"Thinking?" Ivy's eyes sparkled with amusement. "That sounds dangerous."

Betony, not bothering looking up from her work, giggled. "About time you noticed something is amiss, Ivy. Perhaps you will have better luck than I at getting an explanation from her."

Juniper felt her cheeks warm. How could she ever tell her sisters about the turmoil Jack Sterling stirred in her heart? How could she explain the weight of her concern for him and his family, or the way her heart and mind quickened whenever she thought of his hand brushing against hers?

Before she could respond Máthair spoke, her tone calm and measured as always, her Irish accent beautifully genteel. "Whatever it is that preoccupies you, Juniper," she said, folding her pamphlet neatly in her lap, "remember this: life is too short to worry over things that may never come to pass. Best to face your thoughts head-on. Who better to help you face them than those that love you most?"

"Quite true." Ivy closed her book on her finger. "I am always here to listen to your thoughts, Juniper."

"As am I," Betony said, carefully putting her needle in the cloth of her gown. "No matter how ridiculous they are."

Juniper looked from one woman to the next, finding all three of them with sincere smiles, waiting for her to speak. Silently giving encouragement with their eyes and expressions. *Face your thoughts head-on*, Máthair had said. Very well.

She sat back in her chair, her mind still spinning with worry and doubt, but beneath it all, something else took root: an idea, a resolution. She had spent days caught in her own head, worrying over things she could not control—Jack's family, her feelings for him—but perhaps it was time to do more than simply worry.

Perhaps it was time to stop avoiding what was truly on her mind.

Juniper sat in silence for a moment, staring down at the book in her lap as she bit her lip. The warmth and support in the room wrapped around her like a blanket, but still, her heart fluttered nervously. *How could she possibly admit it out loud? Where could she even start?*

"I have been thinking," she began, her voice quieter than usual, her fingers still toying with the edges of the book. "About someone."

Betony's eyes lit up immediately, her smile widening as if she had been waiting for this exact moment. "Oh, have you indeed?" she teased, setting her beadwork aside with a knowing glint in her eye. "I believe I know of whom you speak—but perhaps you had better clarify who this 'someone' is for Ivy and Máthair's sake?"

Juniper bit her lip, her cheeks flushing, but she didn't look up. "A gentleman," she said softly, feeling the weight of their expectant gazes upon her. "Of our acquaintance."

Ivy, ever perceptive, leaned forward slightly with her book now completely closed in her lap. "It sounds rather serious, dear," she said, her tone gentle but encouraging. "Why not tell us who it is?"

Juniper's heart raced, her throat tightening. She could feel her sister's curiosity, and even Máthair's quiet, knowing gaze from across the room.

How could she admit it? Saying his name aloud would make everything real—more real than she had ever allowed herself to imagine.

Betony moved closer, her hand touching Ivy's arm. "You might as well say his name, Juniper. I know exactly who you are talking about, and I feel certain it will not hurt things in the slightest for the others to know."

Juniper's head snapped up, her eyes wide with surprise. "Truly?"

Her younger sister laughed lightly, folding her hands neatly in her lap. "Of course not. Besides, I think at least Ivy has her suspicions. Do you not, Ivy? It is quite obvious, is it not? There is only one gentleman who has made Juniper fidget like this." She gave Juniper an encouraging nod, her smile softening. "Go on, say his name. It is just us."

Juniper hesitated, her heart pounding. Her gaze flickered between her sisters and Máthair, all of them watching her with such kindness, still she couldn't bring herself to say Jack's name aloud. Not yet. "I don't know if I should."

Ivy leaned forward at that, her expression gentle. "Juniper, darling," she said softly, "you don't have to tell us if you are not ready. But sometimes, admitting something to yourself is the first step to making sense of your feelings. We are your family. All three of us are here for you, no matter what."

The tenderness in Ivy's voice made something inside

Juniper relax. She knew her sisters wanted what was best for her, and even Máthair—though reserved—seemed quietly supportive. They were not here to judge her or laugh. They were offering to listen.

Her chest tightened with emotion, and she drew in a breath, trying to steady her racing thoughts. "It is Jack Sterling," she finally whispered, her voice so soft she wasn't sure if they would hear her. But the moment she said his name, an odd sense of relief soared through her, as if a weight had lifted from her shoulders.

She looked up, meeting Ivy's eyes.

Her older sister smiled warmly, no surprise in her expression. "I thought as much," she said gently. "Mr. John Sterling is a good man."

Betony, who had been grinning broadly, clapped her hands together softly. "Oh, Juniper, this is wonderful. I am relieved I no longer have to keep this secret with you. It has been torture."

Juniper smiled weakly, her cheeks still flushed. "I was not quite sure how to talk about it—or if I should."

Máthair, who had remained silent throughout the exchange, finally spoke up, her voice serene. "You have done well, child. Feelings of the heart can be the most confusing things of all. But now that you've spoken them aloud, perhaps you can begin to make sense of what is in your heart." She offered a small, approving nod. "And I believe your Mr. Sterling is worthy of such thoughts, given what I know of him."

Juniper's heart swelled at the sound of his name spoken so kindly. Perhaps she wasn't being foolish after all. The relief in admitting her feelings felt like the first step toward something new—something hopeful.

Her chest still felt tight, her heart pounding now she had spoken Jack's name aloud, but instead of the awkwardness she had feared there was only warmth in the room—understanding, even a sense of quiet joy from her sisters. Yet with that small relief came a new wave of doubt.

"I have no idea if he feels the same," she admitted quietly, her fingers twisting the handkerchief in her lap. The vulnerability in her voice surprised her, but once she started, the words kept tumbling out. "Though we have shared moments that felt particularly warm, I do not know if I am imagining things. And I am afraid to hope for more, because..." She let the thought remain unspoken, unsure how to encapsulate her flickering thoughts.

Betony's expression softened, her teasing smile fading. "Because...you do not want to get your hopes up only to be disappointed?"

Juniper nodded, looking down at her hands again. "Exactly. What if I have misunderstood everything? What if he does not at all feel the same way? Perhaps he sees me as nothing more than a friend to him, or perhaps not even that—only as a friend to Lady Emily."

Ivy leaned forward, her voice as soothing as ever. "Oh, Juniper, it is *not* strange to hope for something like this. You are certainly not foolish for wanting to believe there could be something between you."

Betony nodded in agreement. "Hoping for love—there is nothing wrong with that. Love is what we all want, truly."

Máthair had been quietly listening and wore a thoughtful expression. "Hope is never foolish, child," she said, her voice calm. "Hope is the seed from which the greatest joys and even the deepest loves grow. It would be stranger still if you were to shut yourself off from that hope, to deny yourself all possibility of happiness."

Juniper blinked, absorbing those words. The way Máthair spoke made it sound so simple, yet her doubts continued to assail her. "What if his feelings are not the same? What if I have misread everything?"

Ivy's smile was perhaps a little knowing, but was full of sisterly affection. "That is the risk we all take when we let ourselves fall in love. But from what I have observed, Jack Sterling is a man who cares for you, deeply. Even without knowing for certain, there is no harm in *hoping* for a future where he feels the same."

Betony leaned closer, her eyes sparkling with excitement. "And really, Juniper, why wouldn't he adore you? You are lovely, kind, you have always admired him. It is not at all strange for you to hope for something more. I would think it quite natural."

Juniper looked between her sisters, the weight of their reassurances sinking in. Could it be true? Could she dare to hope that Jack might see her the way she was beginning to see him? The thought sent a flutter through her chest, a tangle of fear and anticipation.

"Perhaps," she whispered, more to herself than anyone else. "I think he must at least like me. A little."

Máthair's kind smile preceded her reassurances. "You ought to build on that, dear. And then, o'course, you know Teague is quite ready to give his blessing to the man, do you not?"

Juniper's cheeks warmed and she put her hands on them to cover the blush. "Oh, no—Teague told you about that?"

Ivy laughed. "He told me about it, too. He was terribly disappointed he did not have the opportunity to interrogate Mr. Sterling as to his intentions toward you. I think he is looking forward to that moment far too much."

The other two women laughed, and Juniper's own smile twitched upward again. Her family loved her, supported her, and they liked Jack. Jack, who she adored. Admired. *Loved*.

For the first time in days, Juniper allowed herself to hold on to that feeling. Perhaps it was new and fragile, but it was hers, and she was not ready to let go of it any time soon.

Despite the comfort of her sisters' words and Máthair's reassurance, a small knot of anxiety remained tight in Juniper's chest. Her thoughts drifted back to the things she had overheard at the charity meeting—the cruel remarks about Jack's family, the insinuations which still stung to remember. She bit her lip, her gaze lowering to the book in her lap, and that familiar unease crept back into her heart. She could not ignore it all.

"There is more at hand to concern me—more than my own feelings," she confessed softly, breaking the brief silence which had fallen over the room. "People are saying such unkind things about the Sterlings. They think his family is undeserving of their place in Society." She glanced at Ivy and Betony, her voice dropping to a near whisper. "What if the gossip turns vicious? What if it affects them in ways they cannot overcome?"

The room grew silent for a while, each woman pondering in her own way. Juniper's lungs tightened—there were no instant words of comfort here, the challenge insurmountable if the *ton* truly did take against the Sterlings. What could anyone do against such a tide of opinion?

Ivy's brow furrowed with concern. "People can be very unkind when they do not understand something—or when they feel threatened by it."

"Or when they are simply too bored with their own lives that they must go poking about in someone else's," Betony added, a touch of anger coloring her tone. "Trying to stir up scandal where there is none, that's scandalous in itself!"

Juniper grimaced as she nodded. "I know," she whispered. "I wish there was something I could do to protect them."

"I am all too familiar with the *ton*'s attempts to keep out those they deem unworthy." Máthair set her pamphlet aside, her expression one of sympathy. "Sometimes the best way to protect those you care for is simply to stand by them, openly and without hesitation. The truth has a way of revealing itself in time, and those who matter will come to see the Sterlings for who they are."

Máthair's words did not quite dismiss her concern, though a flicker of something came to life deep within her. The worry still lingered, stubborn as ever. She would have to find a way to do more than simply stand by—she had to think of something that would truly help Jack's family navigate the treacherous paths of Society.

Uncertainty gnawed at the edges of her hope; but hope remained.

CHAPTER 16

Hyde Park was at its liveliest during the fashionable hour, the lanes crowded with carriages, riders, and walkers, their bright clothes and cheerful voices filling the air. Jack rode beside Emily, keeping his gaze ahead, but his awareness stretched outward to every nod, glance, and murmur which came their way. The sun had come out to brighten the gray March day and glinted off the shining carriage wheels, but despite the cheerful setting, there was a distinct chill in the greetings they received.

A nod here, a faint smile there, but the warmth had waned since the last time they had taken a ride through the park. Emily had evidently noticed it, too; her expression grew more subdued as they made their way through the park and her posture, usually so upright and confident, seemed a touch less assured. Jack could sense her discouragement, even as she maintained her composure, her gloved hands holding the reins with a calmness that belied her true feelings.

"That was Lady Westcott and her daughter on our left," Emily said quietly, her gaze flicking back to a pair of women they had just passed. "She looked as though she might speak, but then changed her mind."

Jack's jaw tightened. "Perhaps she was simply distracted," he offered, though he knew that wasn't the case. The coolness in the air had nothing to do with the weather or the distractions of others. He had noticed it in the way people stepped out of their path, their nods curt rather than cordial. It was subtle, but unmistakable—a shift from the polite curiosity that had greeted their family's entry into Society, to something more dismissive.

Emily gave a small, resigned sigh. "It seems as though we are to be outcasts after all," she said, attempting a smile, though it didn't reach her eyes. "I suppose it was bound to happen eventually."

Jack shook his head, a surge of frustration making him clench the reins. His horse snorted and shook his head and he patted the beast's neck to reassure him. "Nonsense. They have no reason to look down on us. We've done nothing to merit it." His tone was sharper than he intended, and his sister flinched slightly at the edge in his voice.

He gentled his tone, giving her a sidelong glance. "Let them have their airs. We belong here as much as anyone now." Even as he spoke, the words felt hollow. His mind flashed back to the gossip Juniper had mentioned—the unfounded whispers about their family's sudden rise. It stung to see Emily affected by it, even as she tried to hide her pained disappointment.

Yet this was what their lives were to be, it seemed; within the *ton*, but distant from it.

They continued along the path, and Jack noticed every sidelong glance. The fashionable hour had fully arrived and the park was as crowded as usual, the paths bustling with people. It was then, as Jack's frustration simmered, that he felt a shift in Emily's attention.

"Oh, thank heavens. Look, Jack."

Jack glanced up and saw the cause of her good cheer; three

women on horseback approached, weaving through carriages ahead of them. The leading rider, with her bright eyes and tall riding hat, was none other than Lady Juniper Amberton. Beside her rode Lady Dunmore, and the third woman, dressed in fine Italian silk, was the Contessa di Atella. The trio cut an elegant figure, their presence causing admiring glances to follow them along the path.

Jack's pulse quickened, and he sat straighter in his saddle. Juniper, looking radiant atop her chestnut mare, drew his gaze as effortlessly as the sunlight drew the eye. He watched her approach, a sense of relief coming over him despite his promise to ignore his nascent feelings for her. The quiet longing he felt whenever she was near was becoming far too familiar.

As if in answer to his uncertain feelings, Juniper raised a gloved hand with a crop gripped in it, her face brightening as she drew nearer. She inclined her head in greeting, her smile warm and genuine, and for a moment the chill in the air faded.

As Juniper, Ivy, and the contessa drew nearer, the lively din of the park seemed to grow a little quieter, as all of Jack's attention went to the woman at the center of the trio. Juniper, riding at the front, reined in her mare with an effortless grace, her cheeks slightly flushed from the exercise and her eyes glowing as they met his.

"Good afternoon, Mr. Sterling, Lady Emily," she called out warmly, her smile brightening as she inclined her head. A touch of cheerful familiarity in her tone seemed to defy the chill surrounding their afternoon thus far. "It is such a pleasure to see you both. What a lovely day for a ride."

Emily's shoulders visibly relaxed at the friendly greeting. "Good afternoon, Lady Juniper. It is indeed," she replied, her own smile emerging with renewed confidence. "And you are in fine company, I see." She nodded toward Lady Dunmore and Lady Atella, who rode alongside Juniper with easy smiles of their own.

Jack inclined his head, his gaze drifting between the three women. That was it, he could not merely look at one of them... "Lady Dunmore, Lady Atella," he greeted them, his tone polite but carrying a hint of relief. "It is good to see all of you out enjoying the day."

The baroness returned the greeting with a nod. "It is good to see you as well. The park is simply too beautiful to be tucked up indoors today," she said, her voice full of affection as she glanced at Emily. "It has been too long since we last saw you, Lady Emily. I hope all is well?"

Emily offered a polite smile. "All is well, thank you. The fine weather has kept the park from being quiet today."

Lady Atella laughed lightly. "Ah, but it is never truly quiet, is it? Not when so many come to see and be seen." Her gaze flickered over some of the onlookers, who quickly turned their attention elsewhere. "It seems like the attention is always ready to find those who least wish for it."

Juniper glanced at Jack, a subtle concern in her eyes as though she sensed the tension lingering in his heart. "I hope we are not intruding on your ride," she said softly, her voice carrying a note of sincerity that made Jack's pulse quicken. "We happened to see you both, and I could not let the opportunity to greet you pass us by."

Jack shook his head, managing a brief smile. "Not at all. Your company is always welcome." He glanced at Emily, whose spirits were noticeably lifted by the arrival of familiar faces. "In fact, I believe you may have brightened our afternoon considerably."

The words were light, but he meant them. The presence of these women—especially Juniper—pushed back against the chill which had followed them since they'd entered the park. He watched as Juniper and Emily exchanged a few more words, and his gratitude for her public kindness increased tenfold.

As the group continued to converse, Jack's gaze drifted to

the people around them. Though some still cast glances in their direction, there was a change in the air. It was subtle, but the cold stares were fewer and less certain, as if the open friendliness of the other respected ladies gave people reason to pause in their judgment and suppositions. Still, Jack felt the need to be on guard, sensing that the park held more than idle chatter.

For a moment his gaze met Juniper's again, and he was struck by the warmth in her eyes. It wasn't a casual expression in the least; it was a look which said, *I see you, and I stand with you.*

The conversation continued, and though the talk was light—weather, recent events, a concert last evening and plans for the coming week—there was an unspoken understanding that something was different. Jack could feel it in the way Emily's smile softened, the way her spirits rallied with each passing moment in company with the other ladies. He was grateful for it, but he couldn't entirely shake the underlying unease which still clung to him, like a shadow on a bright day.

As Lady Dunmore and Emily spoke of a new gallery exhibition opening in Mayfair, Juniper guided her mare a little closer to Jack's. "You look as though you are carrying the weight of the world on your shoulders," she murmured, her tone low and meant for his ears alone. "Is something amiss, Atlas?"

Now it was her turn to tease him, it appeared; he did not miss the name of the Titan known to hold the entirety of the globe on his back.

Jack glanced at her, his pulse quickening at the concern in her voice. It took him a moment to find the right words, and they had to be the right words. "It is nothing," he said quietly, though even as the words left his lips, he knew she would feel the lie in them. The cold nods and whispers of the past week weighed on him more than he cared to admit. "Or perhaps is only that—" He shook his head. "Some of the attention we have received of late has not been entirely welcoming."

Juniper's brow furrowed slightly, her gaze flickering to the nearby riders who were keeping their distance. "I wondered if it would continue after the ball you told me of," she said softly. "I am sorry you are going through this. The vagaries of Society are many and unpredictable, and universal approval from its quarters is rare and fleeting."

A tightness gripped Jack's chest, and he tried to brush it off with a faint, humorless smile. "It appears we have not found that illusive approval," he replied, his voice betraying a hint of bitterness. "Perhaps we will regain some sort of notice, though likely it will not be positive, depending on how one views scandal."

Her eyes widened. "Scandal?" she echoed, her tone incredulous. "But there is no scandal."

"True," Jack said with a nod, "but that has never stopped those who wish to find something to gossip about. And it seems that now we are the favored topic."

There was a pause as they both took in the implications of his words. Then, with a determined upward tilt of her chin, Juniper spoke. "It is not fair," she said quietly, a touch of steel in her voice. "None of you deserve to be treated this way. Your family has done nothing but conduct itself with grace and dignity. If others cannot see that, then perhaps it is they who do not belong."

Jack's heart gave a faint, almost painful throb at her defense of his family. "You are very kind, Lady Juniper," he said, his voice low. "I only hope you do not find your own name tangled in this mess simply for associating with us."

Juniper's lips curved into a small, defiant smile. "Let them talk," she said, a quiet fire in her eyes. "If the worst they can say is half-truths and rumors, then I shall not lose any sleep. Your family members are all good people. Things will turn out all right."

The simplicity of her words, the strength behind them, gave

Jack a small measure of comfort. He had never sought to rely on others for reassurance. Reinforcement, yes. But not a soothing of his heart with gentle words. Something about Juniper's presence made it easier to bear the weight of things far beyond his control. Her belief in his family—her belief in him—felt like the arrival of the calvary in a battlefield of uncertainty.

"Thank you," he said, the sincerity of his gratitude saturating those two words as much as he could manage. "Your support means more than I can express."

Juniper's smile softened and she gave a slight nod, as though to say that there was no need for thanks. "You do not have to bear everything on your own, Jack," she said gently. The way she said his name made a shiver of pleasure course down his spine, despite the vow he had made to put his feelings for her aside. "Even the strongest shoulders need a bit of help now and then. No one would expect you to face an enemy on the battlefield alone."

Her words stayed with him as Lady Dunmore, Lady Atella, and Emily's conversation drew to a natural close and the moment passed, but the warmth of it lingered. As he and Emily continued on with their ride, Jack was struck by a realization that had been slowly dawning over the past weeks—Juniper wasn't merely a friend of the family or a kind acquaintance. She was someone he could see himself leaning on, someone he could trust with the deepest parts of himself.

And as the group rode on, Jack found that some of the weight pressing down on him had lifted. It was a small reprieve, but it was enough to let him breathe a little easier.

JUNIPER AND IVY STEPPED INTO THE ENTRY HALL, THEIR riding boots clicking softly against the marble floor.

Ivy took off her hat with a flourish and held it out to the maid waiting to collect their things. "I am marvelously glad that we went for a ride when we did. It was lovely to see Lady Emily and her brother, especially after our recent conversation about your interest in him."

Hettie bustled into the entry hall, and Juniper handed her gloves and crop to the maid with a grateful smile, her thoughts still lingering on the ride in the park—on Jack's steady voice and the way his gaze softened every time it rested on her.

She tucked her hand through the crook of her sister's arm. "Do you think such little public meetings will be enough to quiet the gossip and unkind things others are saying about the family?"

"In time, yes—and when people have something newer or more scandalous to sink their fangs into." Ivy patted her hand gently. "We will win them over in time. Once his family is more settled, I have no doubt Mr. Sterling will turn his attention to a formal courtship."

A pleasant warmth remained in Juniper's cheeks, even as she tried to push aside the foolish flutter in her chest. The air of the house, with its familiar scents of polished wood and fresh flowers, did nothing to pull her from her daydreams. She turned to make her way upstairs when a bright voice interrupted her thoughts.

"Ivy, Juniper! You've returned!" Fiona came skidding into the entry hall from the rear of the house, her cheeks pink and her eyes wide with excitement. She held a handful of skirts in one fist to keep from tripping as she ran toward them. "There's a visitor waiting for Juniper in the front sitting room."

Juniper's eyebrows arched in surprise, and she cast a glance toward the closed door of the sitting room's closed door. "A visitor? For me?" she echoed, amusement coloring her tone. "I hardly expected to have company today."

"Oh, but you do." Fiona nodded eagerly, her dark curls

bouncing. "It's a gentleman—or so he says. He's been waiting for nearly half an hour." She lowered her voice to a stage whisper. "I think that *he* thinks he is important. I told him you were out riding, and that Teague wasn't home, and—"

"For goodness' sake, Fi." Ivy laughed and fondly rustled her young sister-in-law's hair. "Who is it?"

"His name is Mr. Waldegrave."

Juniper's amusement shifted to alarm, a small jolt running through her. Mr. Waldegrave? The unpleasant gentleman who had been so persistent in his attentions toward Emily? What on earth could he want with her? She bit back a laugh at the absurdity of it. "Mr. Waldegrave, you say?" she asked, keeping her voice light as Fiona stared up at her. "Well, that is a surprise."

Ivy's brow furrowed. "He is the one who followed Emily about, is he not?"

"Yes." Juniper shook her head and heaved a sigh. "What could he want with me?"

Fiona looked between the adult ladies with interest, clearly relishing her role as bearer of strange news. "He's the grandson of an earl, you know. He told me so himself, and said that it is important that he speak with you. He must have a pressing matter to discuss."

"Indeed," Juniper murmured, her lips curving into a wry smile despite the flutter of unease in her chest. "Thank you for telling me, Fiona. I suppose I had best not keep Mr. Waldegrave waiting any longer—and you should be in the schoolroom."

Pulling a face but clearly resigning herself to the end of enjoyment, Fiona skipped toward the stairs and ascended them.

"Would you like my company?" Ivy folded her hands in front of her with a serious expression. "I do not think you ought to see so unpleasant a gentleman on your own, whatever his reasons for visiting and asking for you may be."

"I will leave the door open and keep one of the footmen in attendance. I know you have a meeting with Lady Jersey within the hour, you had best prepare for that. I think she is a more exacting companion than Mr. Waldegrave will be for me."

Ivy chuckled and gave Juniper's hand a squeeze before going toward the stairs where Fiona had disappeared.

As Juniper made her way toward the sitting room, she couldn't help but feel a mixture of amusement and wariness. What could have prompted Mr. Waldegrave to turn his uninvited attentions toward her, after it had been made plain that Emily was not interested in him? She could hardly imagine anything good coming from his unanticipated visit.

Juniper paused at the doorway of the sitting room, her hand resting lightly on the latch as she took in the scene before her. The room was just as it always was; soft March sunlight peeping through lace curtains, casting delicate patterns on the floral wallpaper, and the faint scent of lavender lingered in the air.

Mr. Waldegrave stood as she entered, his back stiff, his hands clasped behind him with an air of self-importance. He offered a practiced smile, the kind that looked more self-satisfied than truly pleasant, his gaze sweeping over her with the kind of appraisal one might give an object of interest in a shop.

"Lady Juniper," he greeted her, his voice smooth and polished. "A pleasure, as always. I do hope I am not intruding."

Juniper inclined her head in a courteous nod, though a sense of unease stirred in her chest. "Not at all, Mr. Waldegrave," she replied, keeping her tone light. "Though I admit, your visit is rather unexpected. Given that you have waited for me this past half hour, I must either suppose it either important in nature or that you have a particular fondness for our sitting room."

"Ah, yes." He gave a slight chuckle, which felt condescending rather than true amusement. "I suppose it is important. I have hoped for the opportunity to speak with you at greater length since the last time we were in company together." His gaze flicked toward the open door where the footman stood, as though ensuring they were truly alone, before returning to her with a faintly conspiratorial air. "There has been much talk in Society recently—about the Sterlings."

Juniper felt a small jolt of alarm, but kept her expression neutral as she sank into the nearest chair. "Yes, I am aware the family is often a topic of discussion," she said cautiously. "I do not see why that should concern you, Mr. Waldegrave."

His brows lifted ever so slightly and he leaned toward her a little, as though to impart a secret. "It is not myself that I am concerned for, Lady Juniper. It occurred to me that with all the unfortunate rumors surrounding that family, you might wish to reconsider your association with them." He gave a slight shrug, as if to suggest it was merely a passing thought. "It is not unheard of for young ladies to find themselves inadvertently embroiled in a scandal simply by associating with the wrong people."

Juniper's fingers tightened around the arm of the chair, though she kept her tone steady. "I am aware of the rumors, Mr. Waldegrave," she replied, her voice cool. "I see no reason to distance myself from my friends simply because others choose to gossip about inaccuracies. The Sterling family is intimate with my own, including Lord Dunmore and the Duke of Montfort, and they have done nothing to merit such treatment."

"Of course, of course," the unwelcome visitor said quickly, his smile widening, though the gleam in his eyes suggested he was unconvinced. "I meant no offense, my lady. I merely wished to express my concern for your well-being. It would be a shame if you were to be...tainted by association, shall we say?" He spread his hands in a conciliatory gesture. "Naturally, I would not presume to tell you who to befriend. I merely thought you might appreciate my friendly advice."

Juniper's amusement faded entirely, replaced by a cold resolve. Was this truly his intention—to cast doubt on her friendships in order to further his own interests? She drew herself up straighter, her gaze steady. "Your concern is noted," she said, her tone edged with politeness. "However, I prefer to judge people by their character and conduct, rather than by the idle chatter of others ill-informed."

Mr. Waldegrave's expression flickered, a brief shadow crossing his features before he smoothed it over with another blatantly insincere smile. "A noble sentiment," he murmured. "I can only hope that the Sterlings prove worthy of such loyalty."

Juniper's fingers tapped lightly against the arm of the chair, a small, irreverent impulse stirring within her. It was difficult not to find the situation rather absurd—Mr. Waldegrave, with his perfectly polished shoes and self-important air, standing there as though generously bestowing his great wisdom upon her. His tone was that of a tutor offering advice to a wayward pupil, and she was tempted to laugh at the sheer ridiculousness of it all. Did the man think she had no knowledge of such things?

But then he continued speaking, and the absurdity of the situation gave way to something else—a faint unease, like a shadow creeping across the floor.

"You see, Lady Juniper," he said, settling himself onto a chair across from her without invitation, as though they were old friends, "a young lady of your standing must take care with whom she associates. A good name is swiftly lost, and though one might sympathize with the unfortunate circumstances that bring about a rise in social rank, there are those who would question whether it was truly deserved." He gave a slight, dismissive wave of his hand, as though indicating the nebulous 'those' who held such opinions.

Juniper's amusement dimmed further, and she straightened in her seat, tilting her head to regard him more closely. "Are you implying that the Sterlings did not earn their place?" she asked, her tone laced with polite skepticism. "I was under the impression that an inherited title is a matter of birth, not of merit.

Their lineage was proven by the king's own investigator to take up the Benwaith earldom. You wish to disagree with the king?"

Mr. Waldegrave gave a thin-lipped smile, and this time she saw the expression for what it was—one of triumph. "Oh, it was proven, my lady. But you must agree that not all families are equally prepared for the responsibilities that come with a title. It takes more than mere inheritance to maintain one's standing among the true nobility." He leaned back in his chair, crossing one leg over the other. "Connections are paramount, you know. One must have the right sort of friends, the right sort of alliances, the right supporters. Our new Lord Benwaith had no such connections...though as you say, John Sterling was quite intimately connected with the Duke of Montfort's family."

"Indeed. I met him first when he was employed by them," Juniper said boldly, chin lifted. This man was not going to cow her. "He was everything that was proper, as befitting a trusted servant to His Grace. I see no reason to hold that past against him, however. Many a man or woman has been elevated by chance in the past."

"Do you not find it strange that the family has so many of the Duke of Montfort's closest friends and acquaintances hovering around them, while His Grace himself remains in the countryside?"

"Not at all. We are in close contact with the family, given that my sister-in-law is due to produce a child for the family. You may not know this, Mr. Waldegrave, but I am well aware of why His Grace remains at Clairvoir Castle." She curled her fingers tighter around the arm of the chair. She would not lose her temper. "His Grace sent letters of introduction to his friends and family in London on behalf of the Sterling family while he awaits his grandchild. Why should such a thing be a surprise to anyone?"

"A duke recommending his former footman to his friends and relations is rather odd." Mr. Waldegrave shook his head.

"Especially given the number of mistakes they have made since coming. The laundry out the ladies' windows, the way they choose which parties to attend, the sons of the new earl making spectacles of themselves in clubs by speaking about farming with such gusto—the way they have thrown the unmarried Lady Emily into Society yet allowed her to snub whomever she pleases."

That comment gave away more than he likely knew, but the sneer on his lips clearly told Juniper more about his true motives than anything. He was upset he had been spurned by a lady he considered beneath him, by virtue of her upbringing. Was that all?

"They do not belong in London," he said, viciousness entering his tone, "moving among the elite as they wish. They may not for another generation or two. Despite legally inheriting the title, they have no couth, no education, no refinement. They do not belong, and people are beginning to see it. They are not the right sort of connection for one such as yourself, Lady Juniper."

"I wonder that you are issuing this warning directly to me in private, rather than speaking openly with my brother-in-law, Lord Dunmore, who is my legal guardian." She forced a smile and lightness of tone to keep from giving offense, as a lady ought. "It seems like that would have been a more respectable course of action."

He sat back in his chair, his expression relaxed again. "I will certainly speak to him on the matter at a future opportunity, but I am aware you have a certain fondness for Lady Emily. You deserve better friends and connections, my lady."

His words hung in the air between them, and Juniper felt her faint unease deepen into something more definite. There was an underlying implication in Mr. Waldegrave's tone which went beyond mere gossip about the Sterlings—as though he were threatening something, or positioning himself to offer something. What exactly, she could not say, but there was a glint in his eye that suggested he thought he was being quite clever.

"I see," she said slowly, allowing just a hint of dryness to seep into her voice. "And I suppose you would consider yourself among those 'better' connections?"

The man's expression brightened, as though she granted him a tremendous compliment. "Why, yes." He inclined his head with false modesty. "My family, as you may know, has long-standing ties to several prominent families, including the Howards and the Ardens. It is always prudent to align oneself with respectable connections, especially when newly navigating the intricacies of London society. Even for one so fortunate in birth as yourself."

Juniper barely resisted the urge to roll her eyes at the sheer pomposity of his speech. Grandson of an earl, indeed. It seemed that Mr. Waldegrave was rather fond of his distant pedigree and fancied himself an expert on social maneuvering, but beneath his affected politeness there was an unmistakable undercurrent —a hint that he was offering himself as a more suitable acquaintance, one whose association would come without the taint of suspicion or questionable connections.

"I appreciate your concern," she replied, her tone deceptively light. "But I have never been one to choose my friends based on their titles or family connections. I find that one's character is far more important a thing than the state of birth, wouldn't you agree?" She raised her eyebrows, her gaze steady as she regarded him.

Mr. Waldegrave's smile faltered for a moment, but he recovered quickly. "Naturally, Lady Juniper," he said, though there was a faint burr of irritation in his voice. "But you must admit that one's character is often judged by the company one keeps."

"Indeed," she agreed, her own smile sharpening. "And I have always found Lady Emily Sterling to be excellent company, and so has my family. I am quite content with my friendships, Mr. Waldegrave. So while I will thank you for your advice, I must assure you it is most unnecessary."

His expression tightened and there was a flicker of some-thing darker in his eyes—displeasure, perhaps, or frustration at her refusal to be swayed. "Well," he said, with a forced air of geniality, "I am glad we had the opportunity to speak. I only wished to ensure that you had considered all aspects of the matter."

"I shall certainly reflect upon our conversation," Juniper replied, standing and inclining her head graciously. "Thank you for your time, Mr. Waldegrave. I trust you will convey my regards to your family."

The thinly veiled dismissal in her words did not go unno-ticed, and his expression hardened slightly as he rose. "Of course," he said with a stiff bow. "Good day, Lady Juniper."

As he departed the sitting room Juniper let out a slow breath, though the tension in her shoulders did not ease until she heard the echo of the front door closing behind the unwanted visitor. She could not say what exactly Mr. Walde-grave had been hoping to accomplish, but his conversation left a sour taste in her mouth. There was something unsettling about the way he had spoken of alliances and respectable connections —as though he saw friendships as little more than chess pieces to be moved about for his own benefit.

She met the eyes of the footman who remained standing near the door, finding his concerned gaze on hers.

"Have you need of anything, my lady?" the young man asked.

"Not presently. But thank you, Henry." She smiled at him, calm and collected, then rubbed at her forehead. "You may go about your other duties."

For all Mr. Waldegrave's attempts to plant seeds of doubt, he had only succeeded in strengthening her resolve. Whatever others might think or say, she would not abandon her friends to suit the whims of those who placed so much stock in naught but social status.

And she would certainly not let a man like Mr. Waldegrave convince her otherwise.

CHAPTER 17

J ack paced restlessly across the sitting room, his shoes thudding dully against the polished floor. The early afternoon light streamed in through the tall windows, casting long shadows across the room. His mother, Lady Benwaith, sat in her favorite chair near the hearth, needle in hand as she worked on mending one of his father's shirts. Her fingers moved deftly, and the rhythmic motion of the needle should have been calming—but it only heightened Jack's irritation.

A countess should not mend shirts...yet he could not begrudge her the familiarity of the task. She much preferred it to embroidery.

"No callers again today," he muttered, pausing near the mantelpiece and glancing toward the door, wondering when it would admit guests for his sister once more. "Just the same as yesterday. And the day before that. It is as though they have all forgotten us."

Lady Benwaith didn't look up from her stitching. "Not forgotten, dear. After all, everyone cannot visit everyone every day. People are simply distracted with other matters, I am sure."

"Distracted," he repeated with a bitter edge to his tone. "It is not distraction, it is their precious reputations they are worried about. The same people who once flocked to us with curiosity are now avoiding us entirely." He resumed his pacing, hands flexing at his sides as though searching for something to do.

His family did not seem nearly as concerned as he was. They acted as though they had but to weather the storm, rather than meet the trouble in battle. Truthfully, he did not know which method was best. He had hoped, after the ride in the park at the height of the popular time for it, with ladies of standing speaking happily with Emily, things would have improved.

They had not.

His patience had utterly fled him, likely because Emily was involved. He wanted—*needed*—to protect his family.

Lady Benwaith's needle paused for a fraction of a second before she continued her work. "You know how Society is better than I do, Jack. You said they were fickle. So we are seeing it—the novelty of our family's elevation has worn off, and now some are waiting to see if we truly belong." She glanced up, a gentle smile tugging at her lips. "Our new friends stand by us and invited us to their homes. As for the rest, they will come around in time."

"They had better," he grumbled. "I have had enough of seeing Emily's disappointment every time another day goes by without a single caller or invitation from the ladies who ought to be her peers." He gestured toward the shirt in her lap. It was a mark of his irritation that he spoke of it at all, given how he knew she felt about it. "And that mending is not going to change their minds, either. We could easily have one of the servants take care of it—what if someone were to call, and they saw you acting the part of maid?"

Lady Benwaith considered him with a calmness that belied his own frustration. "I prefer to do it myself," she replied, her tone placid. "And I do not think the state of your father's shirts is the problem we need to solve." She threaded the needle through the fabric again. "But if you are so eager to be of use, I have a favor to ask of you."

Jack arched an eyebrow, the prospect of a distraction more pleasant than it ought to be. "What sort of a favor?"

She glanced toward the small bookshelf near the window where a few worn volumes of old poetry and dry historical texts sat untouched. "Go out and find me something interesting to read," she said, folding the shirt in her lap and considering the hem. "Something new. Not the stuffy old things we have in this house. I am quite tired of the dry topics of history and etiquette."

He frowned. "A book? That is all you want?"

Lady Benwaith chuckled softly. "Yes, a book. If you are determined to brood, you may as well do it while on an errand." Her gaze softened as she looked up at him. "It would be good for you to get out of the house. Go on, Jack. Get some exercise."

Jack hesitated, but his mother's kind expression made it difficult to refuse. At least it would give him something to do, a distraction from the slow, silent collapse of their social standing. "Very well." He gave her a resigned smile. "I will find you something entertaining to read."

"Good." She resumed her stitching with a satisfied nod. "And perhaps, while you are out, you might also consider finding something interesting for yourself. One can never have too many distractions at times when the only thing to do is practice patience."

"Yes, Mother." Jack sighed before heading toward the door, determined to make the most of this errand. If nothing else, as she said, it would get him out of the house—and he already had a thought for the sort of book he would like to find for himself.

Hatchard's wasn't the only bookstore in London, but it was the most popular. He betook himself there, on foot, as it was less than a mile away.

At first, the brisk walk did little to ease the knot of frustration coiled tightly in Jack's chest. As he strode along the busy London streets, he struggled to push his dark mood aside. It seemed so pointless to keep circling back to the same problem: the coldness they were facing from Society, the curt nods, and stilted greetings. Emily's waning invitations were only the latest symptom of a deeper issue: their family's struggle to find a place among the nobility when whispers about their origins and recent actions hung like a fog in the background. He could practically feel the stares pressing against his back as he walked, the burden of judgment and exclusion.

He scowled at himself for allowing his thoughts to fester. He hadn't always cared so much for the opinions of strangers. But then, he hadn't always had something—or rather, someone— to lose.

His thoughts turned inexorably to Juniper.

Her warmth had been like firelight in the gloom these past weeks. Her smile had lifted Emily's spirits during that ride in the park and she had spoken with such easy kindness, not a hint of condescension in her manner. She had a way of looking at him that made him feel seen and understood, as if she knew the weight he carried and did not judge him for it. Her words in defense of his family against those cruel whispers had lingered in his mind ever since.

He let out a breath, his steps faltering as he crossed the street. How many times had he reviewed that conversation? The moment their gazes had met and he'd seen the fire in her eyes when she'd spoken in his family's defense? A part of him dared to hope, even to imagine, that she might share his feelings. For a moment, he entertained the idea. A connection to her, to her family, could prove a boon of respectability to the Sterlings. Juniper would help him, too. He knew she would. And yet...

Jack shook his head and quickened his pace, as if he could outrun the longing he felt. No. He could not think like that. Not while his family's standing was so precarious, not while his sister's prospects hung in the balance. He couldn't afford to pursue his own happiness at the cost of Emily's, or their family's reputation. Not when any false move could set tongues wagging anew. And there was always further to fall in Society, and if the cold distance from others became outright scandal, then Juniper would be dragged down with them if she were to attach herself to him.

He wrestled with himself, torn between his growing affection for Juniper and the voice of reason that warned him to keep his distance. There would be time enough to think of her once they steadied their footing. He repeated the words like a soldier's mantra. Still, they rang hollow.

Jack had no thought for how long it would take matters to 'settle.' How many months—or years—before the whispers about his family ceased? What if the opportunity to pursue Juniper slipped through his fingers while he waited? There had to be other potential suitors for such a woman. At the thought, his chest tightened painfully.

No. He would not dwell on it. It was his duty to look after his family first, to protect them from the scorn of the Society they meant to join. Juniper deserved more than a man whose family stood on such uncertain ground.

And yet, a voice whispered in the back of his mind. She had already seen the trouble, and still she stood beside him.

Jack stepped into Hatchard's, the familiar scent of paper and leather-bound volumes filling the air. The shop was quiet today, with few patrons and fewer clerks. The quiet atmosphere ought to have soothed his mind but as he made his way to the counter, waiting for a clerk to be free, his thoughts circled back to the persistent worries which clung to him like fog.

He stood at the counter, glancing absently at the nearby shelves while a clerk assisted another customer. His thoughts wandered, wrestling with the conversation he'd had with his mother and the tumultuous feelings he harbored for Juniper.

Before he could dwell too long on those thoughts, a familiar and most welcome voice floated through the doorway at the back of the shop.

"Henry, you take those to the clerk. Tell him to have them added to Lord Dunmore's account and sent to his residence."

The sound of Juniper's voice cut through the silence like a ray of sunlight breaking through clouds. Jack's heart gave a sharp kick as he turned toward the back rooms, where the stacks of books reached almost to the ceiling and the narrow aisles wound their way among tables heaped with volumes.

He hesitated for a moment, standing beyond the threshold of the doorway. There she was: Lady Juniper Amberton, her back partially turned to him as she handed a modest stack of books to a young footman. Her gown was a soft shade of blue which suited her perfectly, and her hair, tucked mostly beneath a prim bonnet, framed her lovely face. She was the only patron in this room at the rear of the store.

She spoke to the footman with an easy, unhurried grace, as though she had all the time in the world. "Be sure they are properly wrapped. The last time, one of the books was slightly damp when it arrived."

The footman bowed and came toward Jack with the stack, nodding respectfully before stepping around him.

Jack's pulse quickened. What were the odds that he would run into her here, of all places, on his mother's errand? He was torn between the impulse to step forward and greet her, and the need to steel himself against the rush of longing that always accompanied the sight of her. It was absurd, really, to think that a mere chance meeting could bring him this kind of relief, as though her presence alone lifted the clouds that pressed on his mind.

Then, as though sensing his gaze, Juniper glanced over her shoulder—and her eyes met his. For a moment, her expression was one of mild surprise, then her lips curved into a smile, warm and unmistakably genuine.

"Mr. Sterling," she greeted him, her voice carrying a hint of delight that made his heart ache. "What a pleasant surprise. I did not expect to see you here."

Jack took a step forward, unable to suppress the small smile tugging at his own lips. "Nor did I expect to find myself here," he admitted. "I was dispatched by my mother to find a new book for her. Apparently the selection available at the house is too dreary for her taste."

Juniper's eyes brightened with amusement. "Well, that simply will not do. We cannot have Lady Benwaith suffering from a lack of interesting reading material."

She turned fully, her attention completely upon him, and Jack felt the familiar tug of attraction and something deeper... something he dared not name.

He approached her, maintaining a respectful distance. "And what brings you here today?" he asked, glancing over at the stack of books Henry had taken from her. "Stocking your own library, or are you on an errand as well?"

"A little of both, I suppose," she replied, tucking a loose strand of hair behind her ear. "I was selecting some volumes for Lord Dunmore's collection. He has been encouraging his sister Fiona to read more novels and poetry, but I could not resist choosing a few for myself as well."

Jack nodded, taking a moment to admire the way she spoke with such fondness for her family. "As I know you to have excellent taste, perhaps you could recommend something suitable for my mother? She specifically asked for something interesting— nothing dry or overly serious."

Juniper tilted her head, considering the question. "Let me think," she said, glancing around the shelves nearby. "There is a new volume of romantic poems that I was tempted by myself—it might suit your mother's tastes, if she enjoys a little sentimentality. Or there's a rather thrilling Gothic novel that I finished reading myself last evening. Dark, mysterious, and just the right amount of suspense to keep a reader up late. You may in fact know the author."

Jack couldn't help but smile at the ease with which she made suggestions, her enthusiasm shining through her words. "I think the poems might be what she needs," he said, his voice soft. "And perhaps the novel for myself, if only to see what it is that keeps you up late reading."

He was flirting. Outright. In public. With Juniper.

Juniper laughed quietly, a sound that made his chest tighten. "Then I certainly hope it does not disappoint," she said, her eyes meeting his again, a hint of something like affection in them.

The bustle of the bookshop faded from Jack's perception as they stood there, the two of them in a moment of unexpected connection. His earlier frustrations were forgotten, replaced by a warmth that was as unfamiliar as it was welcome. Even as the moment lingered, he knew his duty to his family remained unchanged. He could not forget the duties waiting for him at home.

Yet, standing there with Juniper, he found he wished to never leave her side.

She turned away, picking up a book, and held it out to him. He took it mechanically, his hand covering hers. Despite the gloves they both wore, a thrill passed through him at the touch. He met her gaze and his heart stuttered.

They were so close.

And he might not get another chance like this ever again. Jack drew her closer, holding both Juniper's hand and the book, looking down into her beautiful, upturned face like a man starved for the sight of her—the taste of her. Madness must have overtaken him in that far too public place.

Because taste her, he did.

JUNIPER'S BREATH CAUGHT IN HER THROAT, THE WORLD narrowing to the sensation of Jack's lips on hers. The kiss was so unexpected, so bold, that it took her a moment to catch up with the joy that surged through her chest at the press of his lips to hers. Her pulse fluttered wildly, and she leaned into him without thinking, her hand splayed against the warmth of his coat. She felt as if she were tumbling into something both thrilling and terrifying.

As quickly as the kiss started, he ended it by drawing back. It was over far too soon, leaving her lips tingling and her heart racing with exhilaration—and then falling with disappointment. She stared up at him, breathless, aching for more. There was a look in his eyes she hadn't seen before: wild and unguarded, so different from the composed, stoic gentleman she had come to know. It was as though a storm raged behind his gaze, a tempest that defied all the careful restraint he usually displayed.

"Jack?" she whispered, barely recognizing her own voice. It came out tentative, like a plea. She wanted him to kiss her again, to chase away any doubts, to show her that the connection between them was real. That she hadn't imagined any of it.

Jack didn't move. He merely stared down at her, his breath coming quickly, his expression a mixture of longing and something darker—regret, perhaps, or conflict? The wildness in his eyes faded as he looked away, his jaw tightening as though he struggled to regain control over himself.

Juniper felt a pang of disappointment, sharp and swift, as if a cool wind had blown between them. She had thought—no, she had hoped—that this moment would unfold differently; that it might be the beginning of something beautiful. Yet here he was, keeping himself from her when everything in her wanted him to draw closer.

She took a small step back, her hand falling away from his chest though her fingers ached to stay. "I—" Her voice faltered, and she searched his face for some hint of his thoughts, some sign of his thoughts. Then she gave up the search, taking hold of her courage instead. Why not be bold? "Why did you stop?"

He winced, but met her gaze again. "I shouldn't have done that in the first place," he said, his voice rough and low as though the words pained him. He reached out, his fingers brushing against the edge of her sleeve: unable to quite let her go, yet unwilling to take her hand. "You deserve better than this. Better than a kiss stolen in a bookshop."

Her disappointment deepened, mixing with frustration. "Better?" She shook her head, a faint, rueful smile tugging at her lips. "And what if I enjoyed that kiss, Jack? What if I want even more?"

The words hung in the air between them, daring him to respond, to take the leap she so desperately wished him to—but even as she spoke them, she saw his expression change, doubt crossing his features.

"Juniper, I..." He broke off, his gaze sliding away from hers as if he couldn't bear to look at her. When he spoke again his tone was gentler, though still edged with a doubt she found so uncharacteristic. "I cannot ask you to take such risks with me. My family's position is too uncertain, and I cannot allow my feelings to jeopardize your reputation. You deserve more than I can offer at this time and if someone had seen—"

A flicker of hurt flared in her chest, but she quelled it. "Do not presume to decide what is best for me, Jack," she said, her tone firm. "You are not protecting me by holding back whatever it is you wish to say. You are only making us both unhappy."

The raw emotion that flashed in his eyes at her words sent a shiver down her spine. For a heartbeat, Juniper thought he might step forward again, close the distance between them and kiss her as she longed for. But instead he heaved a sigh, as though the incumbrance of all his responsibilities were pressing down upon him.

"I must think of my family," he murmured, almost to himself, as though reminding himself of his duty. Then his gaze flickered back to her, and there the regret lingered. When he spoke, it was with an unfamiliar formality. "Lady Juniper. I did not mean to make this difficult. My actions were inappropriate. Inexcusable. Please, forgive me."

She swallowed the bitter disappointment that threatened to choke her. "Very well," she said, forcing a small, brittle smile to her lips. "But do not expect me to simply forget what happened, *Mr.* John Sterling. I am not one to let a moment like this slip away without a fight."

For a long moment, he simply looked at her, and she thought she saw the faintest glimmer of hope in his eyes.

And then he took a step back, the distance between them a chasm. "We should return to the front of the shop," he said, his expression far too composed. "I would not wish for anyone to suspect ill of you."

"Very well." Juniper looked at the shelves and plucked up the book of poetry for his mother. She handed it to him, a challenge in her eyes. "Do not forget this."

He took the slim volume, avoiding touching her this time, and added it to the novel in his hand. "Thank you. My mother will be grateful."

As he turned to lead the way to the front of the shop, the sting of their almost-happily-ever-after lingered in her heart. This was not the end. She would not let it be. She would not act like those silly heroines in her novels who remained silent when it would only take a word to win the day. Just one word...

"Jack?"

He immediately paused in the doorway, glancing over his shoulder at her.

"The Atella ball is tomorrow. Your family is still attending, yes?"

"Of course."

"Good." She lifted her chin. "I expect you will ask me to dance?"

He stared at her, then gave the slightest of nods before he continued on his way.

Juniper took in a deep breath, buoyed by the small victory, and followed behind him. If he did not cut her from his life completely, she could perhaps convince him that it was she who knew best in this matter.

Because his kiss had revealed something she had barely dared hope for before: he cared for her. As more than a friend. She hadn't imagined anything so wonderful; Jack *wanted* her.

And she very much wanted him, too.

CHAPTER 18

Agonizing over a kiss wasn't precisely how Jack expected to spend the rest of his day—or the day after in the many hours leading up to the ball. Yet the memory of Juniper's lips on his, and the way she had looked up at him with longing and confusion, resurfaced no matter how he tried to banish it. It was both a torment and a reprieve, for it momentarily replaced his worries about his family's uncertain standing.

Unfortunately, everyone else had noticed his distraction.

"What?" George asked when Jack climbed into the carriage to attend the ball, peering at him. "No lecture on proper behavior this evening? No reminders to keep my hands off my cravat or avoid treading on a woman's overlong skirts? No censuring reminders about farming, or—"

"George, stop that." Susan tapped her husband lightly on his shoulder with her fan. "You can see the poor man is anxious. Leave him be."

Jack gave her a grateful smile as he settled next to Emily on the rear-facing seat, then folded his arms across his chest. "I trust I have delivered enough lectures. If you cannot remember them now, I see no reason to give more."

Their parents, Lord and Lady Benwaith, were in a second carriage with Richard and Katherine, all of them bound for the grand hotel where the Conte and Contessa di Atella were hosting the evening's ball. The event was to be a lavish affair, given all the attention surrounding it in the newspapers. It was a gesture of goodwill from the Kingdom of the Two Sicilies, whose government had been technically overthrown by Austria the year before. King Ferdinand hoped to win European-wide support to regain true sovereignty over his country. It was all delicate political maneuvering—precisely the sort of thing Jack had little patience for, given his preference for physical battles over verbal ones.

"George will behave himself," Susan promised. "But will you manage, Jack?"

He glanced up sharply, feeling his ears warm as he recalled that stolen kiss. The memory stung with both sweetness and regret, but surely none of his family knew of it. He certainly hadn't been behaving himself when he took it. "Of course."

Emily poked his arm. "I think what Susan means to ask is whether you will be all right this evening, given how we were slighted at the last ball we attended."

"Ah. That." He cleared his throat, forcing his thoughts away from Juniper. "There are more interesting things to discuss this evening than our family. That we are guests at all for such an event ought to go a long way toward showing our respectability."

"I still cannot understand how things turned bleak so quickly," George muttered, tugging at his cravat. "We have done nothing truly foolish. A few mistakes here and there are surely no reason for this much coldness."

Jack had to date refrained from sharing the darkest of the rumors—that he was blackmailing the Duke of Montfort. Such an accusation would only serve to upset his family further, and there was little he could do to disprove it without His Grace's presence. Writing to the duke for help was out of the question, the very thought chafing at his pride.

No, they would have to wait it out, as the rest of his family believed; hope that time itself would ease the whispers and warm the stares. But waiting and hoping had never sat well with him. It rankled now more than ever.

The carriage drew to a halt outside the grand hotel, its façade gleaming in the light of the gas lamps lining the street. As Jack stepped down, he cast a glance over the building's impressive entrance, with its tall windows and polished brass fixtures. The night air was crisp, carrying the faint hum of London's endless motion, but soon after they stepped through the hotel doors they were greeted by the warmth and splendor of the ballroom.

The room before them was dazzling, lit by sparkling chandeliers with crystals scattering the gaslight like stars. The high ceiling was adorned with gilt moldings and clusters of flowers arranged in tall vases lined the walls, their rich fragrance making the air heady. Everywhere he looked, there were silk gowns and gleaming jewels, the elegance of the guests' finery blending together in a riot of color.

Jack's gaze swept over the scene, taking in the polished marble floors, the sweeping staircase at the far end of the room, and the musicians seated in a balcony above playing a lively reel. The swell of music and the rise and fall of voices filled the air. For a moment, it was easy to forget the troubles troubling his mind. Here, everything gleamed, and the world was full of laughter, light, and gaiety.

Yet even in such splendor, Jack remained on his guard. As they entered the ballroom, Emily on his arm, he was keenly aware of the watchful gazes turned toward them. He could sense the undercurrent of curiosity and speculation rippling through the crowd like a distant echo, softened by the grandeur of the setting but no less present.

"Stay close, Emily," he murmured to his sister, his hand resting protectively on her arm. "And smile as if you haven't a care in the world."

Emily obeyed with grace, her expression smoothing into a composed, pleasant look. She glanced up at him with a small nod. "I do hope there will be more dancing this time," she whispered back, her voice carrying a note of wistfulness that pierced him.

"There will be," he promised, though inwardly he could not be certain. It was a risk, coming here with the air still thick with rumors about their family—but they needed to be seen, to prove they belonged among these people, no matter how the whispers swirled.

As they moved further into the room, Jack caught sight of the Conte di Atella, the evening's host, greeting guests with warm enthusiasm. His Italian accent was thick, but his English courteous as he exchanged pleasantries with the arriving nobility. Nearby, the Contessa herself presided over a group of ladies, her gown a deep rich shade of green that stood out even amidst the brilliance of the ballroom.

"Ah, Mr. Sterling, Lady Emily," came a familiar voice. Jack turned to see Lady Ivy Dunmore, her eyes bright as she greeted them. Her husband, Lord Dunmore, was just a step behind, a glass of champagne in his hand. "How splendid to see you both."

"Good evening, Lady Dunmore," Emily replied, dipping into a curtsey. "It is a lovely event."

"It is indeed," Jack agreed, though his gaze roamed the room, searching for a familiar face which wasn't there. He had not seen Juniper yet, but with so many people filling the room, it was possible he had simply missed her.

"Lady Atella will be most pleased that you've come," Lord Dunmore said with a nod. "She has spoken highly of you, Lady

Emily, and your sisters-in-law. There was the smallest concern you'd not wish to come, given...well, some of the less than mannerly behavior of our peers."

"Not at all," Jack answered, posture stiff. "We would not have missed it."

Lady Dunmore took both Emily's hands in hers, examining his sister's gown, asking questions while offering up compliments.

The Irishman gave Jack a knowing look, as though sensing the strain he kept hidden from his family beneath his outward composure. "Good," he said, stepping closer. "And if anyone should act less than welcoming, send them my way. I've already had words with a few sharp-tongued gossips this evening."

Jack felt a rush of gratitude at the man's support even as he glanced toward Emily, hoping she had not overheard that last remark. "Thank you, Dunmore," he said, his voice low. "I will keep that in mind."

He offered his arm to his sister once more, leading her toward the open space near the musicians where the first sets were already beginning to form. As they walked, Jack scanned the room again, seeking out familiar faces and keeping a watchful eye for anyone who might look askance at them. He could feel the pulse of anticipation rising within him, mingled with a lingering tension that he could not quite shake, much as he had felt before many a battle in his years of soldiering.

And then, amid the shifting throng, he finally spotted her: Juniper, standing at the edge of the dance floor, speaking to another lady. His breath caught for a moment as he took in the sight of Juniper. She was resplendent in a gown of pale lavender, the color bringing out the dark richness of her hair and the vibrancy in her eyes. There was a smile on her lips as she spoke, and even from this distance, he could sense the warmth in her expression.

The memory of their stolen kiss returned with startling clarity and his chest tightened. Here she was once more, in the midst of Society, surrounded by admirers and friends. Did she think of that moment as often as he did? Or had she, after his clear request for distance and refusal of a repeat, managed to set it aside and carry on as though nothing had changed?

His sister's voice broke into his thoughts. "Jack, are you all right?" she asked, her brow furrowing slightly as she followed his gaze. "You look as though you have seen a ghost."

Jack forced a smile and gave a faint shake of his head. "I am well," he replied. "The room is rather crowded, is it not?"

"Yes, it is," Emily agreed, casting a glance over her shoulder. "But that's a good sign for the conte. Perhaps his king will have the support he needs after all. Besides, we might not attract much attention when there are so many other people to look at and speak to."

Jack wanted to believe that and as his gaze drifted back to Juniper, he found that hope stirring anew. He would speak with her tonight, if he had the chance, dance with her if he dared. It was too soon to know what he would say, but he could no longer avoid the truth—not to himself, nor to her.

The music swelled as the musicians played a new melody, and Jack took a steadying breath. Whatever the evening held, he would face it. For his family's sake...and perhaps, if fortune favored him, for his own as well.

Lord Dunmore appeared again, and this time the Irishman swept a bow for Emily. "My lady, would you do this old married man the honor of standing up with him? It would please me to be the first to lead you about the dance floor this fine evening."

Emily laughed at his overly chivalrous words, but accepted his hand at a nod from Jack. As they joined the forming lines, he turned his attention back to where he had seen Juniper—only to find her already a mere three steps away from him, her gaze holding steady on his.

"Mr. Sterling." She curtsied. "Good evening."

Jack's breath hitched and his heart gave a quick, uneven beat. He bowed in return, the action smooth but his pulse far from steady. "Lady Juniper," he greeted her, his voice coming out deeper than he intended. "It is a pleasure to see you this evening and looking so...so well."

She rose from her curtsey, her eyes never leaving his. There was a light in them, a sparkle that seemed to carry answers to all his unspoken questions. For a brief moment, he wondered if she was thinking about the kiss, too—if it lingered in her memory as it did in his. Her gown, the pale lavender hue, cast a glow about her, and he struggled to keep his gaze from drifting to the curve of her lips.

"I am glad your family came tonight," Juniper said, sincerity within every word. "I look forward to speaking with all of them."

Jack's chest tightened at her words. The way she looked at him, the way her gaze held a kind of quiet encouragement, made him wish he could act on his impulse to take her hand.

"We would not have missed it," he replied, his tone more restrained than he felt. "It was an honor to be invited."

The music swirled around them, and the dancers were taking to the floor. Jack's gaze flickered to the lines of couples, then back to Juniper. He hesitated a moment before he spoke again, his voice softer, almost intimate. "Will you do me the honor, Lady Juniper, of joining me for this set?"

A pause followed, long enough that Jack's pulse quickened with uncertainty. She had demanded the day before that he ask her, had she not? Why did she now hesitate? His chest tightened as he waited for her response, a touch of doubt creeping in.

Then Juniper's lips curved into a warm smile, and she extended her hand toward him. "It would be my pleasure," she said, her tone holding a softness that sent a thrill through him.

He took her hand in his, his fingers curling around hers as

he led her toward their place in the line. The feel of her hand, warm and delicate in his own, stirred something deep within him, a yearning he had tried in vain to keep at bay. As they came to a halt, he released her hand and faced her. As they stood there, staring at one another, a sense of rightness settled over him, even as Jack's heart raced.

As they danced the motion came naturally, each step falling into place as though they had partnered together a hundred times before. Jack's hand tightened brushed slightly at her waist and his gaze locked on hers, the rest of the room fading into a blur of colors and motion. Here, in this moment, there was only Juniper: her nearness, her grace, the quiet understanding that seemed to pass between them without words.

"Mr. Sterling," Juniper said softly, her voice barely carrying above the music. "You seem somewhat distracted."

The question caught him off guard, and he met her gaze, pulse quickening at the way she watched him. Did she know what she was doing to him? The turmoil he had felt since that kiss in the bookshop was only worsened by being so close to her now. He wanted nothing more than to confess that she had occupied his every thought, that he had been tormented by the memory of her lips on his...

"I am," he admitted, his voice rougher than he intended. "More than you can know."

Her brow arched slightly, a hint of amusement sparkling in her eyes. "And what is it that distracts you so, Mr. Sterling?" she asked, her tone light and teasing.

Jack hesitated, the truth pressing against his restraint. How could he tell her that it was her—that she was the distraction? That it had been impossible to forget the feel of her hand pressed to his chest, the taste of that all-too-brief kiss? His grip on her hand tightened a fraction, a surge of longing making his voice unsteady. "It is difficult to explain."

Juniper's expression softened, and the teasing light in her

eyes faded into something more earnest, more vulnerable. "I think," she murmured, her gaze dropping to his mouth for the briefest of glances before lifting back to meet his eyes, "I might understand better than you realize."

The subtle implication behind her words sent a shiver down Jack's spine. Could it be that she had thought of him as often as he had of her? That the kiss had stirred something within her as well? His breath came a little quicker and he leaned closer than the steps called for, the music rising and falling around them echoing the beating of his own heart.

"Juniper," he said quietly, the intimacy of using her given name in such a setting as this forbidden and yet so sweet. "I..."

But even as the word lingered on his lips, a sudden swell of laughter from a nearby group of dancers brought him back to reality. The crowded ballroom, the watchful eyes of Society—it all came rushing back, reminding him of the dangers of being too familiar, too honest. He was not free to pursue her without risking both of their reputations. The words he had almost spoken stuck in his throat, and he stiffened, his jaw tightening as he struggled to compose himself.

Juniper's brow furrowed slightly as though sensing the change in him, the hesitation which had replaced his longing. "Jack?" she whispered, a faint note of concern in her voice.

His breath hitched at the sound of his name on her lips—a familiarity that wrapped around his chest and tightened, making him feel more exposed than he had since that kiss.

He forced himself to assemble his features into a more appropriate, solemn expression: a mask of his emotions similar to the one he'd worn as servant and guard. "Forgive me, Lady Juniper," he said, his tone deliberately light. "I'm afraid my thoughts wandered."

She nodded, but the curiosity—and something more—remained in her gaze. "Distracted and wandering. Perhaps you ought to learn how to better focus on what is right in front of you, Mr. Sterling," she replied, with a curve of her lips.

When he made no reply, her smile wavered, as though she wondered if she had spoken too boldly. But there was still a challenge in her eyes, a question she was silently asking him to answer.

Jack's pulse thudded in his ears. Focusing on what was in front of him was all he'd been doing. It had led to that kiss.

And now, he wanted so much more.

As the final notes of the dance faded, Juniper felt the gentle pressure of Jack's hand ease away from hers. The warmth of his touch lingered beneath her glove, and she struggled to maintain her composure as she dipped into a curtsey. Her pulse fluttered, still racing from the dance. Every movement, every glance, had seemed fraught with unspoken words, as though the air around them was charged with emotions neither dared to voice.

Her gaze flitted to his face, searching for some sign of what he was thinking, of what he was holding back—but his expression had settled into that familiar guardedness, his eyes giving away little.

Jack held out his arm to escort her from the dancefloor, neither of them saying a word until they were within a few feet of Ivy, where politeness dictated he must leave her.

"Thank you, Mr. Sterling," she murmured.

"The pleasure was all mine," he replied, his tone steady, almost too composed. The hint of formality in his words made something in her chest tighten, a pang of disappointment she hadn't expected.

Juniper took a half-step back, forcing herself to wear a

pleasant countenance. "I hope you will continue to enjoy the evening," she said, her voice a touch too bright. "There are many others who would be glad to dance with you, I am certain."

He inclined his head, the polite gesture somehow a dismissal. "And you as well, Lady Juniper," he said, using her title with a detachment that made her heart sink a little farther.

For a moment neither of them moved, as if both reluctant to be the first to step away. But then someone brushed past Juniper —a young lady she vaguely recognized—and the spell broke. She turned, telling herself that she must not look back as she walked away, even though the urge to glance over her shoulder tugged at her with every step.

Juniper managed to keep her composure as she made her way to Ivy, where her sister was engaged in conversation with a few acquaintances.

The second she had lost sight of Jack her expression faltered, and she pressed a hand to her heart to steady its uneven beat. *It hadn't been enough.* The dance, the words exchanged— they had felt so close to something more, and now she felt farther from him than ever.

As she reached Ivy's side, her sister glanced over at her, a knowing look flickering in her eyes. She did not address Juniper until the lady she had been speaking with turned away. Then she said, with a hint of teasing in her tone, "You appear quite flushed, Juniper. I suppose Mr. Sterling dances with as much intensity as he does everything else?"

Juniper tried to summon a laugh, but it sounded hollow to her own ears. "He is an adept dancer," she replied, glancing down at her gloves and tugging at the fingers to straighten them as she continued, "Though I fear his thoughts were elsewhere."

"Were they indeed?" Ivy's tone was curious, her gaze searching her sister's face. "It looked as though the two of you had much to discuss as you danced, and the color in your cheeks suggests it was not all unpleasant."

Juniper's cheeks warmed further. "I am merely warm from the dance," she said quickly. "There is nearing a great crush in here." But even as she spoke, she felt the truth pressing at her—Jack's hesitation, the way he had drawn back, had left her with more questions than answers.

And the ache in her chest told her she wanted those answers far more than she was willing to admit.

From that moment forward, Juniper tried to immerse herself in the evening, dancing with other partners and joining conversations with acquaintances, but no matter what she did she remained acutely aware of Jack's presence. Whether she was gliding through a waltz or standing beside Lady Emily, she sensed the man's gaze on her, as if his eyes were drawn irresistibly back to where she stood. It was a quiet, persistent pressure that followed her around the room, and though she made every effort not to meet his gaze, the awareness of him never left her. It were as though an invisible thread connected them, and with every glance that flickered across the distance, it tightened, pulling her back toward the memory of that kiss and the longing that still lingered, unspoken, between them.

Juniper slipped into the ladies' withdrawing room, relieved to be away from the crowded ballroom if only for a moment. The quiet of the room was a welcome change from the music and chatter outside. She moved to a mirror to check the pins in her hair, then took a deep breath, willing herself to regain some composure. She'd been too aware of Jack's presence, too preoccupied with the longing she had no business indulging. A few moment's to ground herself would do her good.

The faintest sound broke the stillness—a soft, muffled sob. Juniper turned, frowning. The room appeared empty, save for a few elegant chairs and draped windows. She heard the sound again, coming from behind the heavy curtains framing one of the tall windows.

Without hesitation, she approached the drapes and pulled

them gently aside, revealing a figure huddled in the corner, her face buried in her hands.

It was Lady Emily, her pale blue gown crumpled around her as she tried to stifle her tears with a gloved hand.

"Emily?" Juniper's voice was quiet with concern as she immediately crouched down beside the young woman. "Oh, my dear, what has happened?"

Emily started at the sound of her name, lifting her tear-streaked face to meet Juniper's gaze. She wiped at her cheeks, but her eyes remained red and glistening. "I-I'm sorry," she whispered, her voice breaking. "I did not mean for anyone to see me like this."

"There is nothing to apologize for," Juniper replied, keeping her tone soft and soothing. She took Emily's trembling hands in hers, giving them a reassuring squeeze. "But you must tell me—what has upset you so? I saw you a scant while ago, and you seemed perfectly fine."

Emily shook her head, fresh tears spilling over her lashes. "It is nothing," she insisted, though her voice lacked any conviction. "Someone said something to me, something...awful."

Protectiveness flared in Juniper's chest. "What did they say?" Her brow furrowed with concern. "Who was it?"

Emily merely shook her head again, as if too ashamed or hurt to repeat the words. "I have no wish to talk about it," she said, her voice small and fragile. "I just... I want to leave. I cannot face them all again, not after—" She broke off, another sob escaping her.

Juniper's heart clenched, and she stroked her friend's back to comfort her, wishing she had entered with one of her sisters to similarly offer support. "You need not explain if you do not wish to." Her heart ached for her friend. "But you are not alone, Emily. I will not let you face this without someone by your side."

Emily nodded, but the look of despair in her eyes was

unmistakable. It made Juniper's temper rise to think that anyone had spoken cruelly to the sweet-natured woman she considered a friend.

"I will find one of the ladies in your family," Juniper said gently, rising to her feet. "They will know what to do, and then they can take you home, if that is what you wish."

Emily nodded again, looking both grateful and relieved as she wiped at her cheeks with a trembling hand.

Juniper gave her one last reassuring pat on the shoulder before leaving the withdrawing room. She slipped back into the crowded ballroom, searching the throng for any sign of Lady Benwaith, Lady Tenby, or Mrs. Sterling. As she moved through the guests, she simmered with anger at whoever had dared to insult Emily. The audacity!

What had come over the *ton*, to say something so vicious to someone so innocent and kind as Emily—and in public?

She found Lady Tenby and Mrs. Susan Sterling first, studying a floral arrangement together. "Ladies," she said as she approached, voice low and tone urgent. "I need your help. It is Emily—she is terribly upset and in the withdrawing room. Someone said something awful to her, and now she wants to leave."

Both of them turned to her, eyes widened in alarm.

Susan spoke first. "What happened? Is she all right?" Her voice concerned.

"She would not tell me exactly. Only that someone said something awful."

"Who would dare?" Katherine glanced quickly around the room as if expecting to see the culprit revealed by some malevolent and telling expression.

Juniper touched Katherine's arm. "She is very distressed. She needs to leave."

Susan's lips tightened into a thin line, her expression hardening. "Thank you for coming to find us." She squeezed Juniper's hand. "Take me to her."

Katherine nodded curtly. "I will find her brothers," she said, her tone decisive. "We will take her home at once."

"Please do," Susan agreed, her expression taut with worry. "And then we will find some way out of here without causing more of a scene." Katherine nodded and swiftly departed, her steps purposeful as she went in search of one of the Sterling men.

Juniper took Susan's arm and guided her toward the withdrawing room, trying to appear normal and unhurried. As they walked, she couldn't help but glance around the ballroom, searching for any sign of disapproving looks or whispered words. If someone had insulted Lady Emily so cruelly as to reduce her to tears they might linger nearby, smirking behind a fan or trading smug glances. The thought made Juniper want to rail against the entire room, but to what end? She did not have the ability to clip the wicked tongues with her mere reputation. Not even Lady Atella and Ivy's friendship had managed it.

When they reached the doorway to the withdrawing room, Susan squared her shoulders and took a deep breath, as if bracing herself for what was to come. Juniper pushed open the door, and they entered to find Lady Emily exactly as Juniper had left her—curled up behind the curtain, dabbing her damp cheeks with a handkerchief.

The moment Emily saw her sister-in-law, a fresh wave of tears sprang to her eyes. "Oh, S-Susan," she whispered, her voice breaking. "I—I cannot stay here. Please, may we leave?"

Susan rushed to her side, wrapping an arm protectively around Emily's shoulders. "Of course, darling," she said, her tone soothing. "We will leave this very moment. But first, you must tell me who said those dreadful things to you."

Emily shook her head, her expression anguished. "It does not matter. Please, I want to leave."

The two other women's gazes met over Emily's bowed head, and Juniper saw the anger flash in the older woman's eyes. It was clear that Susan wasn't going to let this matter rest—but for now, all that could be done was to comfort Emily and get her safely away from the prying eyes and whispers of the ballroom.

Juniper glanced back at the closed door of the withdrawing room, her thoughts racing. If Emily was to leave the hotel unnoticed, they would need to avoid the main exits. An idea struck her, and she turned to Susan.

"There is a servants' door at the back of the withdrawing room." She pointed to the panel in the wall near the windows, with its difficult-to-see latch in the wainscoting. "It likely leads to the hotel gardens. We could get Emily out that way, where there are fewer eyes. There will be a path around to the drive to find your carriage."

Susan's gaze flickered toward the hidden door with relief. "That would be ideal. Thank you, Juniper. Could you find Jack and let him know? He should be waiting in the gardens when we come out."

Juniper nodded, leaving her sobbing friend with regret and slipping quietly out of the room to make her way back down the corridor. As she neared the ballroom, she spotted him emerging from the crowd, his expression dark and worried.

"Mr. Sterling," she called as she approached, just loud enough to catch his attention.

He turned quickly, his eyes searching her face as he approached, clearly bracing himself for the worst. "Where is she?" he asked, his voice low and urgent. "Is Emily all right?"

"She is in the withdrawing room with Susan," Juniper replied, stepping closer to ensure they weren't overheard. Who knew who their enemies were? "We have found a way to get her out without drawing attention. There is a servants' door that leads to the gardens. If you could wait there, Susan will bring Emily out to you."

"Thank you, Lady Juniper." Jack's shoulders relaxed a fraction, though his expression remained grim. "I cannot tell you how much I appreciate your help."

She offered him a faint, though she hoped reassuring, smile. "I am glad I could be of some assistance. Emily deserves better than this. All of you do."

He nodded, his jaw tightening as if steeling himself for what was to come. "I will go to the gardens," he said, his gaze steady. "And I will see to it that Emily is taken home safely."

With that, he turned and strode purposefully down the corridor, disappearing around the corner which led to the side entrance and the path to the gardens. Juniper watched him go, her heart aching for both Jack and Emily, before she hurried back to the withdrawing room. After she reassured both Sterling ladies of Jack's agreement to wait for them, she opened the door and watched them disappear into the dimly lit servants' corridor.

Though she wished to go with them, it was not her place. Juniper had played her part in the drama, and she could do no more than return to the ball. She wanted to find Ivy, or Teague, someone she could tell the whole story to and find help. If only her late mother's cousin, the Duchess of Montfort, was present. Her Grace would know what to do.

Returning to the ballroom, she had barely taken a step along the wall, alert for any sign of her family, when Mr. Waldegrave appeared before her with a smug little smile on his pompous face.

Suspicion instantly sprouted in her heart. "Mr. Waldegrave. I did not know you were here this evening." How had he secured an invitation to an event of such note?

"I am accompanying my mother, *Lady* Elizabeth Waldegrave, of course," he said with a smirk. "As my uncle the Earl of Kepton could not come, I am here in his stead. Though I cannot blame you for missing my presence earlier, Lady Atella's guest list was not exactly exclusive, was it?"

She blinked at him. "I beg your pardon? Whatever could you mean, sir?" If he meant what she thought he did...

"I speak, of course, of your rather unfortunate friends, the Sterlings—who else? I believe I just saw the Lord Benwaith and his wife leave, and the rest of their upstart clan has mysteriously disappeared." The gleam in his eye made her think it was no mystery to him why they had gone.

Could Mr. Waldegrave be the person behind Emily's distress? Juniper had to find out. Unfortunately, she hadn't time for any of the tricks that worked in her favored novels. She could not spy upon him, nor root through his belongings for his secrets, nor bribe a servant or disguise herself as a footman. No, it was direct words that were needed here, not deceit.

Juniper stepped closer to him, lowering her voice. "Did you speak unkindly to my friend, Mr. Waldegrave?"

Surprise flickered across his expression before he frowned, bottom lip protruding in an absurd pout for a fully grown man. "What an accusation, Lady Juniper. Hardly a polite thing to ask a gentleman of my prestigious rank."

Her eyes narrowed. "A lady of rank has asked you a direct question. Did you speak to my friend this evening, Mr. Waldegrave?"

His chest puffed out. "Ask her yourself."

"You did," she whispered, shaking her head in disbelief. "What did you say to her? Tell me this instant, or I will report your ungentlemanly conduct both to my guardian and to Lord Atella—who is a close family friend, I need not point out, and he might feel required to ask you to leave. Publicly."

"You are making a scene, Lady Juniper."

No one was looking their way, yet she continued bravely, "I do not care in the slightest. This is the last time I will ask you, sir, before I act in a way which will humiliate you much more than it will me."

Mr. Waldegrave glanced about, tension at his temples, then hissed, "Fine. If you must know, I told her that all of Society would soon be aware of her callous ways, leading men on and casting them aside to find bigger and better prospects—acting above the station to which she was born, when she is undeserving of the title of lady."

At last she understood. Oh, it was so clear now. "You. You have been the one telling lies about the family."

"Suppositions," he corrected with a pompous sniff. "My family has influence—standards. We will not stand to see the peerage brought low by those who do not belong."

Never in her life had Juniper been so tempted to strike someone, and though her anger was righteous, she balled her gloved hands into fists at her side and did nothing but glower at the man for several long seconds. Then she heaved a shaking breath. "I suggest you leave at once, sir, as I am reporting your ungentlemanly conduct to our hosts immediately." She turned on her heel and stormed through the crowd without another word or glance at him.

Mr. Waldegrave deserved no more of her notice.

Juniper made her way to the head of the ball room, where she had last seen Lord Atella, giving heed to nothing along her way—until a gentle hand took her forearm, stilling her. She looked sharply at the person who had touched her, hackles risen thanks to her unpleasant interaction with that brute, but froze. "Mrs. Grey?"

The wife of Juniper's favorite author stared at her with wide eyes. "Lady Juniper, my dear, are you all right? You look quite distressed. Please, may I help you?"

Tears suddenly pricked at Juniper's eyes and she shook her head slightly. "I do not know that you or anyone else can." Her words sounded far more helpless than she meant them to, her throat quivering.

Mrs. Grey took her hand and brought her to stand beside a large potted tree. "You looked like an avenging angel, going through the crowd. Please, tell me what I can do. Shall I fetch someone for you? Are you unwell?"

In the face of such unexpected kindness, Juniper's strength faltered for a moment. She was not a heroine in one of her books, nor was she especially wise. She certainly wasn't powerful. And as the helplessness closed around her heart, she found herself pouring out the story of Lady Emily's unmerited distress to the kind woman before her.

To her credit, Mrs. Grey nodded and did not interrupt. She absorbed all of Juniper's words. Then she pursed her lips. "I think I might be able to help you, my dear. It sounds as though what the Sterling family needs is a stronger line of support than what even your kind friends and family can provide."

Juniper raised one gloved hand to rub at her temple. Her head ached from trying to keep back her tears, and from her repressed rage at the unfairness of it all. "Who would even bother themselves with such matters? I know of no one, not until the Duke of Montfort comes to London. He may not even appear at all this Season, depending on the birth of his grandchild."

"The Duke of Montfort is not the only duke in the realm, my dear." Mrs. Grey smiled almost mischievously. "Do you know, my husband's books are quite popular. There is a guest here this evening who is especially fond of reading his Gothic tales. Perhaps you should meet her. I mean, of course, Her Grace the Duchess of Bedford."

Juniper's mouth fell open. Everyone knew Her Grace, Georgiana Russell, a patron of the arts and a first lady of fashion. A queen in Society, if only a duchess by rank.

Mrs. Grey's expression turned to one of determination as

she said calmly, "Compose yourself, my dear. I am going to introduce you, and your dear friend's problem, to Her Grace this very minute."

Hardly able to keep up with such a whirlwind of an evening, Juniper nodded at once. It could not hurt to seek the help of Her Grace. Perhaps the esteemed woman would have advice, if nothing else, that would provide guidance. Taking a deep breath to steady her nerves and wiping her damp eyes, Juniper followed Mrs. Grey back into the throng—this time, in search of a duchess.

CHAPTER 19

The next afternoon, the sitting room of the townhouse was quiet, the kind of silence that deepened with each passing second, pressing down on the occupants like an unseen weight. Lady Benwaith's hands lay idle in her lap, her sewing forgotten, while her husband stared into the hearth, though the fire offered little warmth to the somber mood. Richard and Katherine sat close together, her hand resting on his arm as though to offer comfort, while George absently turned a book in his hands without opening it. Susan's expression was tight with concern as she sat beside Emily, who had barely spoken a word since returning home from the ball the evening before. Her pale cheeks were a stark contrast to her reddened eyes.

The family had gathered without meaning to, each of them wandering into the room which felt the most like home since their arrival in London. Silently supporting one another with their presence, none of them knew of a solution to the problem at hand.

By the window Jack stood with his back to the room, watching the people outside go about their business. The muted murmur of London's streets drifted through the glass, the distant sounds of carriage wheels and laughter a painful reminder of the world that had turned its back on them. It should not matter —gossip, cruel words, Society's capricious whims. Yet it did matter, more than it should. It mattered because it was his family's good name which had been tarnished, Emily's joy which had been taken...and it mattered because he had promised himself that he would protect them.

Jack flexed his hands at his sides, frustration and helplessness knotting in his chest. How many times had he assured Emily that things would improve? How often had he tried to bolster his parents' spirits, to give them hope that the whispers would fade, that Society would come around? It all felt like hollow promises now. The scene at the ball, the tears on Emily's cheeks—those were the only truths that mattered.

And he had failed.

His jaw clenched as Jack turned from the window, his gaze sweeping over his family. They were strong, each of them in their own way, but at that moment they felt fragile, as if even the air was too heavy to breathe. It fell to him to restore their spirits, to find a way through this tangled web of rumor and resentment and ruin. As he wrestled with the words he might say, he found no comfort in any variation.

He didn't know how to look after them this time.

A knock at the door interrupted the oppressive quiet, the sound almost startling in the stillness.

A footman entered, his expression as composed as always, but there was a hint of curiosity in his eyes as he announced, "My lord, my lady—Her Grace the Duchess of Bedford and Lord John Russell have arrived and wish to speak with you."

The words hung in the air for a moment before they could fully sink in. Jack's brow furrowed in disbelief, and he exchanged a brief glance with Richard, who looked equally bewildered.

The Duchess of Bedford and her stepson? What could she

possibly want with them, especially after such a disastrous night?

Lady Benwaith straightened in her chair, her composure returning with remarkable swiftness. "The Duchess?" she repeated, her tone a blend of surprise and curiosity. "Well, by all means, show them in at once."

The footman bowed and withdrew, Jack's pulse quickening as the murmurs of conversation beyond the door grew louder. He glanced at Emily, who looked up with wide eyes, the faintest glimmer of hope flickering across her face. For the first time since they had returned home, a sense of urgency stirred in him —an awareness that something unexpected was about to unfold.

As the door opened again and the Duchess of Bedford swept magnificently into the room, Jack found himself taking a step forward, wariness gripping him. The rest of his family had stood as was right—thank goodness some of his lessons had registered—to greet her with bows and curtsies.

Her Grace was the picture of poise, her dark hair elegantly arranged, her gown a deep blue that gave her an aura of quiet authority. Beside her Lord John Russell, her stepson, was less imposing but carried himself with an easy grace that suggested he was not unfamiliar with difficult social situations.

"Your Grace," Lady Benwaith said as she rose from her deep curtsy as the rest of the family followed suit. "It is an honor to welcome you to our home."

The duchess inclined her head graciously. "Thank you, Lady Benwaith," she replied, her voice warm but measured. "I apologize for calling unannounced, but I felt it was important that I speak with your family as directly as possible."

Jack's gaze flickered toward Lord John Russell, who stood a half-step behind the duchess. The man met his eyes with an understanding look, as if sensing the question that lay unspoken in Jack's mind. *Why are you here?*

The man was unable to answer it, however, as Her Grace

continued, her expression softening as she looked toward Emily, whose eyes remained downcast. "I hope you will forgive the intrusion, but after the events of last evening, I thought it only right to offer my public support to your family."

A ripple of surprise passed through the room, and Jack felt his heart give a cautious thump of hope. "Support, Your Grace?" he echoed, his tone uncertain. "I confess we could never have expected such a kindness." It ought to have been his father who took the lead, or even Richard as the heir. Jack had become so used to his family's reliance on him, he'd spoken without thought.

No one seemed surprised by the impropriety. Not even their guests.

The duchess's gaze settled on him, and there was a glint of determination in her eyes. "There is no kindness, nor honor, in remaining silent while good people are wronged, Mr. Sterling," she said. "I have heard what has been said about your family, and I do not believe any of it is just or fair. It is time we put an end to such talk." She lifted her chin. "The Duke of Montfort has put his faith in all of you. That is enough for me to do the same. So let us begin at once. It is nearly the fashionable hour for riding through Hyde Park. Lady Emily, allow me to introduce my stepson, Lord John Russell. John." She nodded to the duke's third son, a much sought after bachelor.

Lord John stepped forward and bowed deeply to the youngest Sterling. "Lady Emily, would you do me the honor of accompanying my mother and me on our ride through Hyde Park today? With your parents' permission, of course." He looked to the earl and countess with a smile that was bright and genuine. "In fact, if Lady Benwaith wishes to join us, I am certain my mother would enjoy her company."

Emily looked to her mother and father, and they nodded. Jack stood in some shock as arrangements were made quickly, but calmly, and both his mother and sister left the room to change for the carriage ride. His father smiled with the good manners he had always possessed, and did what he would have done should the duchess have arrived at his cottage door: he warmly invited the duchess to sit, and she graciously engaged Jack's rather startled sisters-in-law in conversation about the ball the evening before.

Lord John came to stand next to Jack, a polite expression of interest on his face. "Mr. John Sterling, it is a pleasure to meet you at last—though I believe I have caught glimpses of you before, while visiting Lord Farleigh at Clairvoir." His naming the Duke of Montfort's son and heir did not surprise Jack in the least. In his time as a guard, he had seen many members of the Duke of Bedford's family visit with the Duke of Montfort's family, but having one of such high rank remember him made Jack take in the lord with greater interest.

"Indeed, Lord John. I am surprised you would remember a servant."

The other man's smile changed from polite to amused. "But you were no mere servant, were you, Mr. Sterling? Farleigh told me the secret, you know. I was worried for the safety of my own family at one time, and I spoke to him openly of the concerns I shared with my father. Farleigh suggested we mimic Montfort's use of former soldiers as footmen. It was sound advice."

Jack didn't know what to say, though his eyes darted to his family to ensure none of them had overheard the conversation. When he turned back to Lord John, he said quietly, "My family does not know the particulars of my employment."

"Ah. I see." Lord John gave a succinct nod. "I will be discreet then. But I do wish to tell you that I admire your dedication and loyalty to those in your care. You are a rare sort, Mr. Sterling. I hope to come to know you better, in time."

What could he do but accept the compliment? "It would be an honor, your lordship."

"It is interesting, you know. To see how your family, though its origins are humble and unlooked for, has inspired such loyalty and friendship in those who know you." Lord John's expression turned contemplative. "Lady Juniper spoke with much determination and vigor on your behalf."

Jack's head turned so sharply his spine protested. "Lady Juniper spoke to you? Of me—us?" Shock sparked through him, followed closely by a feeling of longing and warmth. "But when?"

"Last evening, at the ball. Mrs. Erasmus Grey introduced her to my mother, and from there we took a private room to have a most in-depth conversation on the state of your family's repu-tation. As both Lady Juniper and my mother are avid readers of Mr. Grey's work, they found much in common in their admira-tion for honoring those who are good people." Lord John's smile turned crooked. "If I had such a lady looking out for my inter-ests, Mr. Sterling, I would certainly let her know of my appreci-ation for such a kindness."

At that moment Lady Benwaith and Emily returned, ready for their ride through Hyde Park. The duchess and her stepson went out with them, and the rest of the family trailed behind them to wave them off as though in a dream.

As the carriage pulled away, Jack turned to the footman nearest the door. "Ready my horse at once."

"Oh, are you going to the park too, Jack?" his father asked blithely, evidently still in shock.

Jack shook his head. "I am going to pay a visit to Lady Juniper."

"It is about time," Susan muttered.

Jack kissed her on the cheek, then Katherine, and did not waste a moment more.

He had been such a fool, putting distance between himself and the most admirable woman he had ever met. He loved Juniper. He ought to have had more faith in her resilience, in her abilities to help his family, to help *him*. Never had anyone taken up his burden as their own before.

Juniper had done so from the moment she realized it existed.

He loved her. He wanted to share everything with her—the good, the bad, and everything in between. He only hoped he wasn't too late; that he hadn't made too much a fool of himself the evening before, hadn't disappointed her to the point she would view his change in attitude with cool suspicion.

Hope flickered in his heart. But of course she would not! This was Lady Juniper Amberton, an intelligent, compassionate, beautiful woman to whom he owed every pleasant thought he'd had since coming to London.

And he needed to see her.

Jack arrived at Lord Dunmore's townhouse with a sense of mounting urgency. He knocked on the door, and when the young footman Henry answered, Jack peered beyond him to see servants hurrying about, the household clearly in a state of disarray. The boy's round face was flushed, and he looked as though he needed to sit down.

"Good morning, sir," Henry greeted him with a quick bob of his head, his expression one of surprise. "I'm afraid you've just missed them."

Jack frowned. "Missed them? What do you mean?"

"The family, sir," Henry replied, wiping his brow. "They left at dawn—in quite a hurry, actually. Headed for Clairvoir Castle." He paused, then added in a rush, "Oh, but Lady Juniper left a note for Lady Emily, in case someone from your household came looking for her."

A flicker of surprise passed through Jack, hastily chased by his stomach dropping in disappointment. The news of their sudden departure sent his thoughts racing. What had happened to make them leave so abruptly?

It could only be one thing: Lady Farleigh had birthed a

healthy child, and the family was summoned to meet the new heir to the dukedom. As Lady Farleigh and Lord Dunmore were brother and sister, it was no wonder he would rush to be at her side, their mother in his company.

"Where is the note?" he asked, trying to keep his voice steady, though his heart pounded with some urgency.

Henry gestured for him to wait, then disappeared inside for a moment before returning with a small folded paper, unsealed. "Here it is, sir. I was to take it to your household, but I suppose you may deliver it instead."

Jack took the note, the weight of the paper feeling heavier than it should. As there was no seal, after all, the contents were not private. He unfolded the paper and quickly read the tidy, looping hand of Lady Juniper.

My dear Lady Emily,

I hope you will forgive our sudden departure. We received word last evening that Lady Farleigh, sister-in-law to my sister, is safely delivered of a boy. His Grace has summoned the family to Clairvoir with all haste, and there was nothing for it but to leave at once. I am deeply sorry to depart so abruptly, especially given the troubles which have befallen your family. Please know that I shall think of you often, and I am certain that things will soon be put right—and I hope you accept the presumption of a continued correspondence between us. I have faith that those we count as friends will find a way to bring an end to these cruel whispers. Your brother Jack will know what to do, too. He is far more capable than even he knows.

Yours in friendship,

Lady Juniper Amberton

Jack read the note twice, his gaze lingering on the line about himself. She believed in him, even after everything, even after he had kept his distance and allowed the distance between them to grow. A strange mixture of relief and regret coursed through him. She had left, but not without leaving a sign of her faith in him, however small. He could not fail her, nor his family.

He folded the note and slipped it into his coat pocket. There was only one thing to be done: he would go to Clairvoir Castle himself. If Juniper and her family had gone there, he would follow. Not for his family's sake, but for his own.

With a sharp nod to Henry, he turned on his heel and strode back toward his horse, already planning the quickest route to Clairvoir.

CHAPTER 20

The day after their hasty arrival, Juniper sat in the statue gardens at Clairvoir. She had escaped there after a crowded and noisome breakfast, hoping the fresh air and familiar surroundings would ease the tension that had settled between her shoulders since the moment they had left London. The crisp morning air rustled the leaves and carried with it the faint scent of the flowers beyond the stone walls. She tried to focus on the novel in her hands, but the words blurred together, her thoughts drifting back to London. London, and all she had left there.

She wondered if the Sterlings had yet learned of her family's sudden departure. Had the Duchess of Bedford carried out their plan? Had it helped? Anything could have happened in the three days it had taken to travel to the castle.

Inside the castle, there was nothing but joy as Lady Farleigh doted on her newborn son, the future Duke of Montfort. The baby, with his chubby cheeks and dark curls, had brought an air of happiness to Clairvoir that touched everyone around him. Lady and Lord Farleigh looked positively radiant with their new child, and the young family's contentment seemed to promise a bright future for the duchy. Juniper found herself cheered by the sight of their joy, even as she carried her own uncertainties.

Despite the serenity inside the castle and outside in the gardens, she felt restless, a quiet ache settling in her chest.

The pale stone statues around her stood watchful and silent, casting long shadows on the gravel paths. It was a place she had often retreated to when she needed solace during past visits to Clairvoir, but today it provided little comfort. How could she be at ease until she knew what had happened to Jack's family? She had already written a letter to Lady Emily, beseeching her friend to write to her at the castle. She would have to wait for her letter to arrive in London, then in turn wait for a response to return.

But patience was in short supply for her.

Juniper turned a page, scarcely absorbing the passage, when a familiar and unexpected voice broke through her wandering thoughts.

"Has the hero rescued the heroine yet?"

Her breath caught and she looked up sharply, her heart thudding in her chest. There, standing at the edge of the garden path, was Jack. He wore a coat that was travel-worn and dusty, and there was a weary look in his eyes, but the sight of him was like the sun dawning, chasing away the dark uncertainty she had carried since her hurried departure.

"Jack," she breathed, rising from her seat as she dropped the book upon the bench.

"More likely," he said as his expression softened, "the heroine has saved the rather distressed hero." He did not come any closer. "I hope I haven't startled you," he said, his voice rough with exhaustion. "I thought it was past time I thanked you. For everything."

She took a step toward him, then another, until she was close enough to see the strain in his features, the signs of a long and difficult journey etched in the lines around his eyes. "You shouldn't have come all this way," she said, her voice trembling with a mixture of joy and worry. "You must be exhausted—"

Jack shook his head, stance firm and soldier-like. "It doesn't matter," he said, his gaze steady on hers. "I had to see you again As soon as I could." He paused, a shadow of regret crossing his face. "I owe you an apology, Juniper. For being so blind, for keeping my distance when I should have welcomed every moment by your side."

Before he could say another word, Juniper closed the remaining steps between them, her hands reaching for his shoulders as she threw her arms around him. The moment she touched him, her heart lightened. She felt him stiffen in surprise, then his arms came around her, holding her tightly against him.

She tilted her face up toward his, her voice breathless with relief. "You needn't apologize," she whispered. "You are here now, and that is all that matters."

The warmth of his breath ghosted across her lips, and then Jack was kissing her. It was an eager, desperate kiss, as if all the words they hadn't spoken found their expression in that single, fervent moment. She melted into him, her hands sliding up to the back of his neck as his fingers threaded eagerly through her hair. The world around them faded, the only thing in existence was the press of his lips against hers, the way he held her as if he would never let go.

When they finally drew back, both of them were breathless and Juniper's heart raced with joy. She searched his eyes, which had lost some of their weariness and were filled instead with a quiet resolve.

"You truly came all this way," she murmured, her fingertips brushing against his cheek. "For me?"

"For you," Jack answered, his voice hoarse but steady. "And I would do it again, a thousand times over."

Her heart swelled at his words, and she reached up to kiss

him again, this time slowly, savoring the moment that felt like a promise—a promise that this was only the beginning.

He rested his forehead against hers. "I love you, Juniper. I have loved you for far longer than I ought to have, before I had any right to, when I was curious what it would mean to love a woman like you."

Though she wanted to burst with joy, she could not resist teasing, "And what is it like, pray, to love a woman like me?"

"Blissful," Jack answered immediately with a grin. "I have never known such despair as when I thought I could not be worthy of you, and I have never known such joy as the moment I allowed myself to hope that we might have a future together. Please, my lovely Juniper, will you allow me to pay court to you?" He spoke with desperation and such an earnest look in his eyes that she did not hesitate again.

"I love you, too. With my whole heart. Please, court me. Please, love me and wed me."

He laughed and pressed his lips to her forehead. "I am supposed to ask that of you, my lady. *After* a proper courtship."

"Sometimes," Juniper whispered, heart aching with happiness, "I sneak a look at the last page of my book, to be certain I will like the ending. That is what I wish to do now. I want to be certain this story ends the way I wish it to end. With us, happily ever after."

"That is my wish, too." Jack's lips brushed hers again. "Yes. I will court you, marry you, and love you ever after."

She could not think of a better way to end, or to begin, a story for the both of them.

EPILOGUE

The little house Jack had found stood nestled on the edge of a quiet, wooded glen, its ivy-clad walls and steep gables lending it an air of mystery which was entirely befitting of the Gothic tales Juniper so adored. The tall, narrow windows gleamed in the summer's Yorkshire morning sun, and a faint mist curled around the grounds, giving the place an almost ethereal quality. Jack paused by the gate, glancing back at his wife who stood beside him, her gaze sweeping over the house with unfeigned delight.

"It is exactly as I imagined," she murmured, her eyes alight with excitement. "I knew it would be wonderful, but this—" She gestured toward the stone façade, with its weathered carvings and the arched doorway that seemed to beckon them inside. "It is absolutely perfect."

Jack couldn't help but smile at her enthusiasm. "I hoped you would say that." He took her hand in his and lead her up the path to the front door. "I remembered how your eyes lit up the first time you came to Clairvoir, and I thought...why not give you a bit of that magic to call your own?"

She squeezed his hand as they stepped over the threshold

into the narrow entryway, where the dark wooden paneling and deep blue walls created a warm, inviting atmosphere. "You know me far too well already, Mr. Sterling," she teased, glancing up at him with a playful glint in her eye. "I shall have to attempt to keep some secrets, to maintain an appropriate air of mystery."

"Too late for that, Mrs. Sterling," he replied with a grin, closing the door behind them. "You have already revealed your fondness for all things Gothic. I daresay I know what kind of novels I will find tucked under your pillow at night."

She laughed softly, the sound filling the little corridor as though it belonged there. "And you will read them with me, will you not?" She moved farther into the house to admire a stone niche where a small statue of a knight in armor had been set.

"Only if you promise to stop reading when it gets dark," he said, his voice dropping to a mock-serious tone as his heart sang. "I would rather not have you frightening yourself with ghostly tales before sleep."

"Oh, I am not so easily frightened," Juniper replied, casting him a sidelong glance as she moved into the sitting room, where the mullioned windows framed a view of the trees. "Besides, I have you to protect me. My very own shepherd dog."

Jack followed her into the room, contentment settling over him as he watched her take in the details of their new home—the carved mantlepiece with its intricate designs, the slightly crooked bookcase that he was sure she would soon fill, the alcove by the window where they might take tea and watch the seasons change. It was a small house, humble by some standards, but it was theirs. It was a place where they could build their life together, away from the pressures and expectations of London Society.

"Do you like it, truly?" he asked, needing to hear her say the words though her expression had already told him as much.

Juniper turned to him, her smile softening as she reached up to brush her fingers against his cheek. "Like it? Those words are not enough, Jack. I love it. This house is *everything* I could want." She paused, her gaze sweeping over the room again. "It feels like a place where stories could be written—where adventures will begin. And to think, it is *ours*."

He took her hand, raising it to his lips, unable to stay away from her any longer. "Then I am glad I did not wait another day to bring you here," he said, voice thick with emotion. "I know it isn't a grand estate, and not nearly as impressive as Clairvoir—"

"It is far better," she interrupted, fierceness in her tone. "Because this house is ours. It is our home. Our beginning."

Jack's heart swelled at her words and he wrapped his arms around her, pulling her close. "Our beginning," he echoed, the weight of it sinking in as he held her.

He had spent so long trying to prove himself, to earn the right to happiness, but in this moment he realized that it had always been simpler than that. It wasn't about titles or Society's approval—it was about this, about the woman he loved, and the life they had chosen to share.

As they stood there in the quiet of their new home, Jack's gaze drifted to the window, where the mist was dissipating around the trees. The house seemed to breathe with a life of its own, the shadows in the corners fading as the light outside grew brighter. It was exactly the kind of place Juniper had loved to read about—the kind of place where a Gothic heroine might find herself swept up in adventure and mystery. He couldn't wait to explore it with her, to create a life filled with moments like this: small, unassuming, and perfect in their way.

Juniper pulled back slightly, her fingers tracing the line of his jaw. "Now, where shall we begin?" Her eyes shone with mischief. "Shall we explore every nook and cranny, or would you rather sit by the fire and discuss our plans for the future?"

Jack's lips curved into a slow smile. "I think," he said, drawing her closer once more with a familiar gleam in his eye, "I would much rather start with a kiss. The rest can wait."

She tilted her head up, her smile mirroring his. "A most excellent idea, Mr. Sterling," she murmured, and then his lips met hers, sealing the promise of their new life together.

As the shadows diminished outside, the little house grew warmer, welcoming them into the comfort of its walls—a place where love, and all its stories, could truly begin.

THE CARRIAGE ROLLED TO A GENTLE STOP OUTSIDE JACK and Juniper's new home, and Lady Emily Sterling peered out the window, taking in the sight of the little Gothic house nestled amongst the trees. It was charming, with its ivy-covered walls and arched windows, like something out of one of the novels Juniper loved so dearly. As Emily descended from the carriage, a flutter of anticipation filled her chest. It had been a month since her brother's wedding, and she was eager to see how the newlyweds were settling in.

Her brother and new sister-in-law stood at the door waiting to receive her, along with no more than four servants.

"Emily," her brother said, inclining his head with a smile. "Welcome."

Juniper reached out to take her hands as Emily's maid started gathering together her trunk. "I am so glad you have come. You must be tired from the journey. Do come in and make yourself comfortable."

The warmth in her voice and the genuine happiness in her expression left no room for doubt—Juniper was truly delighted to see her.

The ease and affection between the happy couple was palpable. They seemed to exist in their own world, even in this small house where space was shared and rooms were close. It was a subtle thing—the way Jack's hand brushed Juniper's as he moved past her, the soft look in Juniper's eyes as she watched him speak. There was a tenderness there, an understanding that spoke of a deeper connection than Emily had imagined for herself.

She found herself glancing away, a twist of longing catching her unawares. It was a beautiful thing, this kind of love—steady and true, the kind that endured long after the whirlwind of heady courtship had settled. Her brother had found it, and it had transformed him. She had never seen him so content, not even in the happiest days of their childhood. And Juniper—Juniper positively glowed with joy. Emily couldn't help but admire the way they complemented each other: two halves of a whole, their love evident in even the smallest gestures.

"I must confess," Emily said lightly, "I was expecting a grand tour of this house from the moment I arrived."

Juniper laughed, her arm linked with Emily's as she led her farther inside. "You shall have it," she promised. "Though I will warn you, it is not grand in the slightest, but it has character."

As they wandered from room to room, Emily's admiration grew. It wasn't that the house itself was particularly impressive —no, it was the way it felt. Every corner, every niche had been thoughtfully furnished, with a blend of Juniper's favorite touches and Jack's simpler tastes. It was a place that spoke of two people coming together to create something new, something that belonged to them both.

When they reached the small library, Emily lingered by the window, looking out at the gently sloping hills beyond. "It is a beautiful house," she said quietly. "You have made it a true home."

"We have." Juniper's gaze drifted toward the corridor, where Jack's voice could be heard instructing the footman about Emily's trunks. "It is more than I ever dared to hope for."

Emily turned back to her, a wistful smile on her lips. "I am glad," she said sincerely. "You both deserve this happiness."

Juniper's hand reached out to touch Emily's arm, a silent acknowledgment that did not need words. It was a reminder that their friendship had deepened into sisterhood, something more lasting and profound than the circumstances that had first brought them together.

As the day wore on, Emily found herself watching the happy pair as they went about their routines, their hands often finding one another, their gazes meeting and holding with unspoken affection. It was impossible to miss the joy that existed between them—joy that filled the small house with a sense of completeness.

But it also brought a subtle ache to Emily's heart. Though her family's reputation had been mended through the Duchess of Bedford's friendship, and she had indeed received offers that Season, she had decided to end it unmarried. It wasn't that there hadn't been opportunities—there had been. Yet none of the gentlemen who paid her court had stirred her heart in the way she yearned for. None of them had looked at her the way Jack looked at Juniper, or had made her feel the way Juniper's presence clearly brought light into Jack's life.

Emily stepped outside for a moment of fresh air, making her way to the small garden behind the house. The view from there was lovely, with the rolling landscape spreading out like a patchwork quilt. She turned her gaze eastward, where the city of York lay just a few miles away. Her thoughts drifted to a certain gentleman of the neighborhood—Lyness Eastwood.

She hadn't seen him in months, not since their chance encounter during one of the Season's gatherings. There had been nothing extraordinary about their meeting, not really—a few polite exchanges, a shared dance, some flowers received. Yet something about him lingered in her memory. His quiet, steady demeanor, the way he had listened to her with genuine interest, the kindness in his eyes when he had mentioned his love for the countryside and his own home in York.

It was only a passing acquaintance, a single evening's worth of conversation, and yet... she wondered. What was he doing now, she mused, as her gaze lingered on the horizon? Was he still in York, or had he traveled elsewhere? Did he remember that evening as she did, with a faint curiosity of what might have been if either of them had dared to extend the conversation?

Emily shook her head with a rueful smile. It was foolish, perhaps, to dwell on such things. But as she turned to go back inside, she couldn't help but think that perhaps, just perhaps, there was still a chance for a love like the one she witnessed between Jack and Juniper; if fate was kind, and if she was brave enough to pursue it.

For the moment, she planned to enjoy the time with her brother and sister-in-law, content to bask in their happiness.

As she walked back inside, the house seemed to welcome her, its walls warmed by the love that flourished within. She hoped that somewhere beyond the horizon, a new chapter in her life waited to be written.

IF YOU ENJOYED THIS GENTLE LOVE STORY, MAKE SURE YOU check out the rest of the series.

Sign-up for my newsletter to find out all about what's coming next AND receive special bonuses, just for Newsletter Subscribers! (You can do that here: https://geni.us/AuthorSally Britton)

AUTHOR'S NOTES &
ACKNOWLEDGEMENTS

Hello reader! Welcome to one of the best parts of the book. First thing is first, I have to tell you about my fib - or artistic license, as I prefer to call it. The Bell Hotel, mentioned in this story, wasn't built until the 1830's, more than a decade after this story takes place. But I have used this exact hotel before, in another Regency tale, and wanted to bring it back to link those two worlds together a little more...for reasons that will become apparent later in the series.

You also may have noticed that I included two characters in this book from a previously unconnected book, Erasmus and Louisa Grey, from my book A Haunting at Havenwood. My not-scary-ghost-story. After getting to know Juniper better, I realized that the books Mr. Grey writes would be some of her favorites, so I simply had to give him and Louisa a cameo. Perhaps that will be important later. Perhaps not. We shall see.

You met Roman and Lyness Eastwood again, along with Roman's dogs Apollo and Athena, again. Weren't they especially dashing this time around? It's almost time to introduce their series. Which thrills me to my toes!

I hope you enjoyed this gentle love story. It was a joy to write it, and to include so many marvelous places I visited myself this summer. The Tower of London (which has been giving tours since the 17th century), Hatchards Books, Fortnum and Mason, the Burlington Arcade, and Hyde Park. Beautiful places.

Now for my many thanks to all the people who helped me get this book ready, in no particular order: Mindy, Heidi,

Anneka, Laura B., Laura R., Shaela, Amanda, Marilee, Emily, Melisa, Rachel, Joshua, and ALL the lovely people of Bookstagram who helped me iron things out and cheered me on!

To my family: thank you for never giving up on me. It's been a rough go with this book, but we did it! Or...you know. I did it. Mostly, y'all distracted me. But they were GOOD distractions. Love you, darlings.

I hope this story of friendship and love offered you, dear reader, a break from the normal busy things of life. Every time you visit the castle and the people who walk its fictional grounds, I hope you feel like you've come home.

Come again soon!

Sincerely,

Sally Britton

P.S. Some of the great stuff I wrote about the Tower of London at this time period was informed by the book *A Journal of Travels in England, Holland and Scotland*, by Benjamin Silliman, published in 1810. I love the author's name. And the book. I figured he deserves a shout-out.

ALSO BY SALLY BRITTON

CASTLE CLAIRVOIR ROMANCES:

A Duchess for the Duke | Mr. Gardiner and the Governess | A Companion for the Count | Sir Andrew and the Authoress | Lord Farleigh and Miss Frost | Lady Ivy and the Irishman | A Gentleman for Lady Juniper

THE INGLEWOOD SERIES:

Rescuing Lord Inglewood | Discovering Grace | Saving Miss Everly | Engaging Sir Isaac | Reforming Lord Neil

RETURN TO INGLEWOOD:

Romancing the Artist

DEVOTED HEARTS:

Martha's Patience | The Social Tutor | The Gentleman Physician | His Bluestocking Bride | The Earl and His Lady | Miss Devon's Choice | Courting Miss Ames | Penny's Yuletide Wish

STAND ALONE ROMANCES:

The Captain and Miss Winter | A Haunting at Havenwood | Her Unsuitable Match | An Unsuitable Suitor | Mistletoe for Felicity

LOVE UNAWARES

His Unexpected Heiress | Her Unsuitable Match

HEARTS OF ARIZONA SERIES:

Silver Dollar Duke | Copper for the Countess | A Lady's Heart of Gold

ABOUT THE AUTHOR

Since Jane Austen isn't releasing any new titles, Sally decided to try her hand at writing a few stories set in the Regency period. Those attempts led to a happy career doing what she loves most: telling love stories.

Sally Britton, her husband, their four incredible children, their dogs, the cat Willow who tolerates them, and a snake named Basil live in Oklahoma.

Sally started writing on her mother's electric typewriter when she was fourteen years old. Reading her way through Jane Austen, Louisa May Alcott, and L.M. Montgomery, Sally fell love with the elegant, complex world of centuries past.

In 2007, Sally earned a bachelor's in English Literature. She met and married her husband not long after, and they're quite busy living happily ever after.

All of Sally's published works are available on multiple retailers and you can connect with Sally and sign up for her newsletter on her website, AuthorSallyBritton.com.